T0374232

.

MARSHLAND

ALYSTAIR WEST

WESTBOW
PRESS®
A DIVISION OF THOMAS NELSON
& ZONDERVAN

Copyright © 2023 Alystair West.

All rights reserved. No part of this book may be used or reproduced by any means, graphic, electronic, or mechanical, including photocopying, recording, taping or by any information storage retrieval system without the written permission of the author except in the case of brief quotations embodied in critical articles and reviews.

This is a work of fiction. All of the characters, names, incidents, organizations, and dialogue in this novel are either the products of the author's imagination or are used fictitiously.

WestBow Press books may be ordered through booksellers or by contacting:

WestBow Press
A Division of Thomas Nelson & Zondervan
1663 Liberty Drive
Bloomington, IN 47403
www.westbowpress.com
844-714-3454

Because of the dynamic nature of the Internet, any web addresses or links contained in this book may have changed since publication and may no longer be valid. The views expressed in this work are solely those of the author and do not necessarily reflect the views of the publisher, and the publisher hereby disclaims any responsibility for them.

Any people depicted in stock imagery provided by Getty Images are models, and such images are being used for illustrative purposes only. Certain stock imagery © Getty Images.

ISBN: 978-1-6642-9820-0 (sc)
ISBN: 978-1-6642-9821-7 (hc)
ISBN: 978-1-6642-9819-4 (e)

Library of Congress Control Number: 2023907529

Print information available on the last page.

WestBow Press rev. date: 06/01/2023

He is himself the Maker and Creator of the angels: for He brought them out of nothing into being and created them after his own image, an incorporeal race, a sort of spirit or immaterial fire: in the words of the divine David, "He makes His angels spirits, and His ministers flames of fire." He has described their lightness and the ardor, and heat, and keenness and sharpness with which they hunger for God and serve Him, and how they are borne to the regions above and are quite delivered from all material thought. An angel, then, is an intelligent essence, in perpetual motion, with free will, incorporeal, ministering to God, having obtained by grace an immortal nature: and the Creator alone knows the form and limitation of its essence.

—John of Damascus,
Exact Exposition of the Orthodox Faith,
"Concerning Angels"

For many a petty king ere Arthur came
Ruled in this isle, and ever waging war
Each upon other, wasted all the land;
And still from time to time the heathen host
Swarmed overseas, and harried what was left.
And so there grew great tracts of wilderness,
Wherein the beast was ever more and more,
But man was less and less, till Arthur came.

—Alfred, Lord Tennyson,
Idylls of the King

Contents

Characters and Terms

Major Characters

Patrick Armbruster is the managing partner of Winchester & Wells.

Juan de la Cruz Bardero (sometimes referred to as Juan Bardero), whose real name is **John Mirador**, is a former Special Forces officer known as the Watcher.

Harry Dent is a former United States Army Special Forces officer who is currently a paid assassin.

Lance DuFort is an investment banker and acquaintance of Arthur Stone.

El Capitán is the head of a drug cartel operation in Mexico.

El Halcón, whose real name is Javier Velasco, is the leader of a wealthy Mexican family and a former high-ranking official in the Mexican government.

Frank Johnson is the president of Marshland Savings Association.

Solomon Lewinsky, a Houston-area businessperson, is the chairman of Global Savings Association, one of the S&L's involved in the transaction.

Marshland Savings Association is a Texas-chartered savings and loan association.

John Mirador is a former Special Forces officer known as the Watcher

Edward John Mueller, also known as "EJ," is an unidentified American intelligence agency employee.

Don Mendoza is the chief financial officer of Marshland Savings Association.

Maria Mendoza is the daughter of Don Mendoza

Betty Mendoza is the wife of Don Mendoza, the chief financial officer of Marshland Savings Association.

Gwynn Murray is a third-year associate at Winchester & Wells and a friend of Arthur Stone.

Todd Rawlings is the head of the Banking Department at Winchester & Wells.

Albert Renaldi, also known as "Big Al," is a Galveston-area real estate developer and chairman of West Isle Savings Association one of the S&L's involved in the transaction.

Roger Romny is the partner in charge of a transaction involving Marshland Savings Association, West Isle Savings Association, and Global Savings Association.

Arthur Stone is a senior associate at a prominent Houston law firm, Winchester & Wells.

Ben Stone is a retired FBI agent, Bill Stone's brother, and Arthur Stone's uncle.

William "Bill" Stone is the father of Roger Stone and a Presbyterian minister in Texas.

Ahn Winchester is the wife of Stephen Winchester, a partner in Winchester & Wills. She was born in Vietnam, where she met her husband during the Vietnam War.

Jackson Winchester is the brother of Stephen Winchester and the chairman of the board of Marshland Savings Association.

Stephen Winchester is a litigation attorney at Winchester & Wells and husband of Ahn Winchester.

Fred Vixette is a Dallas real estate developer and controlling shareholder of Vixette Savings Association. one of the S&L's involved in the transaction

Watcher. See Juan de la Cruz Bardero.

Specialized Terms

C-4 or Composition C-4. A common variety of plastic explosive, C-4 is composed of explosives, plastic binder, plasticizers, and usually a marker or odorizing taggant chemical that helps to help detect the explosive and identify its source. It is used by militaries, terrorist groups, and others all over the world.

Federal Home Loan Bank Board (FHLBB). The Federal Home Loan Bank Board was created to govern regional Federal Home Loan Banks. As a result of the savings and loan crisis, the FHLBB was abolished, and its functions were transferred to other agencies.

Federal Savings and Loan Insurance Corporation (FSLIC). The Federal Savings and Loan Insurance Corporation provided deposit insurance to savings and loan institutions until its dissolution, whereupon its responsibilities were transferred to the Federal Deposit Insurance Corporation, or FDIC.

Mark-to-Market Accounting. Mark-to-market accounting describes the process by which the assets of a company are valued and recorded on the books of a business at current market value as opposed to historical cost.

Push-Down Accounting. Push-down accounting is the method by which an acquirer's accounting basis concerning the assets and liabilities taken over in a financial acquisition is "pushed down" to its books. In this manner, the acquirer's consolidated financial statements as of the date of the acquisition are adjusted to reflect the fair market value of the assets and liabilities acquired.

Real Estate Limited Partnership. An investment vehicle in which a group of investors pool money to invest in real estate. Limited partnerships have a general partner, who assumes liability for the partnership's business, and one or more limited partners, who are liable only up to the amount contributed to the partnership. Where limited partnerships are publicly traded, the general partner is normally a corporation formed to act as the general partner.

Registration Statement. A registration statement is a document containing financial disclosures a company must make before offering securities to public investors. Such registration statements are filed with the Securities and Exchange Commission. Those preparing and filing registration statements must do due diligence when preparing their registration statement. Misstatements are punishable by law.

Resolution Trust Corporation (RTC). The Resolution Trust Corporation was a federal agency formed to hold and sell assets created by the savings and loan (S&L) crisis of the 1980s. The RTC was essentially a property-management company that held and disposed of assets resulting from the closure of savings and loan associations during the S&L crisis.

Risk-Controlled Arbitrage. A complex form of risk management normally entered into by mortgage-granting institutions, which involves reducing the interest-rate risk of granting fixed-rate mortgages financed by short-term deposits by using various hedging techniques, including swaps, mortgages, dollars, reverse repo transactions, and other financial devices to manage interest rate and prepayment risk.

Savings and Loan Associations (S&Ls). Savings and loan associations are financial institutions that specialize in residential mortgage lending.

Savings and Loan Crisis. In the 1980s, the financial sector suffered a crisis involving the nation's savings and loan industry. As a result of the United States leaving the gold standard and the costs of the Vietnam War and the Great Society programs, inflation and interest rates rose considerably during the late 1970s and early 1980s. This created many problems for the S&L industry. The interest rates that S&Ls could pay on deposits were set by the federal government and were substantially below what could be earned elsewhere. This led depositors to withdraw funds. In addition, S&Ls primarily made long-term fixed-rate mortgage loans. When interest rates rose, these mortgages lost considerable value, which effectively wiped out the industry's net worth. Unfortunately, federal regulators lacked sufficient financial resources to deal with the losses. Therefore, the federal government deregulated the industry, hoping that it would grow and diversify out of its problems. Unfortunately, the problems grew even worse. Ultimately, taxpayers provided a bailout, and Congress acted with significant reform legislation.

Securities and Exchange Commission (SEC). The Securities and Exchange Commission is a federal regulatory agency responsible for protecting investors and maintaining the fair and orderly functioning of capital markets. The SEC requires disclosure by public companies, protects the investing public from fraudulent and manipulative practices, and monitors corporate takeovers. It approves registration statements where public companies are issuing securities to the investing public.

Texas Savings and Loan Department (TSLD). The Texas Savings and Loan Department was established to administer the Texas Savings and Loan Act, which provided for the regulation and supervision of state-chartered savings and loan associations. As a result of the Savings and Loan Crisis, the TSLD was abolished, and its functions were taken over by other state agencies.

Preface

Years ago, while still practicing law, I hit upon an idea for a murder mystery set in a larger law firm. Over time, I often mentioned my desire to write such a novel, but changing careers, raising a family, caring for parishioners, and other tasks (as well as sheer laziness) kept me from undertaking it. When I reached "three score and ten," I made a bucket list. Writing the novel made the list. Eventually, I started.

By seventy, I had left practicing law and had been a pastor for almost thirty years. Since my late twenties, I have admired and been enriched by the work of the Inklings, especially C. S. Lewis, J. R. R. Tolkien, and Charles Williams. One day, I remembered that Lewis once advised Tolkien that they needed to write the kind of things that they enjoyed reading. While, like all authors, I would like to have readers, I wrote the type of story I enjoy reading: a little action, a little learning about something I don't yet understand, and a hero to whom I relate. Of course, it never hurts if there is also a love story. I decided to write the kind of story I enjoy.

My wife likes murder mysteries, spy novels, and an occasional love story. Therefore, I also set out to write something she might enjoy. Nothing made me happier than when she said she liked the first draft. It gave me the impetus to keep on with the project.

The book is dedicated to her and our family.

I restate what is already noted for all our friends and acquaintances over the years: All the human persons in the novel are fictitious, and any resemblance to any person, real or imagined (which I've deliberately avoided) is purely accidental. Our family has many friends and acquaintances in Houston, and we cherish the memories of our time there. I chose Houston as the site of the novel because our family lived and worked in Houston during the time period the story covers.

One important realization of life is that every person one encounters, whether a friend, acquaintance, or foe at the time, embodies a life of infinite meaning and purpose. Human relationships are to be treasured, for we become the people we are through the many relationships we enjoy. Therefore, every human relationship is infinitely important. I thank God for all those who have enabled me to enjoy a rich and meaningful life. Life's most important lessons are not always easy, nor are the most critical and life-transforming relationships always the most positive and pleasant at the time. The One Who Was, Is, and Will Be guides us in mysterious ways.

I wish all readers the best and hope *Marshland* will enrich your life as much as writing it enriched mine.

San Antonio, Texas
Epiphany, 2023

The Storm

ONE LATE SUMMER IN THE mid-1980s, a destructive, whirling mass of darkness, wind, and rain known as Hurricane Fey entered the Gulf of Mexico. Three weeks earlier, just off the coast of West Africa—nearly four thousand miles away—a small thunderstorm developed near the Cape Verde Islands. On a clear and sunny day, dolphins and whales were sporting off the islands when slowly—ever so slowly—a small cloud formed. High above the Atlantic Ocean, dry Sahara Desert air met warm, humid tropical air. What would become a major storm was born in seeming insignificance.

A convection process began, transferring heat from the sun and resulting in strong drafts that lifted the moisture upward. In the high, cold upper atmosphere, the moisture-laden air cooled and returned to earth, where the process

1

repeated itself over and over again until a huge, swirling mass of wind, rain, and waves was created. Prevailing winds pushed the storm west toward the Caribbean Sea. As it traveled, it slowly gained strength and became a tropical storm.

The authorities named the storm Fey after Morgan le Fey of the Arthurian legend. It quickly became a joke among those who named her. As time went by, they were not so sure of the wisdom of their humor. It seemed more a prediction than a mere name. Like a wicked fairy, Fey seemed to have a will of her own. She alternately plunged west, periodically slowing to gather strength, before plunging forward again. As the storm moved across the Atlantic, the barometric pressure fell at sea level, and the heat engine created by the storm intensified. Fey finally became a massive, monstrous, dangerous and highly destructive hurricane. It was as if she was determined to teach the human race that small things can become great dangers.

The course Fey took was almost directly westward. It passed to the leeward of Puerto Rico—where it did moderate damage—and then turned, drifting into the Gulf of Mexico through the narrow passage between the Yucatan Peninsula and Cuba, which missed a devastating direct hit by the storm.

Fey was now large enough to significantly damage South Texas or central and northern Mexico. However, once Fey entered the Gulf of Mexico, she paused again—as if deciding whether to hit the Texas Gulf Coast or Mexico.

There, she gained additional strength from the warm waters. In just a few days, Fey became one of the largest storms ever to threaten Mexico and South Texas.

Oil rigs in the Gulf of Mexico began preparing for a major storm, and crews were evacuated to Louisiana and Mexico. The vast complex of chemical plants along the coast began shuttering their operations, bringing down the hot, lethal chemical reactions at the center of the refining process.

National Oceanic and Atmospheric Administration (NOAA) pilots flew above and into the storm in their Lockheed WP-3D Hurricane Hunters to gather data. They regarded Fey as unusual and dangerous in the extreme. During one particularly dangerous and challenging flight, the pilot and one of the engineers on board cursed the storm as if she were alive. One of their comments was recorded as follows: "We need to get out of here. This storm is out to hurt people. We will be lucky to return home alive today— wherever she strikes, it will be very bad news. I have never seen a storm like this in my entire career!"

Everyone feared a catastrophic landfall, wherever the storm ultimately came ashore. Of course, Fey became the center of a media and governmental guessing game. As one announcer put it, "Everyone is trying to find the answer to two questions: Where will she land, and how much damage will she do?"

For public officials in Washington, Texas, and Mexico, the difficulty was in preparing for the potential damage of such a massive storm. Local and state governments encouraged people to leave before Fey could run ashore and injure local populations. On the other hand, to act forcefully and directly, they needed a clear idea of where the storm would strike—an idea they could not yet conclusively form. All along the border, businesses, governments, and private citizens watched the news, read weather reports, consulted with one another, and considered what to do about the storm.

When Fey finally made up her mind on where to make landfall, she turned toward Mexico, heading toward a point between Tampico and Veracruz. As the massive hurricane neared landfall, it gained new strength. With typical journalistic hyperbole, one Texas weatherman declared that Fey was "a monster storm named after an evil witch, destined to do unbelievable damage wherever she lands."

Then, like the unpredictable fairy whose name she bore, Fey stopped again. She lost a bit of strength before sweeping toward the Mexican coastline. When she hit, she was still a large hurricane and produced a lot of flooding, but the initial damage was much less than expected. As if determined to defy her fate as a great disappointment, Fey hurled across Mexico and emerged on the Pacific side of the nation, but her days of destructive fury were over. She drifted out into the Pacific and slowly disintegrated until she was a thunderstorm once more.

Before and after her disintegration, Fey was implicated in more than a few deaths. Some of those who were part of Fey's story thought that her sudden decline in strength was just one more indication that she was no ordinary storm, nor was landfall the purpose of her wanderings.

The Watcher

THE WATCHER HAD BEEN AWARE of the storm for several days. His handlers warned him about Fey as a part of his briefing before he had been dropped directly into her ultimate path through central North Mexico. Of course, when the Watcher was inserted into Mexico, no one knew where Fey would finally hit land or the exact course she would take. His current location was atop a rise covered with rocks and mountain juniper, above a hunting camp on the other side of a small valley. From this point, he could see the hunting camp and a small landing strip in the valley below. The terrain and his camouflage made it nearly impossible for anyone who didn't know he was there to see him. From his position, he could see clearly and travel closer in the dead of night. His equipment allowed him to see and even hear at some distance.

When he was not watching the hunting camp, the Watcher studied the sky for some indication of when—if ever—the storm would strike his position. He was pretty sure that the hunters in the camp would leave for the United States before the storm made landfall so they wouldn't have to bear the brunt of the storm in Mexico, which was less prepared to deal with hurricanes than its wealthy neighbor to the north.

For several days, the residents and visitors to the camp had followed a schedule, not unlike those of many business-related hunting trips. Prodded by their guides, the group rose early and began their hunt before dawn. They came back for breakfast and then went out again. Around one in the afternoon, they returned to the lodges to eat. After lunch and a rest, the group might go out for a few more hours to catch flights of doves in the late afternoon sun. In the late afternoon or early evening, four men who appeared to constitute the center of the group met. This meeting would last for one or two hours, sometimes longer. Then there was dinner and "entertainment."

Today the schedule was different, and the camp was busier. The hunters stayed in the camp. The group packed and then held a short final meeting. On the landing strip on a little plain below the main lodge, workers loaded luggage—including a few large black containers—into the cargo hold of the waiting, relatively new Beechcraft King Air prop jet.

The Watcher was trained and equipped for this mission, as he had been trained and equipped for many missions in the past. His ancestors had lived not so far from the camp, in the north-central region of Mexico, at the fringe of the great Mesoamerican empires of Central America before the Spanish had come to what they called the New World. These forebears were nomadic tribesmen who had wandered through the great expanse north of modern Monterrey and south of Texas, New Mexico, Arizona, and California. They had lived on the fringes of one of the greatest empires of world history. His specific tribe was known as the Tarahumara, a fiercely independent people known for their physical strength and endurance, symbolized by their tribal sport, *rarajipari*, which involved kicking a ball over the rough ground around the Copperas Canyon area of what is now the state of Chihuahua, near the Sierra Madre Mountains.

His mother and father were proud of their heritage, and some of that pride rubbed off on the Watcher. His grandparents loved Mexico, but poverty and the instability of the Mexican government in the early twentieth century drove the family to make the trek across the border, where they had found work on the great ranches of South Texas. The Watcher grew up on one such ranch.

From his youth, the Watcher knew he was not meant for the life of a ranch hand. He was good with his hands and strong. His quick mind had made it easy for him to learn the trade of those who served on the cattle ranches. He was a hard worker and was liked by those who employed his parents. His quiet, watchful competence was evident, even in his teen years. His glowing brown eyes revealed unusual intelligence. His ancestors' fierce, independent spirit was present in every cell of his body. However, he longed for excitement and to travel and explore vast regions beyond what his eyes could see from the ranch on which he was born.

Disaster struck when his parents were killed in a car accident by a drunken driver on a two-lane country road the summer he graduated from high school. He decided to leave the ranch, join the army, and see the world. The world he saw was called Vietnam. His superiors in the military quickly saw that he was highly intelligent and physically gifted. He was an orphan. No one would grieve his passing if killed on a dangerous mission. He was malleable, meaning he could be convinced to do what the military wanted to be done. He had a tolerance for danger and innate bravery. Eventually, he was offered a chance to join the Special Forces.

He fought in Vietnam and Cambodia, earning a Purple Heart and Silver Star for bravery. As customary, his citation for bravery contained no specifics as to what he did or where he had done it. Soon after, he was transferred home and asked to join an even more elite unit. The fact that he spoke Spanish and English, as well as a smattering of his Native American dialect, meant that he was useful in operations in Central and South America. However, Latin America was only one of many places he served and fought over the years.

Recently detailed to Fort Hood in Texas, John Mirador (the Watcher's actual name) continued to be a part of an increasingly secret unit of Special Forces operatives employed by the United States government. His specialty was known as "close in surveillance." He was a "watcher," which is how he got his nickname.

As a watcher, he was sent close to enemy positions to gather intelligence his superiors could use to plan and execute operations. Over the years, in Vietnam and other places, he spent days so close to enemy encampments that he could smell the food, hear the conversations of men and the groans of the women who often accompanied them, see the enemy in play, and any preparation for action, and feel the tension in the air when there was danger and the enemy prepared for conflict.

His superiors had asked him to take on this particular mission. He knew the mission was not for the military. Neither his location nor the people he watched were military nor of military significance. He had no idea which agency needed the information but guessed it was the Drug Enforcement Administration (DEA) or some other national security agency interested in the drug trade. This impression was confirmed when he arrived at his destination. This was no military or guerrilla encampment. The facility he was watching was a hunting lodge—and a luxury exotic hunting lodge at that. The people were neither military nor likely to be government employees, with one exception.

***

The particular mission involved a hunting camp he was watching in central northern Mexico, near Copperas Canyon, where his ancestors had lived long ago. Below the Watcher, who was hidden in the mesquite and brush of a rocky hilltop, there was a landing strip in a small, flat valley about three thousand to four thousand yards from where he was lying on his stomach, dressed in and covered with camouflage to hide his presence in the desert brush, looking at the hunting camp through a special set of binoculars.

On the primitive landing strip sat three planes, one of which was the King Air. On the crest of a slope farther to the west, there was a large main lodge impressively built of stone and logs. Behind the lodge was an expensive tiled swimming pool where hunters could cool off or sunbathe with wives or girlfriends—in this case, the latter. On one side of the pool area were a cabana and bar.

Surrounding the lodge were smaller cabins, each well-made in the same rustic stone-and-wood style with porches and individual hot tubs for aching muscles at the end of a hunt or entertainment in the evenings. To the south of the main lodge was a stone-and-metal barn where hunting vehicles, four-wheelers, and horses were kept, as were kennels for hunting dogs.

As much out of boredom as anything else, the Watcher gave names to the five men at the center of the small gathering. First, there was a tall, aristocratic-looking man, perhaps a native of Mexico with a Spanish bloodline. He called this man "the Hawk" after his narrow face and long, aristocratic nose. As far as the Watcher could see, he seldom spoke in the meetings, but he appeared to be the most powerful of the group. His piercing black eyes absorbed everything and anticipated most of what was said. It was as if he were thinking, *Whatever is said or done here will fit my purposes and plans.*

The Watcher called the second man "the Jock." The Jock was of medium build and slightly overweight. It was obvious that, at one point, he had been an athlete—a football player, the Watcher assumed. The Watcher had played with similar gringos in his high school days. The Jock was naturally athletic, but years of overeating and too much social drinking had added pounds to his frame. He had clever eyes and often seemed to be joking, but his demeanor concealed a hidden purpose and plan.

The Watcher called the third man "the Number Cruncher." He was shorter, dark (probably Hispanic), balding, and seldom spoke at the meetings. Instead, he periodically ran errands or looked up information for the Jock or one of the others. He would leave the room, returning with some information to answer a question or guide the main participants of the meeting. Most of the time, he looked uncomfortable and out of place.

The fourth man was the most difficult to name. Ultimately, the Watcher named him "the Bureaucrat" because he reminded the Watcher of the many intelligence officials and other officials he'd met in Vietnam and afterward while working in Special Operations. The Bureaucrat was the kind of man one would not immediately notice when he entered a room or remember after he left. In the evenings, he wore faded khaki pants and a blue Brooks Brothers shirt with an open button-down collar. He was quiet, listening intently to what the others said. Although he seldom spoke, when he did speak, the others listened intently to whatever advice he gave.

The final person in the group was a short, powerfully built man in his early forties. He had the same Indian heritage as the Watcher, but his dark eyes were scheming and evil. The others seemed to fear this man, for he was not the sort of man it would be easy to control or with whom reason would necessarily work. This man, Mirador named the "Dark One," for that is precisely what the Watcher felt he was—a violent, dark, and evil presence.

The last meeting of the trip was hurried and tense. Everyone could see the storm closing in on the area where the lodge was located. As servants hurried to load luggage on the King Air, the Watcher could see the discussion but not hear the words, which would have been impossible in any case, over the plane's engines warming up in the background.

It appeared the Jock and the Number Cruncher would be the first to leave, together in the King Air just as they had come. At the edge of the landing strip, the Jock, the Bureaucrat, and the Hawk were conversing. For all the world, it looked as if the Bureaucrat and Hawk were giving directions to the Jock but not necessarily instructions the

Jock appreciated. His pale-green eyes darted to and fro with evident frustration that could not be hidden. The Bureaucrat appeared to be participating in the conversation with minimal attention as if his mind was made up about whatever was being discussed. The Hawk also seemed to be engaged in the discussion with less than full concentration, as if he had decided what should be done and the debate was unimportant.

In the end, the men shook hands, and the Jock, the Number Cruncher, and their pilot climbed into the King Air as it prepared to take off. The Jock seemed content with how the conversation ended, but his frustration showed in his gait and demeanor. *He also,* thought the Watcher, *is not a stable man.*

The Hawk and Bureaucrat moved back toward the main lodge, heads lowered in a deep conversation. The Dark One was nowhere to be seen.

The plane began its takeoff slowly, burdened by its passengers, cargo, and fuel tanks filled to the brim. It gained speed and, in the end, lifted off the runway with only a little room to spare as it began the long flight north, climbing as quickly as possible to its cruising altitude, where it would clear the mountains ahead.

***

The Jock joined the pilot at the controls for the takeoff. Having served in the National Guard during the Vietnam War, the Jock was qualified to pilot the plane, though he

14

seldom did. He did, however, often ride up front. Both the pilot and the Jock looked anxiously at the storm.

"It looks as if we might best have waited. We talked too long on the runway. It was a waste of time."

The pilot nodded. They had waited too long to leave, and whatever was said had been a waste of time—and perhaps dangerous, given the speed at which the leading edge of the oncoming storm was traveling. "We might wish we had not tried to get ahead of Fey. The storm seems to be speeding up a bit."

The Jock nodded and returned to the cabin to be with his assistant, who would have to implement some of the decisions made at the conference when they returned. The plane continued to climb.

***

Ordinarily, the Watcher's job would have been done when the plane took off, and he notified his superiors of the event. According to his instructions, he communicated the fact immediately after the plane took off so that arrangements could be made for intercepting the passengers upon landing. The Watcher believed his agency had sent him as part of some drug interception operation. The large trunks loaded on the plane might conveniently hold a large quantity of drugs which would be discovered when arrests were made.

However, two factors kept the Watcher at his post. First was the oncoming storm. He needed to decide whether to leave and get to the pick-up point for exfiltration to get completely clear of the storm, which did not seem feasible, or find a place to hunker down and ride out the storm. The second factor had to do with the hunting camp, which he could still observe from his place of concealment.

As soon as the King Air lifted off, there was a noticeable and immediate increase in activity in the camp. The trip's business was complete, and everyone was in a great hurry to get as far away as possible as quickly as possible. On the landing strip, another plane was getting ready to leave, and a large black Suburban pulled up to the main house, to be filled with luggage.

Everyone is sure in a big hurry, thought the Watcher. *Perhaps, they are anxious to get ahead of the storm.*

Nevertheless, there was something peculiar about all the activity and the looks on the faces of the people below, so the Watcher continued to observe the preparations until two almost-simultaneous events brought his attention back to the plane.

First, there was a huge clap of thunder and a flash of lightning behind him in the direction the King Air was traveling, followed by a crash of thunder like no other he had experienced in more than twenty-five years in the elements. He turned and observed that the leading edge of the oncoming storm seemed to have leaped ahead of itself in some mysterious way, seeking out the tiny dot that was the plane disappearing toward the horizon and mountains beyond. It looked, for the moment, as if Hurricane Fey was a spectral wraith seeking to attack and devour the aircraft.

As a crash of thunder reached the Watcher, he observed another flash of light as the plane exploded. The great burst of light occurred just as the storm reached out to engulf the plane. Then, there was another crash of thunder, and the dark, almost demonic clouds that enveloped the plane appeared to themselves be enveloped into another rapidly expanding flash of light. Amid the huge expanse of light, which took on the form of great wings of pure white light, there appeared even brighter beams of light set at diagonals with the earth and sky, as if they appeared from some other source unrelated to the storm or the explosion. These beams moved organically but not according to any law of physics. The lights expanded and joined together until they embraced the plane in its extremity.

At least one beam of light left the group, sought out the Watcher at tremendous speed (or so it seemed), and pierced him without causing any pain—an invisible beam of blue-hued light traveling through space at an incredible speed. He had never seen this phenomenon, perhaps a type of lightning unique to this area.

His awareness of the beam of light caused the Watcher to stumble, which saved his life, for as he began to fall, a bullet pierced his arm, a shot that would have killed him had he not lost his balance a moment earlier. When he felt the bullet pierce his body, his military training automatically kicked in. The Watcher rolled to his right, catching his weapon and backpack with his good arm as he slid into the draw behind him. When he reached the bottom, he quickly moved to relative safety behind a few rocks and a tree, where he took time to put a bandage over the flesh wound on his shoulder.

At this point, the Watcher had some choices. Had the person who fired the shots seen the dark fire in his eyes, he might have guessed his decision. Instead of heading away from the location from which the shot was fired, he crawled down the draw until he could move in a circle toward the gunman's likely position. He wanted to know who had done this and why. Then, another facet of his training kicked in, and he slightly changed course, moving away from the site of the injury, carefully leaving signs of his path as he traveled.

A Doomed Flight

ABOARD THE KING AIR, THE lightning, clouds, explosions, and blinding light were no less surprising and confusing than the same events perceived from the ground. A few minutes after takeoff, the pilot gasped as a meteorological event he had never seen in all his years of flying unfolded. As the plane flew north toward the US border, climbing quickly so as to pass safely over the mountains ahead, the pilot saw to the east a large, dark "tube" of swirling black clouds emerge from the main body of the still-distant storm, moving swiftly forward, as if driven directly towards the plane by an invisible intelligence. As the dark cylinder of clouds approached the plane, the black mass of swirling clouds spread out like the wings of a dragon as if to swallow it.

As the clouds rushed onward and outward suddenly, humanoid beams of light (if there can be such a thing) appeared, piercing the gathering darkness on lines unconnected with the orientation of the plane or horizon. One light gray light seemed to go straight into the plane and then expand as the black tube-like cloud was transformed into wings of pure light, engulfing the plane and nearly blinding its terrified pilot.

Surprisingly, given the event, the pilot felt little fear. It was as if the beams of light were a kind of protection from the approaching darkness and fury of the hurricane. A sense of peace emanated from the strange beams of light. The pilot relaxed and concentrated on getting above and away from the approaching storm.

Suddenly, there was an explosion in the cargo compartment of the King Air below the passenger cabin. The force of the blast, which was intended to tear the plane to pieces, was somehow contained by the whiteness that enveloped the travelers and did not wholly obliterate the integrity of the airframe. The aircraft survived, though barely airworthy. Then, as suddenly as the warring clouds surrounded and enveloped the plane, they dissipated amid the flash of light. It was as if, having completed their mission, they returned to some hidden universe from which they had come. There was nothing in front of the plane except blue sky. The storm was left behind, and the sky was just as it had been before the strange phenomena.

The damaged King Air labored north.

Before the pilot could take a breath of much-needed air to recover from fright, the door to the flight deck opened. The pilot turned and growled at the intruder to go sit down. The man did not sit down but instead fell with the force of a dead weight against the back of the pilot's chair. Turning, the pilot was confronted with his client, grimacing in pain and holding his leg below the groin as blood flowed down his pant legs. The explosion had been partly beneath his seat, though his life had been spared.

The pilot stared, then spoke. "I think we should return to the field. The plane made it through what we just now experienced, but it is barely airworthy. I don't know if we can make Houston. Besides, we need to get you medical help."

The client shook his head. "My partners and so-called 'friends' did this. If we return now, they will finish what they began. Make for the field we sometimes use near Terlingua in South Texas. When you get there, if I'm not conscious, ditch the cargo. If I am alive, get me to a hospital before going on to Houston."

The pilot saw the impact of blood loss on his passenger's face. He had seen it before. The man's fleshy cheeks were white and loose. His pale eyes, normally brightly alive and calculating, were slowly becoming dull and lacking the lively intelligence they normally possessed. He wasn't sure his client would make it to Houston, Terlingua, or anywhere else.

"What caused the explosion?" the pilot asked. "Was it that funny lightning or what?"

His wounded client replied, "I don't know, but I'll bet it was C-4 somewhere in the baggage. Whoever did this understood what they were doing. We need to be careful. The explosion came from the baggage compartment."

C-4. thought the pilot. *If that is true, we are in big trouble. It is lucky we are still alive.* Then he turned to ask, "How is Don?"

"Dead. The explosion was directly under his seat. It blew him into the roof. I think he died instantly."

With that last bit of information, the client turned to return to the cabin and rest. He did not make it. He fainted and fell to the floor.

The pilot could not get out of his seat to help. Keeping the plane together and roughly headed in the right direction took all his skill, strength, and energy. The desperate fear that had dissipated in the white light returned. He had a wife and two small children. He'd known the risks when he took the job. There is no hiding from a pilot the business or connections of someone he flies all the time. If you fly someone long enough, you know the score. The pilot had known the score for some time now.

As if speaking to his now-unconscious passenger, he said out loud, "Right now, I don't care whether or not they trace anything. I care that we get out of this alive."

From the plane's present location, there was a closer airfield near the US border between Presidio and Marfa,

Texas, on a large hunting ranch. The owner had hosted the plane on occasion during runs in and out of Mexico. If the plane could make it to the ranch and its field, the pilot could arrange medical care from Alpine or another nearby community. The owner would be willing to dispose of the remaining cargo and hide the plane in an unused hangar until he could decide what to do with it.

The pilot adjusted the plane's course to bring it to the friendly field. For more than an hour—the longest hour of his life—he fought the plane and nursed the plane toward the field.

Unfortunately, the plane was doomed. Over the Chinati Mountains in South Texas, near its hoped-for destination, there was one final flash of light in the evening sky. The King Air disintegrated and fell onto the barren countryside. There were no survivors.

***

As fortune would have it, there were campers near the final crash. They heard the explosion and saw fiery wreckage falling from the sky. The next morning, they found what was left of the plane and reported it to the authorities. The border patrol visited the wreckage that same day. In an unusual move, they called the DEA and FAA to take a look at the site and determine the cause of the crash. Fairly soon, the ownership and origin of the plane were known, as well as the names of those who had perished.

This is where my story begins.

Morning After

I AM NOT BY NATURE a morning person, but practicing law in a major firm demands that a person cultivate the habit of waking early and working late. These traits are important components of success. I learned to work long hours and wake early in the crucible of my first years practicing law for a living. Like most creatures of habit, I have a set of things I do early in the morning upon awakening. During this phase of life, my habit was to rise early, make coffee, read the *Houston Post* and *Wall Street Journal*, eat a quick bowl of cereal, and go to the office. This particular morning, just like clockwork, my eyes were open at 5:45 a.m. on a hot, humid, cloudy, late-summer Houston day.

This day, however, as on a few others recently, it was not the sun or a clock or even my internal clock that opened my eyes. It was fear. I "awoke" to see a black but fiery figure at the foot of my bed. The outline of the form of the body was mine (or at least, possibly so). The figure was black as night, outlined with a fringe of red fire, and filled with dark hate. I closed my eyes and then forced them open again. The figure had vanished.

What is going on? I thought.

I was careful not to wake up the person next to me, though reluctant to lose the warmth of her body. I made coffee, opened the *Houston Post,* and stared in disbelief. The headline on the front page was, "President and Chief Financial Officer of Marshland Savings Die in Plane Crash." The article went on to report that a plane carrying the two had crashed in far West Texas as they returned from a hunting trip to Mexico.

This was bad news on many levels.

Currently, Marshland Savings Association, or MSA, as the documents our firm was preparing normally referred to the entity, was in the midst of an important transaction, and our firm was lead counsel. I was not the lead attorney, a job reserved for the partner for whom I worked. However, I had spent many months on the transaction, which we hoped was nearing completion. Now, as a result of the crash, every document and filing involved in the transaction would have to be changed and amended in some way—if, in fact, the transaction could be completed at all.

I hurriedly finished the news article, learning that the King Air belonging to MSA had crashed near the Mexican border in the Chianti Mountains between Presidio and

Marfa on a flight from Mexico to Houston. I barely knew where either Presidio or Marfa was located. The article did not indicate suspicious circumstances, but there was a tone to the article—as if some things were left out of the story.

I returned to the bedroom, walked to the bed, and nudged the still-sleeping figure. "You had better get up, go home, change, and get to the office. It is going to be a busy day."

Lovely, long, tousled dark-auburn hair moved and a pair of even more attractive deep, dark-green eyes looked up sleepily into mine. "How do you know?"

"The *Houston Post*. Frank and Don died in a plane crash."

"What?"

I repeated myself for the benefit of the quickly awakening figure. "Frank and Don died in a plane crash returning from a hunting trip in Mexico. The *Post* article didn't have many details, but it seems like they were trying to get home before Hurricane Fey reached the area where the hunting lodge was located. They managed to get airborne, but the plane crashed somewhere on our side of the border between Presidio and Marfa."

The lovely face and lovely body attached to it leaped out of bed and began to get dressed. "I'm leaving. See you later at the office."

After Gwynn left, I returned to my morning ritual. The *Wall Street Journal* also covered the crash in a small way, noting that Jackson Houston Winchester, a prominent Houston businessman, and a successful investor with long connections on Wall Street, owned Marshland Savings Association.

Jackson Houston Winchester was the managing partner of San Felipe Investment Partners, or SFIP, a Houston investment firm known to cater to an exclusive group of old family friends and others Jackson had met over the years. He and his investors were the primary owners of MSA.

Our firm frequently represented SFIP, MSA, and Jackson Winchester—though Jackson was careful to spread his business around the Houston legal community to create as much goodwill as possible (and as many conflict-of-interest barriers as possible, so as to make it impossible to find a good firm to sue him). Jackson was, as the saying goes, street-smart.

The *Wall Street Journal* article closed by noting that the rumor on the street was that MSA was preparing to engage in a huge and complex transaction that might become a model for how to rescue troubled Texas savings and loan associations in the future.

***

Marshland Savings Association, MSA, had been in the Winchester family since the 1950s. Jackson's father, Marshall Winchester, became the president and eventually controlling shareholder of Marshland in the early 1950s. Marshall was a banker of the old style whose goal was to follow the 1-2-3 principle of bank management: take in money at 1 percent, lend it at 2 percent, and be on the golf course by 3:00 in the afternoon. The first two numbers might change according to circumstances, but the third number remained sacrosanct during Marshall's lifetime. His prowess on the golf course was legendary at the Houston Country Club, of which he was a lifetime member and former president.

Marshall Winchester was a friend of nearly everyone who counted in Houston, and as a human being, he was well-liked. He had an easy way with people and never made an enemy of anyone. It was rumored that he had the largest Rolodex in the city. He had lots and lots of friends and acquaintances. Not everyone, including his son Jackson, felt Marshall Winchester was a very good businessman, but his bonhomie, good nature, and extroverted friendliness made him many friends and protected him from many mistakes in judgment.

One of the most common comments about Marshall Winchester was, "I never had a better friend or golf partner in my life." This was usually followed by, "We got our mortgage from him, but we never really did business together."

When Marshall died of cancer in the early 1980s, Jackson came home from New York City to take over the family business, which everyone conceded was in trouble. Like most savings and loans formed during and after the

Depression, Marshland initially existed solely to make single-family residential home loans at fixed rates, usually thirty years in duration. After the Second World War and into the 1960s, the growth of the national economy and the Greatest Generation's need for housing fueled a period of growth and prosperity. In particular, Houston grew from a smaller city into the fourth largest city in America, fueled by the national and international growth of the oil and gas business, of which Houston was the center. In that environment, the savings and loan business was a great business to be in and grew rapidly, Marshland included.

Originally, S&Ls, as they were called, were cooperative ventures formed by groups of people who pooled their money to purchase homes. As time went by, savings and loans and savings banks were formed as private business ventures. Almost every town or city of any size in America had a small savings and loan, often owned by local bankers, builders, businessmen, and lawyers. Some of them became quite large in rapidly growing places like Houston, Dallas, and San Antonio.

In the 1970s, in the wake of the United States abandoning the gold standard, the cost of financing the Vietnam War, and other factors, the United States experienced rapid inflation. This inflation exposed a flaw in the structure of the savings and loan industry: S&Ls took in relatively short-term deposits in the form of savings accounts and made long-term mortgage loans to their customers, usually loans of between fifteen and thirty years. When interest rates rose in the late 1970s, S&Ls were forced to pay higher rates to their depositors, while being unable to raise the rates on their mortgage loans. The result was a decline in the value of their financial assets. If this went on for too long, any S&L became bankrupt.

Because S&Ls, like all banks, are highly leveraged, rises in interest rates might destroy their shareholders' equity. By the time Jackson took over Marshland, if all its assets had been sold at any one time, there would not have been enough cash generated to pay off its depositors. This was not just true of Marshland. It was true of nearly every S&L in the nation. Fortunately, MSA was not required to "mark to market" its assets for purposes of regulatory capital.[1]

The federal agency tasked with closing savings and loans and seeing that depositors did not incur losses, the Federal Savings and Loan Insurance Corporation (FSLIC), had only a fraction of the assets necessary to close all potentially insolvent S&Ls in an orderly manner. Congress, therefore, decided to solve the problem by deregulating both the interest that S&Ls could pay on their deposits and the kinds of assets S&Ls could purchase. On the asset side of the balance sheet, S&Ls were permitted to hold other assets besides home loans and mortgage-backed securities.

For a man like Jack Winchester, it was a golden opportunity to borrow huge sums of money from depositors and engage in speculative but potentially highly profitable lending and investing.

---

[1] See the glossary for a definition of "mark to market" and other terms.

Jackson Houston "Jack" Winchester was not the same person as his father. He graduated from the prestigious St. John's School in Houston at the top of his class. From St. John's, he went to MIT, where he majored in physics and mathematics. From MIT, he went to Princeton, where he earned a Ph.D. in mathematics. After a short time teaching at Rice University in Houston, Jackson became restless and went to Wall Street, where he became a legendary bond trader, making millions in the bond market.

In particular, Jackson gained prominence as a buyer and seller of what are known as "junk bonds"; that is, below-investment-grade bonds. He was great friends with Michael Milliken of Drexel Burnham Lambert. Jackson formed SFIP while in New York and operated it as an early hedge fund, using complex algorithms primarily to trade bonds, commodities, and other securities as circumstances permitted. His work ethic was legendary.

It so happened that Marshall Winchester died in 1982, just as the S&L business was being deregulated and able to make different and riskier investments. Jackson, seeing an opportunity, came home and took over the family business. When he took over MSA, Jackson immediately merged it with two other troubled Gulf Coast S&Ls. He began to sell assets and reinvest in other assets, including a portfolio of mortgage-backed securities, which he actively managed, and commercial real estate development loans, which, under deregulation, MSA was now allowed to make.

31

MSA then bid on two other troubled institutions, merged them into Marshland, and Jackson worked his magic on their assets as well. All over Houston, he was seen as a financial wizard, a master of the black arts of making money in the financial markets. Having spent many hours in meetings with the man, I had formed two opinions: he was a genius and the most arrogant person I had ever met.

Jackson's current plan was to securitize MSA's massive commercial and single-family real estate portfolios, together with the assets of any S&Ls the Federal Savings and Loan Insurance Corporation (or FSLIC) merged into MSA, into a huge limited partnership run by MSA (for a fee, of course). The intention was to eventually sell as many of the real estate assets as possible, reinvest in mortgage-backed securities, and then trade and hedge those securities to minimize interest-rate risk in the future.

When Jackson proudly announced the strategy to the investment community, he put it this way:

"For the first time in financial history, a huge portfolio of troubled assets will be divided into investment strips, some paying only interest, some paying only principal, and others paying along different formulas. Over time, MSA will unlock millions of dollars of value trapped in the assets of its partners."

Jackson invented his strategy years before others used it for huge pools of mortgage-backed securities (MBS) and sold the idea to several Wall Street investment firms. These firms would participate in selling the securities of the master partnership that MSA would create. Everyone was going to get rich. The entire strategy was beyond my complete understanding and the understanding of most regulators and S&L operators. Ultimately, this kind of strategy would prove riskier than anyone realized, but that is another story.

***

When I got to the firm, I would immediately need to see Roger Romny, the partner in charge of the transaction. I worked directly for Roger; nothing could be done without his approval. I anticipated that most of the day would be taken up in meetings, making lists of things to do, and contacting those needing to be involved in redrafting documents and restructuring the transaction.

Fully dressed, I grabbed my briefcase, opened the door, and headed for the iron staircase leading to the parking lot. As I left the apartment, I had another in a series of recent unpleasant experiences: I almost fell over, temporarily losing my balance and orientation. It was as if the floor of the walkway suddenly tilted, and my body was no longer vertically oriented toward the ground. After a brief moment, the world came back to normal, and I continued to my car.

These moments of vertigo and the dark dreams of recent weeks had unsettled my normally ambitious optimism. Something was wrong. I did not know what but was scared to find out.

I should see a doctor, I thought, but like most young men of my age, I knew in my heart I would not unless forced to do so, which I devoutly hoped would never occur. On the other hand, troubling dreams and vertigo were not good signs. Not good at all.

The Firm

WHEN I SPEAK OF THE *Firm*, I mean Winchester & Wells, an old, established Houston law firm dating back to the nineteenth century. If any firm in Texas can be said to be "silk stocking," it is Winchester & Wells. After the Civil War, Wyatt Winchester, a Texas Ranger before the Civil War and Brigadier General in the Confederate Army, returned to Houston and began practicing law. His abilities soon made his firm popular and profitable, as railroads and cotton merchants flocked to the firm for representation.

A cultured, self-taught man, Wyatt Winchester traveled widely and made many friends on the East Coast and in Great Britain. The mystique of the former Indian fighter and soldier was attractive to many potential clients (and their wives). Some of the great ranches in Texas, often owned by foreign groups, were represented by the firm. Wyatt

Winchester died in the early twentieth century, leaving the firm in the hands of his son, Jefferson Davis Winchester (J. D. for short), who was just as tough and capable as his father. J. D. formed a partnership with a friend, Wyatt Wells, who eventually expanded the firm into the emerging oil business. The firm grew and prospered, as did Texas.

J. D. Winchester had two children, one of whom was Marshall Winchester, the former president of Marshland. The other had been a member of Winchester & Wells until his death. (In those days, no nepotism rule prohibited children from joining a parent's law firm.) At that point, there were no Winchesters left in the firm.

***

I walked into the firm after a five-minute drive down Allen Parkway and into the garage at the base of the glass-and-steel office tower, where the firm had its offices. Bounding off the elevator, giving an impression of confidence I did not possess, I passed the receptionist on the thirty-first floor, where the Corporate Department had its offices. After a brief wave at the new receptionist (they rarely lasted long), I walked to my office, where Betsey, my long-suffering secretary, was already at work just outside the door. Betsey knew I was not long on social graces or conversation in the early morning or during a crisis. I assumed that, when she earlier heard the news about the crash, she had already mentally prepared herself for a long and not-very-pleasant day.

"Have you heard?" she asked.

"Yes. I read it in the paper this morning. Do you know if Roger is in?"

"He came in early, went upstairs to talk with Mr. Armbruster, and returned a few minutes ago. He asked if you would come by when you got in."

In those days, Patrick Henry Armbruster was the managing partner of Winchester & Wells. Roger Romny was the partner in charge of the transaction. Months ago, the firm had been retained to oversee the important, if complicated, transaction Jackson envisioned. Unfortunately, I never particularly warmed to either the transaction or the lead counsel, Roger Romny. Roger was one of the younger partners at Winchester & Wells, known for his appetite for women, alcohol, mild recreational drugs, and risk—any kind of risk.

Roger loved taking on the most difficult and risky projects in the firm. He personally traded stocks and commodities and engaged in complex investment strategies. Every year, to shelter his not-too-shabby income from the firm, Roger participated in tax-shelter transactions, some of which could only charitably be called "extremely risky." On the weekends, Roger could be found flying restored World War II fighter planes, skiing, or taking a quick trip to Vegas, where, it was rumored, he had a six-figure line of credit. His appetite for risk—physical, mental, emotional, and monetary—was legendary.

I'm being a bit unfair by beginning with this description of Roger's character. He was a fine corporate and securities lawyer, and his abilities were widely respected. His capacity for work and ability to bring difficult transactions to a conclusion were well-known in Houston and beyond. The problem was not so much with Roger as with the chemistry between us. Since Roger and I were completely opposite in every way, it was always unlikely that we could do more than act diplomatically toward each other, which we generally did, though reluctantly.

Everyone in the Houston legal community respected Roger's mind, but not everyone respected his judgment. Over the past years, and especially with regard to the MSA transaction, I had become one of the doubters, an opinion I was careful to hide within the firm.

Jackson Winchester specifically asked that Roger take on the project and hired the firm with the understanding that he would be in charge. Normally, I worked with other partners on somewhat less-complicated transactions, but for some reason, I was chosen to help with this project. Why, I cannot imagine. I was a mid-market merger-and-acquisitions kind of guy. While there were mergers involved in this transaction, they were not the center of the transaction. The mergers were a pretext for the massive restructuring Jackson wanted to do on the MSA portfolio and the portfolios of the other associations that MSA was acquiring.

Recently, I complained to an old buddy about my frustrations. "My experience is not in the type of deal that MSA is contemplating. I have no specific background in the complexities involved, especially in the arcane area of trading mortgage securities and their derivatives. There are plenty of other lawyers in the firm with better credentials. I happen to be a fan of Warren Buffett, and in my investments and legal career, I don't invest a lot of time, money, energy, or brain power in things I cannot understand. The transaction Jackson has concocted fits in the category of Beyond Normal Human Understanding. At least, it's beyond my capacity to fully understand."

Just as important as my dislike of the transaction was that, to my certain knowledge, Roger questioned whether I had what it took to be a partner at Winchester & Wells. I was nearing the point when I would either make partner or need to leave for another firm. In my mind, it was unlikely that I would be elected to the partnership over Roger's objections, and I had taken a few tentative steps to find another place to practice law. Because I was aware of Roger's animosity, I was careful what I said in his presence, sometimes to the detriment of the transaction, the firm, and my self-esteem. In the meantime, my general tactic was to stay as far away from Roger as humanly possible. Whatever future I had at Winchester & Wells depended on a careful balance between helpfulness and respectful distance.

Unfortunately, today was not a day to avoid Roger. After I got into my office and read a stack of messages, I immediately called Roger's secretary to see if he was in and could see me. He could, and I walked down the hall to the door of his office.

***

You might have noticed a similarity between the name of the firm and that of its currently most important client. The similarity is because Jackson Winchester, the chairman of MSA, was the great-great-grandson of the founder of the firm and brother of one of its current partners, Stephen Winchester.

Jackson's father, Marshall Winchester, went to law school before taking over MSA, but he never liked practicing law. The long hours were too constricting on his golf game. "Marsh" Winchester practiced law briefly before the Second World War. After the war, he "retired" into the savings and loan business. His father left him plenty of money, and MSA gave him something to do and a position in Houston society. During his lifetime, until near the very end, the life of a savings banker was easy. Marshall's second son, Stephen, had become a partner in Winchester & Wells a few years earlier—a very important partner, but that part of the story will have to wait.

As I walked into Roger's office, he was sitting at his French provincial desk, dressed (as always) in an expensive Armani suit, an exception to the firm's Brooks Brothers/ Norton Ditto standard. He was intently staring into the darkness of a cup of coffee, possibly contemplating the well-deserved martini he intended to devour at lunch.

He looked up and motioned for me to sit down. "You heard the news?"

"Yes."

"What do you think?" Though he had them, Roger normally never initiated an idea in tense situations. He contrived to allow others to "have the idea." That way, if something went wrong, he had deniability. It was one of the shrewd facets of his personality that I found less than attractive.

"Do you think the transaction will continue after this crash?" I responded this way to buy time to respond to the big question before us. I knew that Jackson and MSA had too much invested in the transaction to let it die due to the crash. The real question was, "What should we do next?"

Roger paused a moment as if thinking about the option of not going forward with the deal, which he was not; then, he replied to my question. "We are all sorry that Frank and Don died, but let's face it—they were not the force behind MSA, nor do their deaths change anything. Jackson is the person everyone is counting on to make the transaction work, and Jackson is just fine."

Frank was Frank Johnson, the president of Marshland Savings, and *Don* was Don Mendoza, its chief financial officer, the two executives who died in the crash.

I continued to try to buy time and get information. "Have you talked to Jackson?"

"Briefly. Of course, he is upset. However, he is already thinking about who might become the president and chief financial officer. The CFO will come from inside. Getting someone from outside up to speed during a complicated transaction would be difficult. The presidency of MSA is more complicated. Jackson may take the title of president of Marshland Savings Association himself until the transaction is closed."

"Perhaps that would make things easier," I replied.

I was always a bit noncommittal with Roger, knowing I might be blamed if any decision went wrong. In this case, though, it would be obvious to everyone that, if Jackson took on the role of president, the confusion and anxiety among investment bankers and regulators would be minimized. What Roger said was true; Jackson was the key to the transaction's success. It was his ability, experience, and reputation that would make it work.

Then Roger asked the question of the day. "What needs to be done to get the deal back on track?"

I was now trapped into making some kind of recommendation. "Once new leadership is in place, the banking section will have to amend every filing MSA has in Dallas and Austin. The people chosen also will have to provide the agencies with their personal information. This almost certainly will delay the transaction a bit while they study the filings and ask questions."

This was an understatement. The FHLB and TSLD were both overwhelmed by problems in the industry, understaffed, and ill-equipped to evaluate and approve or disapprove a transaction as complex as the one Jackson envisioned. The FSLIC was similarly understaffed and did not have the money to close the many insolvent S&Ls across the United States.

No regulatory agency likes complex transactions, especially ones they cannot reasonably evaluate. In such a situation, delay is a common tactic. No one was ever fired from a federal or state agency for delay. Even before the crash, the transaction faced the reality that the regulators did not want to deal with the immense complexity and risks involved in the transaction for fear of making a wrong decision.

"On the SEC side," I said, "the registration statements for the stock and bonds, as well as the interests in the limited partnership, will have to be amended. The SEC will have comments and questions. It will take time to get them to respond to the filings and respond to questions. The corporate documents will not be so difficult. This will mostly involve changing names to get Frank's and Don's names off the documents and the new names on the documents. Of course, we will need information about the new people, and they will have to file forms with the regulators, where needed."

Roger then dropped his impossible request for the day. "Jackson wants the deal done now—as soon as possible."

"How soon?"

"As soon as you can. When will that be possible?" Roger was beginning the not-very-slow process of being in a position to blame someone else, me in particular, for the inevitable delays to come. The "as soon as *you* can" was telling.

The need to work on my résumé was growing moment by moment. "I cannot tell. We cannot make the filings this week because we need names and time to prepare and sign the documents. I can get Gwynn (the redhead from my apartment) and the others to begin reviewing the documents to be sure we are ready to amend them. If you can get Todd (Todd Rawlings, the head of the Banking Department of Winchester & Wells) to have his people look at the regulatory filings and get ready to make amended filings, things will go more quickly when Jackson makes up his mind who will replace Frank and Don. Today, I should make a long to-do list of what exactly needs to be done and think about the timing."

Roger pondered my words. "We will begin as you recommend. I will tell Jackson we are working on making changes in the documents and filings and get him to make some decisions. I will light a fire under the process of getting Frank and Don replaced. I will also talk to Todd and get his people moving."

The words, *I will light a fire under the process of getting Frank and Don replaced*, got me thinking. It was remarkable how suddenly two people we both knew well and had worked with on a day-by-day basis for months were now figures referred to in the past tense.

In a few weeks, they will be completely forgotten, I thought.

The events of the day and Roger's words were a reminder that life is short. *There are no guarantees*, I thought. If, lost in thought after lunch today, I stepped onto Louisiana

Avenue in front of an oncoming car, by Wednesday I would be in the past tense and, in a short time, forgotten. Gwynn eventually would meet someone else, get married, and have a family. I would become nothing more than a long-ago fling. My friends would come to the funeral, grieve, and continue on with their busy lives. Twenty years later, they might have difficulty remembering my name.

"Remember that guy at Winchester & Wells who stepped out in front of a car? What was his name? I can't recall?"

Many of the things I felt so meaningful and important were fleeting experiences in the lives of most of those around me.

I pondered this somber thought momentarily, then asked, "Do you know when the funerals will be?"

"No. Jackson and I did not discuss it. I guess when the bodies are returned to Houston, the families will make arrangements. Next week, probably."

Our conversation went on for a few more minutes, and then Roger waved his right hand and said, "You better get started,"

I left to get to work on the transaction.

The Transaction

AS I WALKED BACK TO my office, I pondered "The Transaction," as we called it, and its many complicated features. A new holding company was to be formed for MSA, into which Jackson, the SFIP investors, and a few other shareholders would exchange their shares in a merger. The new holding company would also issue common stock and high-yield bonds to the public in registrations with the Securities and Exchange Commission, commonly known as the SEC.

When the holding company was formed, two other savings associations would be merged into MSA, substantially increasing its size.

As if that were not enough, the last component involved the creation of MSA Real Estate Holdings, LLP (MSRH), which would house certain real estate development loans and properties of the combined savings associations, so that they could be disposed of in an orderly way and the proceeds reinvested. In this final step, MSRH was going to issue investment units, which units were being registered with the SEC and sold to the public, immediately lowering the risk of those assets to MSA and the FSLIC, had there been a failure of one of the institutions. It was an important incentive for the regulators to approve the transaction.

The transaction involved filings with the Federal Home Loan Bank Board (FHLBB), the Texas Savings and Load Department (TSLD), the Federal Savings and Loan Insurance Corporation (FSLIC), and the SEC, not to mention filings in states where the securities were to be sold.

There were multiple Houston and New York law firms involved. In fact, almost every major firm in Houston had some part in the transaction because several commercial banks, three investment banks, and three savings and loan associations were involved. This was by far the most complex and difficult of all the transactions that Jack Winchester ever concocted in a long life of mystifying Wall Street. It was an enormously complicated transaction, and I was the senior associate overseeing the implementation of the project. If anything went seriously wrong and it was my fault, my career at the firm was over. *I really need to work on my resume.* I thought to myself.

The merger of two S&Ls into MSA to form one larger entity was, in many ways, the center of the transaction and the source of complexity. Jackson had carefully chosen these institutions to maximize the incentive of regulators to approve the transaction as quickly as possible. One of the S&Ls was owned or controlled by an individual the regulators were desperate to get out of the business. The other was highly respected and gave the transaction instant credibility with the regulators and business community, as well as increasing the potential for success.

The first of the two savings and loans to be merged with MSA was West Isle Savings Association, or what we called WISA. WISA was owned and controlled by one of the most flamboyant and colorful characters in the savings and loan industry. Albert "Big Al" Renaldi was well known in the Houston/Galveston area and its business community.

Big Al grew up in Galveston, the son of a middle-class family. As the name "Big Al" implies, Albert Renaldi was physically huge. He attended the University of Texas, where he played right guard. Upon graduation, he was picked up by the Houston Oilers and became one of their most popular players with the Houston audience—a local boy made good.

After his pro career ended (carrying three hundred pounds is not good for the joints), Big Al returned to Galveston, running a small-time real estate operation financed from his football earnings. Over the years, his small operation grew into a pretty big company. Along the Gulf Coast, Big Al was a player in the smaller apartment and strip mall shopping center business before the real estate crash of the 1980s.

Big Al's family was part of a bigger Renaldi family, some of whom still lived in or near Galveston. In the early twentieth century, many Italian immigrants came to Galveston. Its status as a seaport and the distance between Galveston Island and Houston made it a perfect place to conduct gambling businesses, prostitution, and other illegal activities. Over time, Galveston achieved the reputation of a place where crooked politicians, criminal activity, bootlegging, prostitution, protection rackets, and other dubious enterprises flourished.

In this environment, Giuseppe "Pretty Boy" Renaldi made his reputation. He ran one of the two biggest and most profitable gambling and prostitution businesses on Galveston Isle. He built a dinner club across from Galveston Beach that rivaled his more famous competitor, the Maceo family. This dinner club, which was famous for its food, was even more famous for its back room. It was the initial center of the Renaldi business empire.

Pretty Boy's little brother, Albert, who had a flair for numbers, became his business partner. Big Al was Albert's grandson but inherited Giuseppe's size and outsized personality. Unfortunately, Big Al was not easy to get along with, and his reputation for honesty and loyalty was less than stellar.

Another Italian family, the Maceo family, was famous in Galveston for its good manners, loyalty to business associates, and generosity to the community. The Renaldi family was different. It had a reputation for self-centered ruthlessness. Over time, as the economy worsened, Big Al began to have difficulties gaining financing for his real estate holdings from his many friends from his career with the Oilers.

As one of the other lawyers told me, "Big Al was never terribly picky about where he gets money, recently much of which comes from institutions with nebulous connections with the underworld."

When the S&L industry was deregulated, Big Al purchased a small S&L on Galveston Isle, West Isle Savings Association, and ballooned it to over $300 million in assets. Most of those assets were real estate development loans to friends of Big Al who owned savings and loans that did business with Big Al. It was a great arrangement for all concerned—until the loans came due, and there was no way to repay or refinance them.

Hence, his participation in the transaction.

If Jackson Winchester was the most arrogant person I had ever met, Big Al Renaldi was the biggest bully. Early in life, Big Al learned to use his bulk to shatter opposition on the front line. He transferred this tactic into his business career, where it was much less successful or attractive. In negotiations, he was given to yelling, pounding the table, angrily standing in the face of his physically smaller opponents, threatening and generally intimidating everyone in the room.

He had employed this tactic on various occasions against Roger, me, Jackson, the other lawyers and accountants involved, and every single officer of MSA. In recent negotiations, it became obvious that Frank and Don did not like the inclusion of WISA or Big Al in the transaction. During one particular meeting called to address the subject of documentary deficiencies in the real estate files of WISA, there was a big confrontation.

Big Al was indignant at a suggestion that his files were not appropriately documented. He rose from his chair and came after me, screaming, "I will break your skinny neck."

I played a bit of football myself in high school and am pretty decent with my fists, but facing down a frenzied three-hundred-pound opponent was a frightening possibility. I tried to pretend I wasn't scared. But I was.

After cooling down, Big Al eventually agreed to hire a law firm to see that the problem was resolved. Sure enough, he hired one of the best real estate firms in Houston, and after a few weeks, we verified that the files were appropriately documented.

In the process, much of the original documentation was somehow accidentally destroyed so that neither the firms involved nor the regulators could reconstruct the past with complete accuracy.

A few days later, MSA called another meeting with Big Al and WISA about the transaction. This time, the discussion dealt with the financial disclosures in the registration statements with the SEC concerning the real estate of WISA to be included in the transaction. It again became obvious that Frank and Don did not want WISA to participate in the transaction. Again, Big Al blew up, laying hands on Frank before his own employees restrained him. He threatened both Frank and Don personally if the transaction did not go through.

"I know what you guys are up to, and if you try to kill this deal, it's not going to go well for you. Believe me, it is not going to go well at all."

I had heard Big Al blow up on several occasions. I was accustomed to it. This was different. For the first time, I sensed desperation in his voice. He was a man who might do anything to get what he wanted under ordinary circumstances. These circumstances were anything but ordinary. Given that Frank and Don were dead, those threats seemed potentially more than simple bullying.

The other major participant in the transaction was as different from Big Al as possible. Solomon Lewinsky was born in Houston and raised near what is today Meyerland, which at the time was a growing, prosperous Jewish community in the southwest part of the city. Sol grew up in a middle-class Jewish family, attending the Brit Shalom synagogue on Bellaire Boulevard.

When he finished high school, Sol attended Rice University, which at the time was free to any student who could get admitted. Sol was an excellent student, majoring in civil engineering and business. After graduation, he worked in a construction firm for a while and then went into business for himself. If Big Al was my least favorite participant in the transaction, Sol Lewinsky was my favorite. He exuded quiet intelligence and business competence. He was invariably courteous and never raised his voice, no matter how tense the situation. When he spoke, everyone, even Jackson, listened intently.

Somewhere along the way, Sol Lewinsky and Jackson Winchester became friends. Although Sol was older, they initially met socially while Jackson was an investment banker in New York. Since Texans everywhere have an immediate rapport, their friendship was cemented over a late-night dinner at the 21 Club, where Jackson was a frequent and welcome guest.

By the time Jackson moved back to Houston, Sol was the president and chairman of a middle-sized publicly traded real estate company. Lewinsky had begun his independent business career as a successful real estate investor and developer. By the 1980s, his interests went far beyond real estate. His small empire included insurance, a couple of small commercial banks, and a variety of other businesses. In the late 1960s, friends in the Beaumont area decided to sell their savings and loan and retire. Sol made an offer on the savings and loan, purchased it, and changed its name to Global Savings Association, or what we referred to as GSA.

GSA was a traditional savings and loan association. Sol, however, had not made his reputation by being foolish or shortsighted. He was among the first people to realize that the savings and loan business was changing, and its fundamental economics were no longer valid and likely to succeed. He formed a mortgage company that originated single-family residential loans, selling them into the market while keeping a fee for originating the loan and the servicing rights, which were valuable. He carefully took his losses on older single-family loans when he could use the loss to offset gains. Finally, he gradually created GSA's ability to originate commercial loans.

In GSA's home-lending operations, Sol emphasized adjustable-rate loans. In the residential area, he concentrated on the least risky side of the business—large so-called "jumbo" loans to wealthy individuals who made substantial down payments. In the commercial-loan area, he was conservative and careful to whom he lent money and how much equity his borrowers had to lose in the event of a default.

"People with a lot of skin in the game are the best borrowers," he used to say.

GSA packaged most of its fixed-rate loans so that they could be sold to Ginnie Mae or Freddie Mac. Sol did not keep any risk he could avoid keeping. GSA traded Ginnie Mae and Freddie Mac securities, though not on the scale that MSA engaged in the practice. Its hedging operations were mostly directed toward minimizing the risk of holding originated fixed-rate loans until they could be sold into the market.

Each time the federal government gave S&Ls the right to conduct additional businesses, Sol studied the business, and if it would work as a part of his business strategy, he entered it.

Lewinsky's participation in the transaction assured the regulators that a respected, long-term member of their business community would be involved, at least tangentially, in the business after the transaction was approved.

One of the regulators recently said to me privately, "If this transaction is approved, it will be because of Sol Lewinsky."

It had been obvious for some time that Sol Lewinsky held no higher opinion of Big Al than anyone else involved; it was obvious that he did not trust or like Big Al. Unless it was important, Sol was known to call ahead to see if Big Al would be attending a meeting. If the answer was yes, he often sent someone else.

At meetings, Sol sat alone or with those from GSA. A slender, wizened figure with horned-rimmed glasses, he carried a small notebook bound in leather, a ruler, a pen, and an ever-present financial calculator. He took careful notes during any discussion, even if one of his assistants was present doing the same. During the conversation, it often appeared that he was not paying attention. In truth, he was listening carefully, jotting down notes, and thinking ahead.

Jackson initially wanted Sol to take the job as vice chairman of the board of the combined savings and loan, which was to be renamed Texas Global Savings Association. Saul rejected that offer, agreeing only to stay on as a consultant and adviser. The merger agreement made it clear that Sol would have no continuing interest or ability to influence Texas Global Savings and Loan Association. He would only give advice. Jackson had been disappointed at this but understood, once Sol explained that this was part of a retirement strategy.

Sol proclaimed, "I am aging and want to spend more time with my grandchildren and family."

To facilitate estate planning, Sol wanted a third of the purchase price of GSA in cash, roughly its current book value. The remainder he would take in stock.

Only recently did it occur to me that Sol might not think Jackson could successfully manage the combined association and was getting enough cash out for himself and his investors to hedge a future loss. In a sense, Sol was saying goodbye to the savings and loan industry, while appearing to retain an interest in the business.

Interestingly, Sol liked me and appreciated my role in the transaction. He was wary, however, of Roger. During business negotiations, he would sit near me, and we would have a chance to talk. I developed the opinion that Sol thought of me as a genial human golden retriever. In Sol's mind, I was competent at retrieving birds in swampy water that Sol did not want to get into, disinclined to bite strangers, and loyal to my masters—all qualities Sol appreciated.

If I objected to a point, indicating that it didn't make sense to structure the transaction in some way, Sol often looked my way, quietly nodding. If he thought I had made an error of judgment in recommending a course of action, he looked at me quietly, signaling that he wished I would change my mind. During breaks, he occasionally gave me his opinion of the transaction and where it stood.

Recently, Sol had begun to indicate reservations about the transaction. During breaks in negotiations, he asked me questions like, "Do you think the regulators will approve this?" or "Do you think a large savings and loan that is in the business of making loans, trading government securities, and buying and selling commercial real estate is a sound business plan?" In one of our recent meetings, he looked me straight in the eyes and asked, "Do you really think Jackson can pull this off?"

I tried to be convincingly positive.

After a recent blowup, Sol gave his solemn opinion of Big Al. "In my faith, we are warned to have nothing to do with foolish or violent men. You ought to read our holy books."

He walked away without saying more. He had signaled why he was unwilling to be business partners with Albert Renaldi, perhaps warning me as well. My bet was that Sol and his investors would sell any shares they received in the transaction, just as soon as any waiting period was over.

Originally, there had been another participant in the transaction—Vixette Savings Association (VSA), located in a suburb of Dallas. VSA was owned by one Fred Vixette, a flamboyant real estate developer, headquartered in McKinney, Texas. VSA had been a sleepy local institution that made home loans in a rapidly growing area, under the name McKinney Savings & Loan Association. When Vixette purchased the savings and loan, he modestly renamed it after himself and completely altered its fundamental business plan.

When purchased, VSA had approximately $50 million in total assets. Within five years, that number approached $600 million. The vast majority of these loans were real estate construction and development loans, many of which were reaching the point when they would either go into permanent financing or default. For many of them, default was the only option. More seriously, some of the loans had been made in violation of a supervisory agreement that VSA was forced to enter into with the FHLBB after an examination revealed major problems.

Jackson felt including VSA in the transaction gave regulators an overwhelming impetus to approve it. No one in the business felt that VSA would be a survivor. It would inevitably be closed. VSA was a "zombie bank" and could not possibly survive the current restructuring of the industry and the real estate crisis in Texas. Word on the street was that VSA symbolized the excesses that doomed many savings associations.

Vixette himself was a not-so-charming con man. His reputation for lies and business skullduggery was legendary, as was his questionable judgment. He went around Dallas loudly proclaiming that he was "Carl's man in Texas," a reference to the reputed head of the Louisiana underworld.

He also was known to loudly proclaim in restaurants and business meetings that he was associated with the CIA and involved in "important CIA business in Latin America."

In a way, Vixette's behavior, if true, would have given him perfect cover. Everyone believed he was lying all the time. No one believed anyone in authority would trust his judgment on any conceivable matter of national security. Furthermore, no one believed that an organization as shrewd as the Mafia would have such a fool as a partner. If his lies had been true, Fred Vixette would have been the Scarlet Pimpernel of the savings and loan industry and CIA/Mafia partnership, an apparent fool who was, in fact, a deadly and dangerous agent. I thought Fred was an idiot.

Months ago, Roger and I had our first run-in about including VSA in the transaction. Todd and the banking section called me to his office and gave me the following information:

"VSA is a sewer, a black hole of bad loans made to untrustworthy borrowers. Including VSA in the transaction means that we have to estimate the losses on these loans in order to ask for the appropriate amount of assistance and forbearance from the FSLIC. No one in the banking section of Winchester & Wells, or Jackson's accounting firm, or among the investment banking firms involved in the transaction thinks it is remotely possible to accurately gauge the losses VSA might incur on its loan portfolio. VSA has to go if Roger wants the transaction to gain approval."

There was a big confrontation, first between Roger and me, then later with Jackson, about removing the VSA from the transaction. When I went to Roger to give him the same information that Todd had given to me, he initially blew up.

"I don't know why, but I think you are intentionally trying to kill this deal."

My response was denial. "Roger, I am not trying to kill this deal. I am trying to tell you that, if we want approval and avoid the risk of getting Jackson into what could be a terrible situation, we need to cut our losses and remove VSA from the transaction."

After a visit with Todd, Roger agreed to confront Jackson when I was present. Jackson resisted our arguments until his friends from Wall Street threatened to abort the deal unless VSA was removed.

In the end, neither Jackson nor Roger could defend VSA's inclusion in the transaction, and a meeting was called to give Vixette the bad news. Vixette blustered and threatened Jackson, MSA, the other participants, and the investment bankers. He made dark predictions about the results if VSA were not included.

"I know too much. I have friends in Washington, just like Jackson. He cannot afford to cross me."

But in the end, VSA was out.

***

As I walked back to my office through the lovely, picture-lined corridors of Winchester & Wells, I pondered Roger, my reservations with the transaction, and the future. Generally, when a transaction approached that moment in time when it either would close or be abandoned by the parties, there was a sense of excitement in the air. Particularly if a hard transaction finally was coming to a successful end, a kind of elation and feeling of success would develop on the team that was putting the deal together. The MSA Acquisition and Restructuring Plan, as the transaction was described in official communications, was coming to its end with no positive feelings. It was as if the transaction had taken on a life of its own, and great darkness surrounded it. The more we worked, the darker the clouds around us became. Instead of reaching a point of clarity, Jackson's brainchild became increasingly obtuse, complex, and difficult to close. Slowly but surely, the transaction was drawing all participants, human and corporate, into a dark financial and business vortex from which there was no escape.

As far as I was concerned, there was no elation or anticipation. There was only fear, if the transaction were not to close, and dread of what might happen if it did.

Inconvenient Facts

AS I WALKED TO MY office, the doomed King Air crash site, five hundred miles away in Presidio County, was a scene of frenetic activity. People from the border patrol, the National Transportation Safety Board (NTSB), the Bureau of Alcohol, Tobacco, and Firearms (ATF), the Drug Enforcement Administration (DEA), the FBI, and the Presidio County Sheriff's Office—a whole host of investigators—were busily examining the crash site like bees hovering around a blooming flower bed.

The hikers, who saw the flaming plane fall from the sky, did not immediately try to reach the crash site. It was too dark and too dangerous for them to attempt to reach the site at night. When morning came, one of them suggested the group investigate, so they set out to find any remnant of the fiery ball they had seen fall from the sky the night before.

When they reached the site, it was afternoon. They immediately noticed the odor of jet fuel, burned plastic, charred human flesh, and marijuana. They found the King Air scattered down a small valley bordered by mounds of brown and gray rock and cactus, strewn about in a swath of twisted steel and aluminum, shattered plastic, and bits of human remains. At the end of the valley, the plane finally hit the side of a small mountain and completely disintegrated. As they searched, they also found remnants of packages of marijuana and more than a few plastic bags of white powder.

Fairly quickly, their guide suggested leaving.

"We need to get out of here and notify someone. Don't touch anything because we do not want our fingerprints on any of the debris—and put down those plastic bags."

The stench was such that no one disagreed.

When they returned to the main road where they had left their vehicles, they ran into a border patrol agent and reported the crash. The border patrol and the local sheriff went to the site, took one look, and immediately called the NTSB, ATF, and FBI.

***

The next morning, the FBI, NTSB, local authorities, border patrol, and ATF visited the site. By this time, the investigators were operating on the assumption that the plane was what was left of an overdue flight from Mexico to Houston containing two businessmen returning from a weekend hunting. It did not take long to determine that this was no ordinary private plane incident. The presence of cocaine and marijuana was enough to make the crash a drug-related incident. There were other peculiarities at the crash site that the FBI and other investigators noticed.

The presence of prominent businesspersons from Houston on the plane was enough to catch the attention of the FBI and other agencies. One other fact went unmentioned in the news reports: neither the NTSB nor FBI officials thought it likely that the crash was a result of equipment failure or pilot error. They could not be sure without additional investigation, but they felt that there had been more than one explosion, an initial explosion that crippled the plane, a second explosion that ended the flight, and a final explosion and complete destruction of the craft when it hit the rough terrain in the Chinati Mountains.

That evening, the FBI agents went home to El Paso, 250 miles away, and called Washington and Houston. They informed Washington that the El Paso office of the FBI would be happy to continue to monitor the crash site, but the investigation, they felt, should be run out of Houston. Washington would need to be involved, as it was likely that the answers to some of the questions that investigators had would be found in Mexico, not the United States. Washington agreed, and the Houston office took over primary responsibility for the investigation beyond the crash site itself.

***

Miles to the south, the Watcher was hiking toward a small northern Mexican town where he had distant relatives, family about whom no one else would know. He had not seen them for many years—long before his parents died. He knew little about them but thought they would welcome a visit. *They will take me in for a while,* he thought.

He needed time to think and recover from the trauma of the incident. He also needed a place where whoever ordered the bombing of the plane would be unlikely to find him, at least for a while.

After Mirador rolled down the draw into the dry creek bed near the hunting camp, he noticed his shoulder was bleeding due to the failed assassination attempt. The wound was superficial but needed emergency treatment. In order to clean and bandage the wound, he moved slightly to the north of his position into the surrounding rock and brush, away from the hunting camp and the direction of the rifle fire that had wounded him.

Whoever fired the shot eventually would come to examine the site from which he had been watching the camp, hoping to find a body. When the assassin did not find a body, he would try to find the Watcher and finish the job. The assassin would not want to inform his principals that he had failed, and Mirador was on the loose. People who hire a hitman do not like failure or loose ends.

The Watcher was certain the shot that wounded him was fired by a professional using a sniper rifle designed to hit a human target at long distances. Only the flash of a strange light, the crashing thunder, and his momentary loss of balance had saved his life. The assassin would know the Watcher would try to outsmart and find him first. He would be on high alert. The next hours would be a game of cat and mouse.

Mirador intended to be the cat. He thought it best to move away from the site beyond the line of travel the assassin would follow to verify his kill shot had only wounded his intended victim. It was a good idea to take a path in the general direction of the exfiltration site, just in case his principals had not betrayed him and came looking for him. Mirador doubted this would be the case.

I need to choose a course that is not suspicious to the assassin and find a place to ambush him, Mirador thought.

As Mirador bandaged his wounds and planned his next move, on the other side of the valley, the assassin took a moment to gather his thoughts and consider his best course of action. He was sure that the thunder, odd lightning, and Mirador's unexpected movement had put his aim off by just enough to save the Watcher's life. If the assassin was correct, and Mirador was alive, he needed to finish the job he had been hired to do.

My employers will not want to deal with an angry Special Forces operator on the loose—and I do not want to deal with angry and disappointed employers of the kind that hire hit men, he thought. *I need to find Mirador and finish the job.*

The assassin put his rifle strap over his shoulder, though he was fairly sure he would not need the rifle. Unless he was extremely lucky, if he found Mirador, their confrontation would be up close and personal. They were both professionals. He might get a chance to fire a rifle from behind cover in the rocky and rough terrain, but it was more likely he would need his pistol or knife. Mirador had just escaped an assassin's bullet. He was too shrewd to expose himself in a way that would permit a long shot with a sniper rifle.

The assassin worked his way from the site of his original shot toward where his intended victim had been watching the camp. He moved carefully and watchfully, knowing Mirador might be waiting or on his way to find him to gain the element of surprise. It was slow work.

When he reached the site where Mirador had been watching the compound, he saw traces of blood but no sign of heavy bleeding. The assassin noted that Mirador had retrieved his weapons and pack, leaving nothing behind but a few food wrappers. Mirador would have his weapons in any confrontation.

The assassin made his way carefully down the slope to the bottom of the rocky, dry creek bed, where Mirador had stopped, cleaned, and bandaged his wounds and set out down the gulch, veering off to the north.

As he continued the search, signs of blood were absent, meaning that Mirador had successfully stopped the bleeding. This was not good news. The absence of blood meant he would not meet a bleeding, weak, and depleted adversary. He could not easily follow the trail. Mirador was wise enough in the ways of special operatives to leave few clues to his path. (Mirador was careful to leave few clues, so as not to give the assassin reason to suspect he might be walking into a trap, but he left clues enough to keep his adversary on a chosen path.)

Hours passed as the assassin, himself former Special Forces, stalked his prey. By now, the storm was upon him in full force. The wind and rain meant he could only make his way with some difficulty. The weather favored his quarry. Wind and rain would make it much harder for either to see or hear the other approaching. Mirador had the advantage of choosing the place and time of their meeting. The advantage had shifted from the hunter to the hunted, who possibly was already at a chosen site, waiting patiently.

Eventually, the assassin found himself at the mouth of a small canyon. He knew the place from maps he had studied while preparing for the mission. Mirador would have studied the same maps. While a single set of muddy footprints led into the canyon—and the canyon would be a relatively good place to set a trap—the assassin was suspicious. Mirador would find it hard to escape from the canyon, with its steep walls, and would know that he might face his adversary before climbing out on the other side. On the other hand, the assassin would find it hard to search the canyon and might be surprised amid the dirt-gray boulders and rough terrain. On the ridges that formed three sides of the canyon, the assassin might easily be surprised and disadvantaged.

It was hard to find the path Mirador had taken. Concerned about the increasing darkness and the difficulty of tracking his quarry in the night, where Mirador would definitely have the advantage, the assassin determined to backtrack to discover whether his prey might have doubled back.

He paused underneath a seven-foot-tall rock, seeking protection from the wind and rain. Suddenly, a wet, dead weight of bone and muscle fell on his back, and two strong arms pinned him to the ground. A blow to the head caused him to lose consciousness. Quickly, the assassin's hands were tied behind his back, and just as quickly, his feet. Mirador had won a few calf-roping contests in his youth, and the assassin was the victim of that experience, plus many years of Special Forces training.

Mirador turned the man over and stared. He recognized the face from Vietnam. *What do you know. It's Harry Dent.*

Mirador now recognized the truth and the worst of his situation: He had not been shot by a random guard hired by those in the camp. Dent had been hired to kill him. He had been betrayed.

Mirador had heard that Dent had left the military after Vietnam, and there were rumors of his activities as a hired assassin. Dent never had a good reputation in Vietnam or anywhere else. If Dent was involved, the people who hired him were definitely not on the side of the angels. *The only people who knew I was in Mexico and who could have hired Dent and ordered a hit are in the military or whatever agency asked that I be sent to Mexico.*

Mirador was nearly certain the responsible parties were not in the Army Special Forces. It was more likely that he had been betrayed by someone in the agency who had asked for the camp to be watched. That "someone"—or a hireling or higher-up—could have hired Harry Dent. Mirador had not been interested in Dent in Vietnam or thereafter. Now, he was extremely interested in Harry Dent and even more interested in whoever employed him.

Dent regained consciousness and tried to speak, "Mirador, please, I did not—"

The words were hardly out of Dent's mouth when Mirador turned toward his would-be assassin. "Harry, you are going to tell me all you know."

***

In Houston, there was another confrontation. Jackson Winchester had plenty to lose if the transaction failed to close and was unhappy about the King Air crash. He had not been pleased about the hastily called meeting in Mexico. He had not liked the request to send Frank and Don. He especially did not like sending Don, whom he regarded as a goody-goody. He did not like the increasing opinion among his partners that he should consider abandoning the transaction and sell MSA to someone else, perhaps someone from Mexico, of whom the United States government might approve. Above all, he did not trust his partners in Mexico, their friends on the United States side of the border, or his friends in Washington and New York.

His sources in Washington had long ago told him that the FHLBB was not favorable toward the transaction, nor was it inclined to approve such a complex transaction any time soon. His friends in government were not anxious to do any favors that, if something went wrong, might end their political careers, elected or bureaucratic. His friends on Wall Street were similarly cautious. Wealthy, powerful, and influential people did not like negative publicity. An unexplained plane crash involves negative publicity.

In the beginning, everyone involved realized the potential benefits of the transaction for MSA, for the other S&Ls involved, for their investors, and for the investment bankers, as well as for the regulators and for the industry as a whole—if it worked.

If Jackson could find a way to unlock hidden value in the real estate and commercial loan portfolios of Texas's zombie banks, it would save billions of dollars and not a few careers in Washington. There would be plenty of money made by Wall Street and by members of Congress, trading on their exemption from insider trading rules. More importantly, many transactions, which should never see the light of day, would never be uncovered by zealous prosecutors. If Jackson was successful, everyone would win.

In response to all inquiries, Jackson kept "on message," continuing to press his case. His friends on Wall Street, always ready to pocket a six- or seven-figure investment banking fee, supported him as best they could. Nevertheless, Jackson knew it was fish-or-cut bait time for everyone.

Late in the evening, two days after the crash, Jackson received a call he had been dreading. The voice on the other end of the line was matter-of-fact.

"Jackson, the boss-man wants to know if you really believe you can pull this off."

"I do. However, I need support. The FHLBB needs to approve the transaction. Without that, we cannot move forward. If the FHLBB approves the transaction, regulators in Austin will follow their lead. Once the regulators approve the transaction, I think the SEC will prioritize the deal and feel pressured to approve it. We can close in just a few weeks."

"So, what do you want us to do?"

"Get me regulatory approval."

The voice on the other end of the line paused as if to ponder what to say next.

Taking advantage of the silence, Jackson asked his own question. "Tell me about the crash."

"We don't know much. Our sources at the FBI tell us that the agencies involved do not believe the crash was accidental. There were substantial amounts of drugs aboard the aircraft when it crashed. Cocaine and marijuana. Fortunately, everyone was killed, so there are no eyewitnesses for the FBI to interrogate. The folks in Mexico will never be interrogated or seriously investigated. As it stands, based on what we know, we don't think that the investigation will get very far.

"Unfortunately, it may seem to the FBI that your people were in bed with drug lords in Mexico, but it will not go any further. In some ways, it may even be a good thing the way things worked out, as the evidence points toward Mexican drugs as a motive for the bombing and Mexican drug lords as responsible. I am afraid that the former president of MSA will not come out of this looking very good."

Jackson was furious. "What I want to know is this: what in the world were drugs doing on my plane?"

"I can't tell you. I can tell you that the FBI believes they were there. The crash was part of an operation of some sort, we think perhaps involving a rogue Special Forces officer named John Mirador. We don't believe he was supposed to be where he was, nor do we know for whom he worked. Mirador has disappeared, and no one seems to know where he is. The authorities are looking for him. Frankly, I doubt he will try to reenter the United States, at least not if he is smart.

"There will be an investigation but it will not gain traction, nor will it uncover the responsible parties. We will see to that behind the scenes. I would not worry if I were you, though you and your people will undoubtedly be questioned. However, there will be no more to it than answering questions from the FBI."

"Questions?"

"Yes, questions. It is standard procedure. The FBI will want to question you and your top people. They also will visit with people in your legal, accounting, and investment banking firms to see if they know anything, which they don't. Eventually, the regulators will want to visit with you before the deal is approved. You were not in Mexico and obviously do not know anything."

"Shit. OK. I will be ready when they come. I will see that our lawyers and accountants are prepared. Frankly, no one at MSA or any firm involved knows anything about the trip to Mexico. Frank or Don may have mentioned to someone that they were going hunting in Mexico, but that is all. I am the only one who knows that you requested a meeting. Who is this Mirador guy anyway?"

"Mirador was an asset on loan from one federal agency to another. Perhaps drug enforcement investigators were interested in the meeting. Mirador must have planted explosives on the plane for some reason. We are not sure why. In any case, that is the story we are hearing."

Jackson had been around long enough to know a concocted story when he heard one. *Whatever the truth is, this is not the truth—or at least, not the whole truth. For some reason, there were drugs on my plane when it mysteriously crashed, I might be tainted and could end up the fall guy. For some reason, they want to pin the crash on this guy Mirador.*

The story did not pass the plausibility test.

Most importantly, if Mirador or drug lords were found to be not involved, Jackson Winchester would be a prime suspect, suspected of being a drug runner and money launderer. This was not something Jackson wanted to contemplate. It might mean that certain people wanted to bring him down, while at the same time ending the transaction. He needed to be careful. His "friends" might not be friends for long.

Jackson did not want the person on the other end of the line to perceive his doubts about the storyline he was hearing. He decided to end the conversation.

"I can't understand what this is about. It does not involve Marshland or me. What I need is approval of the transaction." With that, he engaged in a few pleasantries and rang off.

After this conversation, one other call was made. A tentative decision was made to take steps to fast-track approval of the Marshland Real Estate–Backed Bond Transaction, as the regulators officially referred to the transaction.

Funerals for Two

A LITTLE OVER A WEEK after the crash, the authorities released what was left of the bodies for burial. Two of the families involved with MSA decided to have a joint funeral. None of the people killed was especially religious. Frank Johnson had been married only briefly to his second wife, Veronica, who was manifestly uninterested in planning his funeral. She was moving on.

The pilot's wife, who belonged to a church in another city, was so distraught at the prospect of raising her children alone that she was frozen by grief. His funeral was held privately in their hometown. She let it be known that she intended to move home as soon as possible to be near her parents and raise her children. MSA made a commitment to help her with the move, and insurance paid enough to get her back on her feet.

Betty Mendoza, the wife of the chief financial officer, Don Mendoza, was a Roman Catholic but only nominally so for many years. She rarely attended mass. His daughter attended an Episcopal church northeast of downtown, near what was called the Houston Heights. The daughter reached out to her mother and to Veronica Johnson, who agreed with her plan to hold the funeral at her church, which had once been a dwindling working-class congregation but was experiencing growth under a charismatic pastor and the gentrification of the Houston Heights area. The funeral was on a hot, humid, early fall day, one of those days when it is almost insufferable to be outdoors in Houston.

***

No one at Winchester & Wells was anxious to attend the funeral, but the firm felt that Roger and I should go. I went with Gwynn. Roger came with his current wife, looking like he wanted nothing more than to leave and find a place to drink. In one of his most uncommon moods, Roger looked worried.

Jackson was there alone, looking grim, bored, and distracted. Many of the staff and employees of MSA also attended. They looked saddened and distraught by the tragedy, especially those close to Don. More than a few congregation members came to support Judy Mendoza, the daughter, and her family. The sanctuary was not completely full, but pleasantly so. A lot of folks liked and grieved for Don Mendoza.

I was brought up Presbyterian. My father was a Presbyterian pastor. His religious parents raised their boys on a small ranch near Kerrville, Texas. Dad's name was William "Bill" Stone. He and my uncle, Benjamin "Ben" Stone, were brothers. When World War II began, Dad entered the Marine Corps, while Ben served in the navy. Ben served on a cruiser, saw only a little action in the European Theater, and came home relatively unaffected. After the war, Ben became an FBI agent and remained so until his recent retirement. In retirement, he formed an agency that did security consulting and private investigating work.

My father was an altogether different case. By the time he got to the South Pacific, the war was winding down, but he saw considerable action at both Iwo Jima and Okinawa, two of the bloodiest battles of the Pacific war. When hostilities ended, he was in training to participate in the invasion of Japan. It was rumored that as many as 500,000 or more Americans might die—and, as always, the marines would be first on the beach and committed to the most desperate and difficult battles. Dad had seen death up front and personal and wanted nothing to do with violence or armed conflict ever again. He was proud of his service but was under no illusions about the nature of war. He had seen terrible violence and death, enough for a lifetime. He decided to become a Presbyterian minister.

Upon returning to the States in late 1946, Dad married his high school sweetheart. Being poor and from Texas, he went to Austin Theological Seminary in Austin, Texas, on the GI Bill. He graduated in mid-1950. I was born a year later, and my brother was born just over a year after me. Mom worked as a schoolteacher before my brother and I were born. After my brother's birth, she worked in the home and supported my father as the pastor's wife for his congregations, a role she more or less loved.

My father's congregations were mostly in smaller, rural Texas towns, and our worship services were definitely "low church." Dad was simple and tried to keep his preaching simple and to the point. He never aspired to be a tall-steeple preacher. He just wanted to love people and help them through life. He loved his congregations, and they loved him in return.

One of Dad's favorite descriptions of his preaching was that he "knew how to put the cookie on the lowest shelf." Children, youth, and ordinary people could understand my father's preaching, appreciate his services, and respond to his obvious love and care for the people of his congregations. More sophisticated congregants also appreciated his intelligence and practical helpfulness. Wherever he lived, he was a much sought-after friend and counselor, even beyond the walls of whatever congregation we were serving.

Dad was of the opinion that weddings and funerals should last thirty minutes, with a reading of scriptures, a few prayers, and perhaps a hymn or two. He felt it should take "thirty minutes to marry 'em and thirty minutes to bury 'em." In rare cases, a family member would speak, giving a remembrance of the loved one. Nearly all the funerals I attended in my childhood were officiated by my father and conformed to his style.

My only wish as a child was that our Sunday worship services—especially the sermons (which I found boring and difficult to understand)—would conform to the same thirty-minute rule Dad applied to funerals and weddings. My brother and mother were the religious ones. I looked forward to Sunday lunch and sports with the guys until dark.

This service was different from those officiated by my father.

The priests met in the back of the congregation, wearing their white cassocks. While they were still in the outer area, we heard familiar words, "We brought nothing into this world, and we can certainly carry nothing out. The Lord gave, and the Lord hath taken away. Blessed be the name of the Lord," together with the assurance, "Neither death, nor life, nor angels, nor principalities, nor powers, nor things present, nor things to come, nor height, nor depth, nor any other creature, shall be able to separate us from the love of God, which is in Christ Jesus, our Lord."

For some reason, the phrase "We brought nothing into this world and we can certainly take nothing out" struck a chord and caused me to continue the meditation that had begun when Roger referred to Frank and Don in the past tense a few days earlier.

I was young and in the stage of life where men and women gather things to take through life. I was busy creating a career; finding a lovely and intelligent girlfriend and hopefully a wife; preparing to buy a house in West University Place, which was desirable for young attorneys and doctors; driving an expensive car to impress clients; and paying for a membership to the Athletic Club to stay in shape. I had a long list of things I wanted to gather from life.

The death of Frank and Don were reminders that the final journey is not always after a long and successful life. Death finds us all, sometimes sooner than we thought possible. In my childhood memory, I recalled a phrase from Psalms, encouraging the reader to "number our days so that we may become wise." The deaths of Frank and Don were a reminder that the verse contained an important truth.

I was comforted by the priest's assurance that nothing, not even demonic powers, could separate me from God's love, though for the time being, Gwynn's love was far more real and infinitely more important to me. Roger's doubt of my abilities and my resulting position in the firm certainly was not demonic, but I worried about the future and feared what might happen over the next months and years. I was troubled by the transaction and my need to impress Roger, who did have some power over the future. Perhaps my dreams and occasional unsteadiness were symptomatic of the pressure I was under at work. Then, there was Gwynn, whom I cared about and desperately wanted to impress. I had things on my mind. Even though I was no longer religious, the idea that my life, with all of its uncertainties, might be in the hands of a benevolent power was not unattractive.

My thoughts were interrupted by the processional and opening hymn. I am not much of a singer, and so I had a moment to reflect on my surroundings. Gwynn sat a respectful distance from me, far enough away to allay any suspicions by clients or members of the firm, yet close enough that I could sense her warmth, distant but silently inviting.

As pastors go, my father was a builder. The American church grew in the late 1950s and early 1960s, and having a pastor who could help renovate and expand was attractive. Some of the churches of my childhood were older, traditional structures, while others were modern buildings with only a few abstract stained-glass windows. One of them was a glorified A-frame with a dark-wood interior, which I loved. In one of our churches, my brother and I would hide before services in an unused passageway under the altar floor that led to the choir loft.

In contrast, this church was old, with ancient and lovely— though not expensive—stained-glass windows depicting the apostles' lives and scenes from Jesus' life. Behind the altar was a window depicting the Resurrection, the importance of which was emphasized by the angle of the afternoon sun streaming through the light of the white, yellow, and red figure of the risen Christ ascending to heaven. It was as if the architect intended the light to symbolize the Spirit of Christ streaming into the room.

I am a natural skeptic. However, in the quiet and beauty of the simple sanctuary, despite my carefully developed cynicism about all things religious, I was touched. I noticed how the sanctuary windows were located and filled with scenes from the Bible. Their alignment spoke of the infinite distance between heaven and earth being eliminated by the life of the Messiah. In this sanctuary, a worshipper was surrounded by the story of the Bible from beginning to end. Light pouring through the stained glass symbolized the Holy Spirit, which seemed, in some way, present in the pastors and congregation.

The pastor went on with words intended to comfort the family, commending Don and Frank to the mercy of God. I was pretty sure that only mercy could prevent some kind of judgment on Frank, at least. Don was a different and more likable sort. We had struck up a friendship over the months of preparing the transaction to close. His death was a personal loss.

There were more readings from scripture, which were chosen to comfort the family. Then, there was a longish prayer, followed by the Lord's Prayer. The congregation said a unison prayer for the families and the departed with bidding by the priest and responses from the congregation. The congregation sang another hymn, and a short homily focused on Frank and Don. Somehow, the pastor, who had known neither of them, made it seem like they had been close friends. Of course, he might have made them seem just a bit more religious and virtuous than they had been in reality, but that was forgivable. The purpose of a funeral is not to judge the departed but to comfort those they've left behind.

The service ended with a short prayer from the Episcopalian Book of Common Prayer:

> Father of All, we pray to thee for those whom we love but see no longer. Grant them thy peace; let light perpetual shine upon them; and in thy loving wisdom and almighty power work in them the good purpose of thy perfect will; through Jesus Christ our Lord. *Amen.*

After a closing hymn, the presiding minister stepped forward.

"The families have asked me to tell you that the burial will be private. Thank you all for coming, and may God bless you."

Simple and sweet. We were all relieved to avoid a long trip to two cemeteries and two more short services. In the Houston heat and humidity, it would have been unbearable.

As we left the sanctuary, Roger and his wife stopped to visit with us, and we visited with the MSA staff. We walked down the receiving line to give our condolences to the families.

When I came to Don Mendoza's daughter, Maria, she expressed her thanks, then looked into my eyes, and spoke unexpected words. "If you ever want to talk to someone, I would love to visit. I am sure that Father White would love to see you as well."

I was embarrassed and could not understand what in the world she meant to say. I had heard this congregation had a charismatic membership and immediately categorized her as a nutcase. It turned out, however, that her words were instrumental in my ultimate understanding of the deaths of Frank and Don and the circumstances surrounding them. At the time, I was just put off by her.

Near the front of the church, I caught sight of two people standing on the outskirts of the crowd, quietly observing everyone, including Gwynn and me. The man wore a nondescript, inexpensive dark suit, and the woman wore a dark dress designed to hide her figure. As the nephew of an FBI agent, I turned to Gwynn and said, "They look all the world like two police detectives in a television murder mystery who have come to the funeral to observe the suspects."

It never occurred to me that I might be included in the group of suspects.

Gwynn and I rode back downtown in silence, each of us lost in our own thoughts. We arrived at the firm in the late afternoon and went our separate ways. By six o'clock, I was tired and ready to quit. The day had been stressful. Besides, I had a good bit to think about and did not really want to stare at documents and make notes about changes any longer. I needed a glass of wine and a long conversation with Gwynn. Fortunately, she agreed.

Dinner for Two

THAT EVENING, I WAS IN the mood for steak. We went to a quiet, dark local steak house near the River Oaks area of Houston. After the past few days, we needed a treat, so I ordered a bottle of Malbec, which Gwynn liked, and I tolerated. As we sipped our wine (which I noticed Gwynn barely touched), it was obvious that we both had things on our minds. I decided to say something mildly diverting, like, "It was a nice funeral."

Gwynn did not grow up going to church or in a religious family. Her parents divorced when she was in junior high school (what today we call "middle school"), which began a period of rebellion that lasted beyond college. Her mother remarried and became somewhat religious, but Gwynn never went to church with her mother, except for Christmas and Easter. Her stepfather, who never attended church except for family events, tried to be nice but never bonded with his daughter. She grew up lonely and feeling unloved by the men in her family.

Her father married a "Derrick Doll" from the Houston Oilers, with whom he had a relationship before the divorce. He was a successful businessman, inclined to ignore his family duties, and his preoccupation with a new young wife created tensions. In the end, Gwynn developed a distant self-sufficiency and intuitively distrusted men. I had learned that she was a tough cookie in negotiations or when crossed but actually somewhat introverted and self-critical. Although outwardly self-confident, inside she never thought she was good enough.

Gwynn's father grew up in Odessa, Texas, working in the oil fields of West Texas before starting his own oil field supply business. In time, the business grew, and the family moved to Houston to take advantage of greater economic opportunity. After the divorce, he continued to grow the business, until recently, when he sold it to an overseas investor group. He spent most of his time with his new wife and family or at a farm he purchased in East Texas. He rarely saw his first child.

Gwynn and I met when she first joined the firm and ended up working with Roger. We had good chemistry from the beginning. I have a natural gentlemanly quality, born of growing up in a home where my father enforced gentlemanliness on his two not-always-gentlemanly sons.

My mother was determined that her boys would treat the girls right. Ultimately, my brother and I developed a kind reserve and regard for women that protected us from the worst possible experiences and attracted many women, especially pretty women accustomed to unwanted advances from men.

In retrospect, I realize that Gwynn found my quiet respectfulness safe and attractive. I was a little older and more experienced in business and law, allowing me to substitute just a bit for the father she wished she had. Over her first and second years at the firm, we worked together on various projects. Then, we were thrown together when Roger asked that I be on the team for the MSA transaction. Over the months we worked together on the transaction, I admired her work ethic, redheaded stubbornness, willingness to take on difficult assignments, and unfailing intelligence. Eventually, we became lovers.

She was not assigned to the transaction with negotiation in mind; she was too new to the firm for such an assignment. In the difficult due diligence period, however, she worked out many problems independently, presenting the partners and me with solutions, not more problems to solve. This was much appreciated. She proved to everyone that she was a good lawyer and deserved success at the firm and elsewhere.

In the 1980s, the rules for relationships between lawyers were not nearly as strict as today. (In my view, that strictness is an improvement in how law firms treat females.) When it became obvious that Gwynn and I were becoming romantically inclined, I took one short look at the Personnel Manual (given to every new lawyer and then ignored by everyone). The manual revealed that, as long as my advances were not unwanted, there was no absolute written barrier to our relationship, as long as our relationship did involve unwanted physical contact or the attempt to receive favors in return for professional advancement. As an associate, I felt I had little or no control over her future success at the firm. Eventually, my advances were definitely physical but also definitely not unwanted. I decided to ignore any potential problems with our relationship.

When I say that Gwynn and I had chemistry, the word *chemistry* should be underlined and in all capital letters. Gwynn had full-figured, athletic good looks that I—and almost everyone in the firm—found irresistible. She was tall, with features that not only involved beauty but also a kind of stateliness. She was normally quiet and a good listener. Her emerald eyes streamed a quiet intelligence that took in everything. Even when listening, she exuded a quiet self-command that drew attention and respect. When I first looked at her, I thought of her as a queen and, most recently, as the queen of my heart. Somehow, I knew almost from the beginning that no one would ever take her place in Arthur Stone's personal pantheon of "lovely women I have known." She was the best of the best.

Gwynn was a woman toward whom every eye turned when she entered a room with her long, athletic strides. Her long dark-auburn hair was striking. Her deep-green eyes had watery, liquid characteristics men found irresistible. For me, one look in those eyes and there was absolutely no one else in the room, making it important in business meetings to avoid that one long gaze that would freeze my mind. Much to my chagrin, my mind regularly went completely blank when she looked into my eyes. It had happened more than once. Sometimes people noticed. People who might use that information.

Looking at her across the table, I was in one of those blank-minded moods, so I said the only thing that came to my barely functioning mind.

"It was a good service. I'm also glad we didn't have to do this two times. It was nice to get it over."

I took time to recount to her my ruminations at the funeral, especially my observation that the things we think are important may not be so important in retrospect. I intended to leave the distinct impression that she was important, eternally so. I had already thought I would ask Gwynn to marry me someday. I was now busy setting the stage and testing the waters.

She took in my thoughts but continued to gaze deeply into the deep-red depths of her Argentinian Malbec, which I noticed that she was looking at but not drinking. Eventually, she looked up as if she had decided that this was the time to share something.

"Art, I need to share a situation with you."

All of sudden, there was a knot in my stomach. Gwynn had many admirers inside and outside the firm. There had been another guy in law school, but it had not worked out. When Gwynn attended law school, there were a lot of men for every female in her law school class. In such a situation, Gwynn would have had many suitors. Around the firm, which included many high-testosterone males, she was an object of many conversations. Trying to be my normal, nonchalant, and carefully overtly unworried self, I asked her to go on, hoping this was not a goodbye talk.

She continued to stare at the glass, then dropped her bomb, one of the last things that I expected to hear from her this evening.

"I am pretty sure I'm pregnant."

Perhaps she expected my initial reaction to be dismay, as this event would have profound consequences. Interestingly, dismay was not at all my initial reaction.

Far from dismay, my initial reaction was one of peculiar joy. Normally, I am pretty careful and plan what I am going to say, but in this case, I said the first thing that came to my nearly non-functioning mind.

"I love you."

In high school and college and even to this day, I had long taken the view that is a big mistake to utter those words to a woman and carefully avoided them. Once said, the word "love" can never be taken back without hard feelings. I was not sure it was wise to utter the word just now. In fact, I did not think about my response at all; the word just came from my deepest heart. I had crossed a bridge that I neither could nor wanted to cross back over.

Unfortunately, that declaration did not seem to rouse Gwynn from her reflection, nor did she respond by falling into my arms, which would have been difficult in a dark steakhouse booth. Seemingly unfazed by my declaration, Gwynn was in a practical, not romantic, frame of mind. "What do you think I should do?"

My response required care and thought. I decided to eliminate a few objections to my intended suggestion before answering. I told her how much I admired and loved her and had for some time. I acknowledged that, under the circumstances, it would be necessary for one of us to leave the firm, which might set back her career if it was her. I reminded her that, as we had discussed in the past, my chances of becoming a partner in the firm were not great due to Roger's opposition. Therefore, she would not necessarily have to leave. I would be happy to do so.

"Gwynn, you know I graduated fairly high in my class in law school. I was on law review, clerked for a federal judge, and worked for the Texas attorney general before coming to Winchester & Wells. I will be able to find a job somewhere in Houston. As to any setback in your career, you are the brightest lawyer in your class and one of the brightest in the firm as a whole. You will soon make up any lost time caused by a pregnancy leave of absence."

Given the situation and the culture of the day, I was not sure this was completely true.

Having set the stage, I gave my solution to the problem.

"Gwynn, will you marry me?"

I never thought Gwynn would give an immediate answer to my proposal when it came. She was intensely careful, especially where men and emotions were involved, so the quiet way she continued to contemplate the mystery of her red wine did not bother me. I waited.

When she looked up, I saw she was conflicted but that the practical, down-to-earth Gwynn I loved was about to give her opinion about the most important suggestion I had ever made to another human being.

Her response was not, however, to my proposal. She gave her response with typical hardnosed bluntness. "I was thinking it might be best to terminate the pregnancy." Gwynn then proceeded, in a most pragmatic way, to set out the problems with each of my points.

"The firm is not old-fashioned, but when it becomes obvious that the baby was conceived before any wedding, there would be talk and most probably consequences. Individual partners would be concerned and offended. While it is true you might be leaving the firm in any case, it is not certain that Roger will prevail in his opposition to your partnership. In the end, it is possible, and even likely, that we would both have to leave."

I listened with only half a mind on her words and the logic behind them. Instead, I remembered a moment from the recent past. Like most lawyers, I took Constitutional Law my first year in law school. I had read Griswold v. Connecticut, with its mysterious "penumbra of privacy," and Roe v. Wade, with its declaration of a woman's right to abortion due to the zone of privacy Griswold had created. I knew the law. I did not know, however, the reality. I had never considered that Roe might possibly apply to me.

The previous week, I had been driving down the 610 Loop to see a client and passed a billboard with a picture of a fetus. I remembered the picture and the first thought that came to my mind when I saw it. My thought was, *That is a baby.* Of course, being a modern person, that realization had little or no impact on my legal or social views concerning the matter. It was just an observation, like, "That is a bumble bee." In this case, my observations of the week were not best communicated to Gwynn just now. Cutting to the chase, I returned to what was on my mind.

"I love you. Will you marry me?"

Gwynn began to tear up and gave me a look women reserve for someone they can hardly bear to live without. I could tell that my proposal was neither completely unexpected nor unwelcome. I was pretty sure she loved me but was less sure she intended to walk down the aisle with me just now. Like me, there were many things on her life agenda, and marriage and children had not been on that agenda until now.

"I need to think."

"Of course you do. You know that I love you, want to marry you, and will support you whatever you might decide."

I also was not sure that was completely true. But it was the best thing to say.

Gwynn obviously wanted to change subjects, so our conversation returned to the day and the transaction. She asked me what I thought about the deal with Marshland.

"Jackson wants it done yesterday. Roger wants to get it done faster than I think it can be done. Honestly, I am not so sure it will ever get done, which puts me in a hard place. There is much work to be done for the deal to close. We have to have a new president and chief financial officer. Then, we have to amend the regulatory filings with the various authorities. You've been working on the registration statements with the SEC and the due diligence. Frankly, I think this deal is too complicated. I wish it were simpler. On top of all that, the FBI will be investigating the crash."

Gwynn thought momentarily and then asked a question I had asked myself. "Have you considered the possibility that this deal is intentionally complicated?"

This concern had crossed my mind in the past. Afraid of the answer, I asked the obvious question.

"Can you give me an idea of what you mean?"

"As you know, most of my role in this transaction is due diligence and packaging the commercial loans into groups within the master partnership that MSA is creating. There are a lot of loans to review and understand, some of which were originated by MSA, but most of which are from West Isle Savings Association, interestingly enough some of which were initiated by other banks in Texas and Louisiana." Gwynn looked down as if summoning the courage to voice her fears. "Some of those banks have unsavory reputations, particularly those connected to New Orleans. The paperwork on all the loans is now faultless, but ..."

My stomach, never in good shape when thinking about WISA's commercial real estate loans, was now definitely upset. In reviewing the documentation during due diligence, I noted that many WISA loans originated in a few savings and loan associations and commercial banks in East Texas and Louisiana. I wasn't a banking lawyer, so the nature and connections of a series of banks were beyond my knowledge, though, like everyone else, I had heard rumors. It now occurred to me that my lack of experience in that area might be one reason why Roger wanted me on the team. I might miss certain things that Roger or Jackson wanted to be missed. In addition, any mistake might conveniently be seen as due to my lack of experience with the banking industry. Perhaps most importantly, things Roger did not want to become matters of discussion might never be noticed. My stomach definitely was upset, but I tried to give a harmless explanation.

"If the regulators, who have access to the loans, don't think there is a problem, I suspect there is no problem. We know that the federal and state regulators are concerned about certain elements in the savings and loan industry, but Jackson would not have anything to do with those guys." I paused, not sure that my last words were true.

Gwynn took the opportunity of my silence to make her final comment. "You might be right, but the complexity of this transaction benefits Jackson and MSA. Very few people can understand the mechanics of the deal, much less figure out the meaning and motives behind it. There might be more going on than we are meant to see."

Our dinner arrived, which gave me time to think about all Gwynn had said.

I had noticed a growing element of desperation in Jackson and his management team to get the deal done as soon as possible. Jackson was no longer the fully rational and self-controlled egomaniac he used to be. He lost his temper with increasing frequency. He made snap judgments, not all of which were wise. He was even more secretive than usual. I had long wondered if there was more to the transaction than Jackson shared with his lawyers or the regulators.

Our dinner continued with small talk, plans for the weekend, and the like. We drove home in silence. I didn't know what to do at her door, so I simply held her in my arms and kissed her as gently as I knew how. Obviously, she needed to think. We went our separate ways in a state of confused silence.

Wise Advice

THE NEXT MORNING WHEN I arrived at the office, I was met with dreaded words from Betsey.

"Mr. Armbruster would like to see you as soon as possible. He said to tell you it was urgent."

Requesting an associate to visit the managing partner's office is always an opportunity for anxiety. Given my status at the firm, I would normally have been anxious. Given the confusing situation with MSA, I felt certain the call to see Patrick had to do with my least favorite subject. My anxiety mostly involved the need to avoid saying something critical that might get back to Roger. Last of all, the word *urgent* is seldom used concerning good news.

When I arrived at Armbruster's office, his secretary told me to go right in and then asked whether I wanted a cup of coffee. At this time of day, the answer to that question was and is always in the affirmative.

"I will bring it to you. Patrick said to send you in the moment you arrived."

I entered his wood-paneled office with its oak flooring and Persian rugs, and Patrick asked me to sit down, which I did. He stared with absent-minded attention to his legal pad, on which he had some notes. Then, he looked up.

"The FBI is here. They would like to visit with you and all the members of the team handling the transaction with MSA."

It took me a few moments to digest this news, though from my experience with the attorney general's office, after learning of the crash, I thought it likely that the FBI and other investigators would want to interview most of the people with a connection to MSA and the transaction. To my knowledge, none of us knew anything about the hunting trip, much less anything to do with the crash. I communicated that fact to Pat, who pondered the information. Then I asked, "Does Roger know?"

"He is talking to them right now."

"How was Roger when they asked to speak to him?"

"His reaction was pretty much the same as yours."

"How many other people do they want to visit with?

"Everyone."

His answer was no surprise. Under standard procedures, the FBI would want to interview people like Roger, Todd, the head of the Banking Department, and others to ensure our stories were consistent, which I was certain they would be.

"When do they want to visit with me?"

"As soon as they finish with Roger."

Patrick Henry "Pat" Armbruster was a trial lawyer, one of the best in Houston. Winchester & Wells had always been known as a trial firm with strong corporate capacities. Both name founders, Winchester and Wells, had been general practitioners, as were almost all lawyers in their day. However, they were best known and considered superior trial lawyers.

As the firm grew and lawyers began to specialize, the firm developed separate departments that concentrated on specific areas of the law. The biggest divide was between those working in various business representation areas and the litigators. In recent years, the litigation section had produced the most business and was respected and recommended everywhere, even beyond Texas.

Armbruster began as an insurance defense lawyer and spent much of his active law practice in that area. Over time, he developed expertise in commercial and business litigation. Given his abilities, it was no surprise when the firm made him its managing partner.

Our relationship had always been cordial. He liked the fact that I had clerked with a federal judge and worked for the Texas attorney general in the past. While at the AG's Office, I tried several cases before working in the appellate area. While working for the AG, I had come to see the influence of corporations and corporate lawyers in government and law and decided I wanted to work with a big firm. At Winchester & Wells, I was assigned to the Corporate Department, which was fine with me. The constant conflict involved in litigation was never my favorite part of practicing law, and I looked forward to a more genteel law practice.

There was some time before I would be called to visit with the agents, and so Armbruster took the opportunity to reach out with a little philosophy of the practice of trial law.

"Art, I've always thought that you could be a good trial lawyer. You have the right background. You are smart, and you speak and write well. You can think on your feet. You're outgoing, friendly, and like people. As a result, people like you. You tolerate people you don't necessarily like, and you can adapt to changing circumstances. These qualities are important to a good trial lawyer. You have a bit of the common touch and could learn to explain things to a jury in ways they can understand and accept."

He paused for just a moment, letting me know that the punch line was just about upon me. "In my mind, litigation is the most interesting part of practicing law. To be good at it, you must learn to think out problems from different angles. The worst mistake a lawyer can make is relying solely on his opinion. The second worst mistake is to rely upon the story and opinion of the client."

"I agree," I said.

"A good trial lawyer learns to see things from many points of view. It's important what the judge thinks about the case. It's important what the jury thinks about the case. It's important what the press and the media think about the case because as often as a judge warns a jury not to look at newspapers or the media, they do. It is even important to contemplate what an appellate court will think about a case, if it reaches that level.

"In the end, there are a lot of folks whose opinions matter. It doesn't take long before a good lawyer understands that it's rare that everyone involved sees a particular case in the same way, and only a fool tries a case based solely on his or her own ideas and opinions. One of the best things about trial law is that it teaches you to be humble and teachable pretty quickly. If you appear arrogant before a jury, you almost certainly lose."

Again, I agreed.

"Most cases never make it to the jury, but you remember that one day, you might have to make your case in front of twelve ordinary human beings. There's a lot of talk today about creating 'a narrative'—that is, a story that the jury will favor. This is true—and every good trial lawyer instinctively knows this truth. A good lawyer has to develop his case like parents telling a bedtime story to their children. It has to be at the right level for that particular jury and convincing enough that they take in and remember the most important points.

"If the story presented in court deviates too much from what the jury is prepared to believe, it's my experience that a jury simply won't accept or go along with the story you're telling. If the story you are trying to present deviates too much from what the judge thinks, he or she will interfere, in subtle ways, to help the jury see the other side of the facts. If the story deviates too far from what the client thinks, the client will not be happy with your representation. If the story you tell the judge and jury deviates too far from what you think, you cannot present a convincing case because jury decisions are from the heart as much as from the facts, and juries sense a conman pretty quickly in most cases."

He paused long enough to let his words sink in. He did not have to tell me that I needed to apply these principles to the transaction involving MSA. It was as if Armbruster knew I had been guilty of allowing Jackson's (and especially Roger's) desires and desired storyline to dictate my arguments to the other parties and to the regulatory agencies during the transaction.

I thought to myself, *I must start thinking about the transaction from multiple points of view, particularly from the point of view of the regulators who have to approve the transaction. I've been afraid to do this because to travel too far down the road of sympathizing with the regulators might lead to the conclusion that the transaction is doomed.*

Subconsciously, my attitude was partially dictated by another unworthy motive. If the transaction failed, Roger and the firm might easily blame me, ending whatever chance I had of making partner.

Armbruster's instincts as a trial lawyer were legendary. He was a large man, well over six feet tall, and had become heavy in late middle age. During the hot, humid Houston summers, he almost always wore cotton or poplin suits. In the office, he was a dedicated, intelligent, and sophisticated trial lawyer. He was well-read and cultured and enjoyed a fine meal and good wine. In front of a jury, he was one of the common folks, sweating profusely in the Houston heat. One could almost visualize him drinking a cold Lone Star after a long day as a stevedore on the Houston Ship Channel, something he had done in his youth.

Armbruster always had a simple theory of the case embedded in a story he presented to the jury. In this story, his client was a well-meaning person or institution, attempting to do the right thing, and if mistakes had been made, well, they were minor and accidental. The opposition, on the other hand (depending on the facts), was subtly pictured as slightly less well-intentioned and perhaps guilty of intentional or unintentional mistakes. All this was said in the spirit of a person who liked everyone, appreciated everyone, and was deeply saddened that someone had to lose the case (the opposition) and someone had to win (his client).

I had watched several of Patrick's closing arguments over the years, and they were brilliant. He never spoke too long.

He covered all the important facts and drew the conclusions required to win the case, all within the framework of a theory of the case embedded in a simple story of what had happened.

If Armbruster's instincts were that there was more to the story of Marshland Savings and the transaction than I knew or than met the eye, this insight was important and not to be ignored. I had an idea that his mind was already looking at the facts of the situation from all possible angles, deciding what was the best story to construct about the firm's involvement with MSA and the transaction if things went badly. If the transaction did not work out, Armbruster wanted to do all he could to protect the firm and begin the creation of that all-important narrative that might someday be shared with a jury.

As if sensing our time together was nearly over and knowing that he'd either been successful or unsuccessful in making his point, Armbruster shifted gears to give me a little advice about the interview to come.

"You know enough to know that you should just answer their questions *yes* or *no* as much as possible. Don't speculate on what might be the case. If you don't know, just say, 'I don't know.' Don't be too quick to answer. Think carefully but not too long, or they will think you are inventing a lie. Above all, be careful how you phrase your answers."

I had heard this advice before. Nevertheless, it was good to hear it again just before the interview.

Armbruster looked down pensively and then looked up for his final word. "Remember that the firm does not want to be involved in a scandal."

I noted that he did not remind me that lying to an FBI agent is a crime.

At that moment, Armbruster's secretary returned with more coffee and the news that the FBI was awaiting my presence in the conference room, next door to the managing partner's office. I made ready to leave.

He looked at me, his pale blue eyes opaque, hiding his thoughts, and said, "When this is over, we will talk again."

I looked as friendly and hopeful as I could manage. "That's fine, and I don't think we need to worry."

With an odd look that I remembered afterward, Armbruster looked me in the eye and said, "I certainly hope you are right, for all our sakes."

Interrogation

THE NEXT HOUR WAS BOUND to be stressful. I took a few moments to go to the restroom and splash cold water on my face. Then, I turned around and went to the conference room next to Armbruster's office, which was sometimes used for private talks and small meetings. As I walked in the conference room door, I saw the couple who had been watching us at the funeral. My instincts had been correct. They attended as part of their investigation. The male agent wore the same suit he'd worn at the funeral. The female agent was dressed more attractively. I suspected she would be the "good cop," charming me, while the male agent played the "bad cop," asking the tough questions. I was not disappointed.

Like any interrogation, it began with a bit of small talk as we introduced ourselves to one another. Then, they began a more formal interview process.

"Can you give us your full name?"

"Arthur David Stone."

"What is your position with the firm?"

"I am a sixth-year associate at Winchester & Wells, what we sometimes call a senior associate."

"Did you ever practice anywhere else?"

"Yes. After law school, I clerked for a federal district judge in San Antonio and then worked for the Texas attorney general's office in Austin before coming to Winchester & Wells."

"Are you familiar with Marshland Savings and Loan Association and its leadership?"

"Yes."

"Can you give us an idea about the level of your familiarity with the transaction?"

This question was designed to evaluate my pride. It might open the door for my own speculation and help them evaluate my level of involvement in and understanding of the transaction. A person with a big ego or a need to be important would try to impress the agents. In so doing, such a person would usually say too much. Therefore, I was precise but understated about my understanding of MSA and its leadership.

"I am one of the attorneys on the Winchester & Wells legal team, representing MSA in a transaction in which a holding company will be formed and MSA merged with two other savings and loan associations. As a part of the transaction, a limited partnership, made up of commercial real estate properties, will be created. Both the holding company and the limited partnership will be public companies."

"Have you represented MSA in other transactions?"

"No, but I have represented persons and entities that own an interest in MSA in the past in unrelated matters."

"Are you the leader of the team?"

"No. The principal person leading the team is Roger Romny, a partner in the firm."

"Would you say that you are the person most familiar with the transaction?"

"No. Roger is the chief coordinator and negotiator. I am his principal assistant, but I am not in charge. There are some meetings and discussions to which I am not invited."

At this point, they decided to interject just a bit of uncertainty as to my situation, no doubt hoping that I would give information prejudicial to some party, perhaps Roger.

The female agent looked up from her notes, smiled, and replied to my statement. "Would it surprise you to know that Roger Romny suggested that you structured the transaction and know more about the transaction than any other party?"

It didn't surprise me a bit that Roger feigned a degree of ignorance about the details of the transaction. It also did not surprise me to know that he had tried to shift responsibility and knowledge on to my back and paint himself as a distant chairman of the board figure, unfamiliar with the details of the transaction. Although I would have liked to turn the investigators against Roger, this was a situation where I had to tell the truth but not incriminate a partner in the firm.

"I doubt that Roger meant to say that he wasn't in charge or knowledgeable about the transaction since he's a partner in the firm, which I am not. Roger probably meant to say that his role was to supervise a large number of people, not just in the Corporate and Securities Department of the firm but in the Banking Department as well. Roger is the person primarily responsible for communicating with the client, other law firms, investment banking firms, and other parties involved in the transaction.

"Roger was correct if he told you that, in the beginning, my first assignment was to outline the business, corporate, and legal steps necessary for the transaction to occur. In that sense, I structured the transaction. The client, however, designed the business transaction that gave rise to the legal business our firm is doing. My job in structuring the transaction was to prepare a list of legal and regulatory steps necessary for the transaction to close. Going forward, a lot of the details have to be handled or coordinated by someone in my position.

"As the senior associate involved, Roger sometimes uses me to attend meetings and convey information that he might ordinarily convey, but he cannot attend or convey due to other matters and commitments. I do make decisions when Roger is unavailable. In those situations, I am representing the firm and Roger, but I report to Roger."

The agent seemed to accept my explanation of the difference between our two statements. I did believe, however, that they realized that Roger had been trying to avoid responsibility. I suspect this meant he would get another chance to visit with the FBI, probably after they interviewed many other people.

It was now time for the agents to seek to understand my relationship with the victims of the crash. "Did you know Frank Johnson, the president of Marshland Savings, and Don Mendoza, its chief financial officer?"

"Yes."

"Was your relationship professional or personal?"

"Professional."

"Can you explain that professional relationship?"

"I think so. My primary job was and is to organize the transaction and keep it organized, participate in the negotiations, prepare some of the documents and revise most of them, review and revise various regulatory filings, and oversee the due diligence team. This means I spent a lot of time with the management of MSA."

"In undertaking your responsibilities did you get to know Frank Johnson and Don Mendoza?"

"From a professional point of view, yes. I could not tell you exactly how many hours we spent together before the crash, but it would be in the hundreds over months. The transaction is complex, and there are a lot of parties and law firms involved. When you spend that much time with people, you inevitably become friends and have a working relationship. In that sense, I guess that you could say that our relationship was personal, but any friendship was based on business, and specifically, our relationship resulted from the transaction we are handling for MSA."

This was absolutely true. I went on.

"One of the things that makes a business practice attractive is the relationships one builds over time. Large transactions take a long time to accomplish, and friendships are developed with the people involved. There's something about being part of a team with a common goal that allows people to bond and share their lives together for a brief period. In such a situation, you get to know all kinds of folks, people tyou might never get to know in private life. The feeling is not dissimilar to the way soldiers in a platoon feel about one another during battle. At Winchester & Wells, I have had the opportunity to represent people from all over the world, from different places, religions, and lifestyles, different cultural backgrounds, and different business practices.

"I also have the opportunity to work with people in various businesses—oil and gas, banking, real estate, ranching, the hotel business, medicine and medical equipment, and even professional athletics. In every case, for a time, short or long, relationships are built and enjoyed. When a transaction is over, there is always a time of sadness, as those friendships dissipate and new friendships develop."

I look back on the days when I did more transactional work than I do today with good memories, not for the businesses themselves but for the people involved. However, at that moment, as the FBI was examining me, I was not so sure.

In any case, the agents looked satisfied and asked another question. "Can you tell us how your involvement began?"

"Sure. One morning several months ago, I got a call from Roger, asking me to attend a meeting the next day at MSA's corporate offices." This was a part of my intention to be sure that Roger was placed in the appropriate spot in the transaction, whether he liked it or not. "We went to a meeting at MSA's offices in Greenway Plaza. It was there I first met Jackson Winchester, Frank, Don, and many other people who are involved.

"At the first meeting, our firm, MSA's accounting firm, and the lead investment firm on the transaction were present. Jackson led that meeting. He described the transaction we were being hired to complete. It was a long meeting. With a break at lunch, it took a day—a long day—to complete the initial briefing. On that day, we got our marching orders and came back ready to begin work."

"What happened next?"

"A day or two later, I received notice that I had been placed on a team working with Roger on the transaction. Fairly quickly, we held a meeting inside the firm to divide up the legal work that had to be done among the sections involved. As I mentioned before, this is a complex transaction. In this situation, people from the Banking Department, the Corporate Department, the Real Estate Department, and the Tax Department were present at the meeting. It takes a big team to complete a deal of this size and complexity.

"To be successfully completed, the transaction had to be negotiated and documented between two, and originally three, savings and loans in the form of an acquisition and merger agreement. A new holding company is being formed for the three savings associations involved. A registration statement is being filed with the SEC for the new holding company being formed. A separate registration statement is being filed with the SEC for a limited partnership being created to hold real estate assets. Finally, the transaction cannot go forward without the approval of both state and federal regulatory authorities. Regulatory filings were filed at the state and local levels. We are at the approval stage of the process right now, or we were before the accident. After the recent accident and deaths, most of the documentation and filings will have to be amended. The process is still ongoing."

When I used the word *accident*, I noticed that both agents looked down at their notes.

This line of questioning went on for some time. By the time it was over, the agents had established the beginning of the transaction, its organizational phase, the negotiation of the initial documents, the filings with state and federal authorities, and the negotiations that had taken place involving the institutions involved, the regulatory agencies involved, and the questions they were asking. Then, the questions began to focus more clearly on the deaths.

"Were you aware of the hunting trip?"

"Yes. Some days ago, either Frank or Don—I can't remember who—mentioned that they would be out of town on a hunting trip for the weekend, and we couldn't have any meetings for a few days. Other than that, I knew nothing. I was surprised when I read about the crash."

"Did you know the business purpose for the meeting?"

"No. As far as I know, it was just a hunting trip."

"Did you know the place where the meeting was to be held?"

"No."

"Did you know who was present at the meetings?"

"No."

"Have you ever traveled on the airplane in question?"

"Yes. Several times. As part of the due diligence process, we had to fly a good deal to locations where the savings and loans have branches. We also flew several times to meetings in Austin and Dallas and often took the King Air. At some point during the transaction, I went on a hunting trip to West Texas on the plane."

I wished I had not mentioned the prior hunting trip because it was too similar to the circumstances surrounding the crash. Unfortunately, it was too late to take back my words. The agents then asked a series of questions about that hunting trip, eventually establishing that Roger, Jackson, Frank, Don, and I had gone hunting at a ranch outside of Amarillo. I didn't like to talk about the trip because I did not have a good time. We did not discuss much business, but the others watched a good many pornographic movies. I'm not a prude, but I don't enjoy that kind of entertainment. My parents would have very much objected, and though I had drifted away from their faith and morals, there were still elements of my upbringing that impacted my behavior.

I went to bed early and read a book the first night. I was afraid that the others would be offended by my unwillingness to be one of the guys. The second night, we cooked the game we had shot during the day's hunt and listened to Jackson's stories of his adventures on Wall Street with Michael Milliken and the junk bond market. I was pretty interested in that discussion, which lasted until after midnight. The next day, we had an early hunt, packed, and flew home.

The agents circled back around to the trip to Mexico, asking, "Do you have any idea what the participants were discussing during the trip to Mexico or why Frank and Don were there?"

"No. In fact, I was surprised they were in Mexico. There are no parties to the transaction located in Mexico and no reason for them to be there that I know of. Of course, our transaction is not the only piece of business that MSA has going on at any given point. It may be that they were in Mexico talking to a potential client or on some completely unrelated matter. Perhaps it was just fun. I don't know. I was surprised when I learned that the plane crashed crossing the border from Mexico into the United States."

This line of questioning continued until I asked a question that had been forming in my mind for some minutes.

"I don't understand why you're asking so many questions about the crash. In fact, I really don't understand why you are here. As I understand it, the crash was an accident."

The agent in the dark suit paused for a moment, looked down, thought for a few moments, and then responded.

"Neither the FBI nor the other government agencies involved currently believe that the crash was an accident. In fact, we are proceeding on the assumption that the crash was not an accident."

Federal agents rarely volunteer information. They get information. They responded to my question and made their surprising disclosure to see how I would react. They could see I was astonished, which probably solidified in their minds the notion that I did not know anything important about the crash.

They asked a few more questions, and I tried to get them to give me more details about the crash, but the interview was almost over. They refused to answer any more questions about why the FBI felt the crash was intentionally caused.

"We understand that there are other persons in the firm who are involved in the transaction. Mr. Romny gave us a list of names, which I am going to read to you. Please tell us whether or not you think the list is complete."

They read a long list of names, which included Gwynn. It was accurate. They then read me a long list of names of the firms and people involved and the other parties to the transaction. It was accurate. After a few more moments of polite conversation and a warning that they would prefer I not talk about the interview with third parties, I returned to my office.

I felt a sick tightness in my stomach, which I recognized as a sign that my suspicion that something was wrong with the transaction and with MSA was probably justified. Gwynn had been correct in bringing it up last night. I did not yet know exactly what was wrong, but something was wrong, and I needed to be careful. Very careful.

12

Intimate Disclosures

WHEN I GOT BACK TO the apartment that evening, I was met by the aroma of a roast cooking in the oven. Gwynn was on the couch, reading a book, in a most fetching cotton bathrobe. It was my opinion that there was nothing on underneath it.

She looked up and gave me her best smile. "It was a lousy day, so I came back early, swam, and sat as long as possible in the hottest bath I could tolerate. I decided to be nice to you and cook for a change, so I bought a roast at Randall's. We are going to have a feast tonight to make up for today."

I grinned in response and sat down on the couch beside her.

"It was a really hard day. Did you talk to the feds?"

"You bet. They asked me 1,001 questions, most of them about the transaction, Jackson, Roger, and other partners at the firm, including you. They seemed to be trying to figure out which one of you was the most likely suspect in some crime. They also mentioned Jackson Winchester and others as people with whom they wanted to visit."

"Did they ask you about the crash?"

"Not really. They asked me if I knew about the trip in advance. I answered, 'I did not.' They asked if I thought you knew about the trip in advance. I told them I didn't think so. They asked if Roger knew about the trip in advance. I told them I wouldn't know because I rarely deal directly with Roger.

"I believe they understood I was being honest. At that point, they stopped the game of twenty questions. Once it was established that I rarely visited with Roger, they understood that I am a junior attorney and know little or nothing about the details of the crash or anyone they intend to interview. Frankly, I think they believe that none of us knew about the trip before it took place."

"So they never mentioned the crash itself?"

"Near the end, before they read me a long list of names of people they were going to interrogate, I asked them, 'Why all the fuss?' They told me they were investigating the possibility that the crash was not an accident. I told them I didn't believe that was possible. They didn't respond."

This was good information. It indicated that the FBI did not believe that Gwynn knew anything important about the hunting trip or crash. I was also probably in the clear. Just to comfort her, I said, "When I walked through the doors of the conference room at the end of my own interview, I also had a feeling that they didn't think that any of the 'worker bees' in the firm knew much about anything, other than the details of the transaction."

Then I changed the subject. "This afternoon, I went back and saw Pat for the second time today. I gave him a general idea of what the FBI had asked. He didn't respond. He just nodded. I don't think Pat thinks that any of us have anything to worry about."

I looked at Gwynn, pondering for a moment whether I wanted to make her privy to my thoughts.

"Gwynn, you were right in your worries. There is likely more to this situation and the transaction than we currently understand. I don't know about you, but I'm no longer certain the transaction can go forward. I've been giving it a lot of thought. Obviously, the FHLBB and TSLD will not want to go forward in the face of an ongoing FBI investigation. Neither will the SEC. As we mentioned last evening, this transaction is so complicated that I'm not sure we can overcome the hesitations they'll have because of the crash and deaths. If any more bad news comes out, I just cannot see how to close this deal.

"There's one more thing: I believe the FBI is working on the hypothesis that Frank and Don were murdered. The FBI agents did not say it in so many words, but they indicated in response to one of my questions that they had some reason to suspect foul play. It seems ludicrous to me, but they may have information we do not possess. When you asked essentially the same question, they indicated that they are investigating the possibility that the crash was not accidental. They are aware of some set of facts that might indicate an intentional downing of the plane. Otherwise, they would not be going to all this trouble.

"On the other hand, who would have any incentive to kill Frank and Don? Certainly not Jackson. He needed them to complete the transaction. Certainly not the firm. We are only interested in closing the deal and getting paid. I don't think Don liked the transaction much, and I suspect that neither Frank nor Don liked Big Al at all, but I still don't see a reason why the FBI would suspect that anyone at MSA or Winchester & Wells had any connection with their deaths. They can investigate for a while, but in the end, the firm will be in the clear. That's what I told Armbruster."

I paused for a moment. It was time to come clean with my deepest thoughts.

"I've been at this for almost six years now, and I think I can usually sense when a deal just can't be completed. I have been in similar situations, though nothing this complicated or with a client as forceful and demanding as Jackson. Nevertheless, I'm coming to the conclusion that this deal can't be closed. It is one thing to disclose in a registration statement that the business is subject to the uncertainties of the real estate markets, interest rate fluctuations, and government regulation. It is quite another thing to disclose that the business is potentially the subject of a murder investigation."

I could tell my thinking had gone beyond where Gwynn had gotten to in her own meditation on the day's events. As I began to unfold the kinds of disclosures that we might have to make to three different regulatory agencies, she began to look pensive and perhaps just a little bit afraid.

"What are you going to do?" she asked.

"I think that tomorrow, I had better visit with Roger. I don't want to do it, and I don't think Roger will agree, but I do think I have to get my fears out into the open. Frankly, I have been tiptoeing around Roger because of his low opinion of me for too long. I may not make partner as a result of our visit. If so, then so be it."

Gwynn was well aware of Roger's and my problematic relationship. "Do you think that a visit with Roger might be premature? After all, the FBI could easily clear MSA, the firm, and all the individuals involved in the near future. If you pick a fight with Roger right now, and then it turns out there was nothing to be concerned about, you are going to look bad. That certainly would hurt your chances of making partner."

There was a certain wifely concern about the consequences of an impetuous act, which I found attractive, touching, and perhaps revealing of her true feelings toward me. She was also right. I was quick to agree.

"You are probably correct, but in the past, I have let my fear of Roger and his potential to block my making partner control how forthright I am with him and others in the firm about a lot of things, including and especially this transaction and its problems. I really do think that this is the time to stop behaving in that way."

Gwynn nodded. "Just be careful and diplomatic."

I decided to change the subject. "We have a lot going on right now. There is a lot of uncertainty. We don't know whether or not I'll make partner this year, next year, or ever. We don't know whether I will stay at the firm. We don't know how this transaction is going to turn out. We don't know how its failure to close will impact our future at the firm. However, Gwynn Murray, there is one thing about which I am absolutely certain. I am certain that whatever future there is, I want it to be with you."

I hoped to see some small indication of agreement in her eyes. Interestingly, her eyes began to draw me in to her innermost mind and heart. It was as if she wanted to say yes, but there was something else on her mind.

"Art, there are a few things about me you need to know. They impact my attitude about marriage in this situation. My mother was pregnant with me when Mom and Dad married. Both of them tried in their own way to make a go of it, but they lacked whatever it takes to make a marriage work over a lifetime. My mother tried hard. Very hard. But it didn't work. She just could not make it work. I don't want it to be that way with me."

She paused for just a moment and chose her words very carefully. "I love you, Arthur. I do want to be with you. I just don't know if this is the right time to marry."

My response was emphatic. "Is it the baby? Do you think I am asking you to marry me because of the baby? Sweetheart, I have been trying to get up my courage to ask you for a long time, for months and months. The baby just provided the right time."

Gwynn looked down again for a few moments before replying.

"In the beginning, I was pretty sure I wanted to get rid of the baby. The other day, I had a little bit of discharge and pain. When I thought about losing the baby, losing that part of me that is also a part of you, I was terrified. I decided there and then, whether or not we marry, I am going to keep the baby. It will probably mean that I will have to leave the firm. It will also mean I will have to practice law part-time, at least temporarily. If you really want us to be together, then the answer is going to be yes. Before making any quick decisions, however, I want to think about my parents and the impact of the past on our future."

It was a long time before I understood the full impact of the words Gwynn spoke that evening.

It was a couple of hours before we ate that roast. As we sat together and ate, we formulated a plan. Without making definite plans, and without Gwynn finally and certainly saying yes, we would not announce our engagement immediately. Gwynn, however, would begin to make plans to leave the firm before the baby arrived. I would test the waters concerning my own departure from Winchester & Wells, just in case.

Gwynn always wanted to do a bit of pro-bono work, perhaps with poor and abused women. This was a chance for her to take a break from corporate law and decide whether or not she wanted to be more involved in a different kind of practice. We decided that I would talk to Roger tomorrow, but I would not push him too far.

In the middle of the night, my dark and flaming shadow returned. As I struggled for consciousness, I saw the shadow standing over Gwynn. It was obvious his intentions were to harm her. I jumped on him, determined to rescue Gwynn. Immediately, I felt two hands pushing me away while screaming with fright.

"Art, stop! You're hurting me, and you might harm the baby."

I woke up for the second time, this time for real. I was lying on top of Gwynn, fighting an invisible enemy. I lifted myself off of her.

She sat up and looked me straight in the eye.

"What in the world is going on with you?"

"I'm afraid that I've been having dreams. In these dreams, I see a figure, a dark replica of myself. In my dream, the figure is black with a fringe of fire, a kind of glowing darkness. The figure never speaks to me. He just stands at the end of my bed filled with hate. Tonight, he was standing above you and our baby. In my sleep, I tried to fight him away from you."

Gwynn had now gone from dealing with a fiancé involved in a troubled business deal and a career going bad to a fiancé with mental problems. I could tell that she was disturbed and thinking hard before she smiled and replied with a grin, "Our baby cannot possibly have a father in a mental hospital. I think you need to go see someone as soon as possible." Then, as if to make light, she asked me, "Do you have any other revelations for the day before we go back to sleep?"

Once again, I had to make a disclosure. "Well, there is one more thing. I've been having odd experiences. This experience only happens as I enter or leave the law firm or get ready to leave the apartment to go to work—at least, so far. From time to time, I have this feeling, a sensation that the world is going topsy-turvy. It's as if what I consider to be up and down is now at an angle with the rest of the planet."

As if to make light of matters, I said, "I think it's one more part of not knowing what to do about our relationship and the firm!"

My quip accomplished exactly what I'd hoped. I had told the truth, but Gwynn did not take it too seriously. She thought I was joking.

Playing along with the joke, she said, "While you're at the doctor, I think you better talk about vertigo as well as little dark men with fringes of fire. In the meantime, I guess we better pray that you are going to be all right."

She gave me one last kiss for my gallantry in saving her from a nonexistent threat and went back to sleep. Gwynn slept through the night, but I was awakened once or twice by a dream in which I saw a pale humanoid figure of light shimmering in the corner of our room, almost invisible to the human eye. Radiating from that presence was a kind of protection. I did not think that my black apparition could find a way through that pillar of light.

A Busy Week

WHEN I ARRIVED AT THE office the next morning, there were two notes on my desk, one expected and one unexpected. The first note was a call from Roger, asking that I come to see him immediately when I got into the office. The second was from Stephen Winchester, asking that I give him a call or come by at some point during the day. This second call was welcome but not exactly expected.

Of all the lawyers in the firm, Stephen was the one with whom I most enjoyed working. Stephen was a Winchester— Jackson Winchester's brother. They both attended St. John's School in Houston. While Jackson was always an excellent student, Stephen was only an above-average student in high school. He concentrated on football and girls. When he graduated, he went to Southern Methodist University in Dallas. At SMU, he played freshman football and continued his high school ways until, for reasons not completely known, he suddenly began to do very well in school. When he graduated, he was accepted to Harvard Law School.

At Harvard, he stood well up in his class and worked on the law review. After graduation, he enlisted in the Marine Corps. His reason for joining the Marine Corps was apparently quite simple: he wanted to be a combat soldier. In the army, navy, or air force, he certainly would have been given a commission and assigned to the Judge Advocate General Corps. In the marines, he had to go through basic training, just like everyone else, and qualify as a rifleman, which he did. He wanted to be a soldier and serve his country.

In the end, Stephen Winchester served as a private in the Marine Corps. He was sent to Vietnam. His career in Vietnam did not last long. He was shot nine months after arriving in Vietnam during the Battle of Khe Sanh, winning a Bronze Star in the process. When he returned home, he brought with him the lovely and exotic Ahn Winchester.

The history of their relationship was the subject of many legends in Houston and at the firm. The first legend had Ahn as the daughter of a high Vietnamese official who left Vietnam with unlimited stolen wealth. This legend had her as the advance guard for her family's eventual escape (which did happen). The second had her as a high-class prostitute, whom Stephen met and fell in love with in a Saigon brothel. This legend portrayed her as an Asian adventuress who latched on to a good thing—a sort of "Miss Saigon" with a happy ending. Finally, the third had her as a nurse's aide in the hospital where Steven Winchester had been taken after his injury. This legend had her as a kind of Florence Nightingale of the Orient, who met and fell in love with a handsome prince in her hospital. There were infinite variations of these three basic versions of the legend, none of which Steven and Ahn made the slightest attempt to correct. They seemed to enjoy the mystery.

Whatever the origin of their marriage, there was no question that they were a devoted couple. Steven had never been particularly religious. Ahn was a devout Catholic, a group that, during the war, made up the majority of South Vietnam's leadership. Upon returning to the States, Stephen dutifully became a Roman Catholic and attended mass regularly with his wife. They attended St. Anne's Catholic Church in Houston, and Ahn was active in the parish.

They never had children. At social functions, Ahn was a quiet, watchful presence. One often saw the two of them visiting together at a table full of other people, gazing into each other's eyes in a world all of their own, a world seemingly populated by lotus blossoms, fragrant tea, and meditative peace. When they were together, Stephen's attention was always protectively focused on Ahn wherever else it might be directed.

Ahn was active in numerous Houston charities as well as in her church. Other than her charitable work, she kept to herself. In fact, both of them kept pretty much to themselves. At some point, her parents had escaped Vietnam and moved to the Houston Ship Channel area, where they had a shrimping operation and a small fuel business near Kemah. If there was great wealth, it was well hidden.

I often compared Gwynn and Ahn. Both of them were smart and beautiful. In Gwynn's case, when she entered a room, every male eye turned toward her advancing figure. She exuded a kind of enticing, athletic sexuality that drew men toward her like a magnet. I was familiar with the constant need to ward off unwanted advances. Gwynn was tall, overtly self-assured, and commanding, a kind of medieval Irish warrior queen returned to earth.

When Ahn entered the room, men also took notice, but it was a different kind of notice. Ahn never radiated sexuality. She radiated a kind of quiet, peaceful feminine light. She did not so much walk into a room as glide into it with no pretensions and no expectation of being recognized. Her dark brown eyes took in everything, but she rarely told anyone except Stephen what she observed.

Stephen Winchester initially worked for Butler, Binion, Rice, Cook, and Knapp, one of Houston's larger and best firms. At Butler-Binion, he made a reputation as a trial lawyer. Along the way, he specialized in commercial, securities, and antitrust litigation. He enjoyed working with commercial lawyers on commercial and securities litigation and eventually wanted to be able to do some corporate practice. In the more or less rigid division of sections at a large law firm, this was almost impossible. About this time, one of the partners at Winchester & Wells approached him, asking if he might be interested in joining a firm with roots in his own family.

Stephen agreed, but not before the firm committed to permitting him to do both litigation and corporate and securities work at his pleasure. In the beginning, he worked with other corporate attorneys until he developed the expertise he needed to work on his own. Over time, he was allowed to develop a legal team that crossed the boundaries between litigation and corporate work. Eventually, he developed a practice group of business law specialists. It was as if he had his own little legal Marine Corps in the middle of the armed forces of Winchester & Wells.

It had always been my desire to work on Stephen's team.

I left word with Stephen's secretary that I would be available whenever Stephen had time, but I had a meeting with Roger in the morning. After leaving that message, I went to see Roger. He was on the phone when I arrived—a call from Jackson. I waited and visited with his secretary, June, until he was available.

When I entered, he looked up and motioned me to sit down, which meant that our talk would not be short. I had forgotten to bring a legal pad and pen.

Looking frustrated, Roger opened a drawer in his desk and gave me a pad and pen. "I just visited with Jackson," he said. "He wants us to put on a full-court press to get this deal done. Now. He thinks we can get regulatory approval if—but only if—we move quickly. Apparently, he has visited with his contacts in Washington. He thinks things can be sorted out, but we need to move fast."

It was obvious that my reason for coming was going to be ignored, but I thought it best to fully and carefully state my case. "Roger, you were interviewed by the FBI yesterday. I was also interviewed, as were most of the folks in the corporate area. The banking and regulatory attorneys are going to be interviewed today. Based on my interview, I think the FBI intends to interview everyone involved, all the law firms, all the accountants, all the investment bankers, all the participants, everyone.

"Those interviews will take significant time. In all probability, the regulatory agencies won't approve the transaction until the FBI investigation is complete. That investigation could take months. I hate to say it, but I don't think that this transaction is going to close any time soon. Perhaps never. Someone needs to tell Jackson the facts of life."

Roger looked startled by my opinion that the FBI was going to continue the investigation for a prolonged period, though he must have realized the truth in my predictions of delay. He decided he needed to pump me for any discrepancies between his story and mine. "I am glad you mentioned the interviews. Can you tell me what was said?"

"They asked me, as I assume they asked you, not to discuss the case. However, I think it is safe to say that they view the crash as unusual, and the agency is committed to finding out if there was any foul play."

Roger quickly replied dismissively, "I assume they would want us to believe there was more to the case than a crash to make everyone nervous and get additional information. In the end, they will realize that there is nothing to their suspicions." Looking at me in the eye, he said, "At least, as far as I know."

Given his obvious opposition to my views, my goal was to warn Roger, not to change his mind about the transaction or its potential to close.

"Roger, we have worked together on several transactions. None of them was remotely as complex as this transaction, and none had as many moving parts. If you add a federal investigation to the moving parts, it is hard to believe we can close this any time soon. If we move forward before the investigations are complete, we will have to disclose something about the crash and deaths and the ongoing investigations of the causes. That alone is going to make investors nervous. The TSLD, FHLBB, and SEC were already nervous. They are probably a lot more nervous now. The FBI either has visited or undoubtedly will visit with them. We need to face reality—and so does our client."

Roger put on his thoughtful look and gazed out the window before replying. I could tell he understood my concerns but was silently considering how to negate them for the sake of our client. "You could be right. I will think about what you have said. I may even visit with Jackson. In the meantime, Jackson wants us to move forward. For our own protection, we need to show our client that we are trying.

"Jackson has definitely decided to take the role of president to minimize delay and investor fears. As to the chief financial officer position, he is going to promote Wendy Ramirez for the time being. Wendy knows the transaction and worked with Don for a long time on its financial details. It will not take long for her to get up to speed. We can begin to get closing documents prepared and amend the filings with that new information."

I was speechless at Roger's failure to at least talk through the various objections raised but had no recourse but to do what he wanted. Nevertheless, I put one more shot across the bow of his plan.

"We still have to decide what to tell the regulators about the investigation and what disclosure to make in the registration statements. You will have to talk to Jackson about the problems and provide the regulators with some language that he can live with and that they will accept. I don't need to tell you that whatever we say has to be palatable to the agencies and accurate if it turns out that the investigation is more serious than we imagine. Neither the SEC nor the banking regulators are going to approve the transaction without some degree of disclosure. We cannot just ignore the crash and related issues."

I had not mentioned to Roger that the FBI had let out that they were proceeding on the assumption that the crash was not accidental. I might have pushed the point right then and there, but I didn't feel that I could make that disclosure quite yet because of the FBI's request not to speak with anyone about the interview. A lot of pain might have been avoided if I had. I wanted to press the point, but I still lacked the confidence to press Roger too far.

***

After I returned to my office, Gwynn called to see how things had gone with Roger.

"As well as could be expected," I told her, "but we are to proceed as if the transaction is going to close for the time being."

We spent a few moments reviewing my ever-present to-do list for the transaction as it pertained to her. Gwynn had her marching orders for the next few days by the time she hung up.

For the next few hours, I redrafted some critical documents. I could have left this to Gwynn or someone else, but I needed to do something routine so that my subconscious mind could wander for a time. When I did this, I often kept a small notebook close beside me so that I could jot down things to do. One of the things that popped up was to call Don's daughter, who had spoken to me at the funeral.

In the early afternoon, I got a call from Stephen's office to come to see him. I had been to his office many times and was always on edge as I entered his office. He was someone

I desperately wanted to impress. Unfortunately, a nervous associate never impresses any partner in the right way.

I walked up the stairs to his office on the floor above mine and was ushered in by his secretary.

It was obvious that Ahn had something to do with decorating the office. There was a simplicity about it, just as there was a simplicity about her. The office, however, also reflected the man. Part of the furniture consisted of family heirlooms, stretching all the way back to Colonel Winchester himself. Stephen used his father's desk, which had been given to him by his brother, who preferred a more modern style. There were a few early pistols and Civil War–vintage rifles in shadow boxes on the wall, all family heirlooms. Despite the Texas frontier character of the office, there was also an oriental flavor to the office that showed itself in the lamps and vases.

As I arrived, Stephen was standing beside his desk, and he motioned for me to sit in one of two cane chairs facing the desk. He used those chairs, which were uncomfortable, to prevent people, especially young lawyers, from staying too long. An hour in one of those chairs seemed an eternity. As if realizing this was not a good idea in this particular situation, he changed his mind, and we sat facing each other in a couple of wing-back chairs separated by a coffee table engraved with a golden dragon.

As he sat down, I noticed he was careful with his back. His injury in Vietnam had left him with permanent stiffness. Other than the stiffness in his back, it was hard to believe this was a man in his fifties. Most men begin to age in their late forties, especially those who do not or cannot exercise regularly. Stephen Winchester still possessed kind of rugged, youthful good looks and vigor. His face, which could be stern and determined, especially when angry, was also capable of a lopsided grin that naturally put people at ease. He spoke as someone who was in control of himself and the situation.

"Arthur, I asked to meet with you because I am concerned about my brother and this transaction we are handling for him. I would like you to tell me what you can about it."

I went through the transaction, which by now was indelibly engraved on my mind in all of its labyrinthian complexity. I outlined the savings and loan associations involved, their ownership, and the nature of their assets. In response to his questions, I disclosed the problems with the assets of West Isle Savings and the relative cleanliness of the assets of Global Savings. I described the unique (at that time) notion of putting certain real estate assets, to be sold after the merger, into a "special purpose" limited partnership, and then selling interests in the partnership, with various rights to future cash flow, to the investing public. I described the regulatory filings and the problems we were experiencing in getting approvals.

From time to time, he asked questions to be sure he understood. After I had gone through the transaction, he reflected for a moment, then made the understatement of the century. "It seems overly complicated to me. I am not sure the regulators have the time, energy, or expertise to evaluate such a complex transaction." He then disclosed that he had met with Roger. "Roger seems to think that you don't like the transaction. He feels that you are, consciously or unconsciously, delaying it in hopes that it will just go away."

Hiding my fury at Roger, I gave Stephen a brief description of the assets of WISA and the problems in dealing with Big Al. Stephen knew all about Albert Renaldi and his reputation.

After another pause, he quietly remarked, "Renaldi is not the sort of person with whom my brother normally would do business."

He left that comment hanging in the air as I pondered its meaning, wondering exactly why Jackson *had* chosen Big Al and WISA to participate in the transaction.

I gave Stephen the answer Jackson gave when asked.

"Jackson feels that the regulators are pretty desperate to get Al out of the business. He feels he will get the maximum assistance and forbearances from the FSLIC if he takes on one of their biggest problems close to Houston, where he can personally oversee the problem. Originally, he wanted Fred Vixette and his Vixette Savings Association in the deal for the same reason. Having VSA in the transaction was more than any of the other parties could tolerate, so he gave up the idea. When I—and others—have asked why he wants to include the other institutions, he always says, 'To give regulators maximum incentive to approve the transaction.'"

I reminded Stephen that the FSLIC was empowered to give assistance to those who purchased insolvent S&Ls. This assistance could be monetary and sometimes was. It also, however, could involve forbearances, by which the buyer did not have to meet, among other things, normal capital requirements for a period of time, often years. In the case of the transaction with West Isle Savings, Jackson was seeking both substantial financial assistance and five years to bring the merged entities into full capital compliance.

My answer satisfied Stephen for the time being. Then, he asked me a question that no one had asked during the entire time the firm had been involved with Jackson, MSA, and the transaction. He asked with the earnestness of someone who wants to know the answer.

"So, what really bothers you about this deal?"

In undergraduate school at UT, I had been a part of what is known as "Plan II," a special program that grants those admitted a lot of flexibility in designing their program of study. I used that flexibility to prepare for law school, study history (which I loved), and learn a bit about economics, which I also enjoyed. I took several business courses. While I lacked the sophistication of lawyers who had accounting, tax, or extensive business backgrounds, I could normally understand the financial implications of a transaction without much trouble.

I replied carefully. "Stephen, to answer your question, I'm going to have to talk a bit about the accounting of the transaction. There's almost no question but that MSA,

WISA, and GSA, like almost every savings and loan association in Texas, are technically insolvent. If you had to sell all of their assets today, those assets would not sell for an amount equal to their deposit liabilities. If that were to happen, the FSLIC would have to make up the difference in cash, which it does not have.

"In the case of WISA, those losses are huge. Its assets are primarily commercial real estate properties, which would be difficult, if not impossible, to sell during the current recession in Texas. I can't be sure, but I think it will be years before those properties will sell for as much as Big Al loaned against them. To get the right forbearances, Jackson and his partners have to accurately estimate those losses, which I think is nearly impossible.

"The case with GSA is different. Its assets are almost all made up of government securities and single-family residential home loans. Sol Lewinsky is a careful and conservative businessman, and his contacts within the Jewish community in Houston and beyond are sterling. He deals with reputable and successful people. To the extent that Sol has made commercial loans, those loans are well-capitalized, made to borrowers who put equity into the deals, and there is a reasonable chance that they would sell for more than is loaned against them. His home loan portfolio is also of high quality.

"In the case of GSA, the problem is not with the loans but with the interest rates at which older home loans were made. If you 'marked to market' those loans today, the majority would not sell for the balance due on the loan. Sol does not have to do this because he is holding them as an investment, hopefully to maturity. Sol is a smart guy, and he knows that while he doesn't have to recognize the loss immediately, he will gradually recognize that loss over the next few years. I think Sol is selling to get out of the business while he can, with at least some of the equity he has in Global."

Stephen followed me with rapt attention, and I could tell he understood exactly what I was saying.

"Here's the final part of the transaction that I don't like," I said, "and it is a problem with all the savings and loan acquisitions done in this environment. When a business makes an acquisition like this, it uses what we call 'push down accounting' to register or 'push down' the price paid and value the acquired company's assets on the combined balance sheet at fair market value. Under accounting rules, if you pay more than book value for assets, the difference is booked in the equity side of the balance sheet in an account called 'Goodwill.' To give you a simple example, if IBM were to purchase a small software company, the value of the physical assets of the acquired company would be less than the amount paid. The physical assets of such companies are never as large as the purchase price because software is not a tangible capital asset. The amount paid for the software company reflects the future earning power of that software, which can be considerable.

"Let me give you an idea based on my example. Suppose IBM purchases a small software company for $10 million, but the business has only $3 million in tangible assets. After the purchase, IBM allocates $3 million of the purchase price among those assets and then books a new asset or adds to an existing goodwill account at a value of $7 million. That $7 million asset represents the future earning power of the software company."

Stephen nodded so I'd know that he was following me.

"Now, let's compare my hypothetical transaction with what's happening in this transaction. Three savings and loans are being merged together. In the case of WISA, new shares are being issued to Big Al, reflecting a value of about $5 million. In the case of GSA, Sol is receiving shares worth about twice the net worth of GSA and cash equal to its net worth. But if marked to market, their assets would be less than their liabilities to depositors. In fact, the amount of the negative net worth is currently estimated to be approximately $40 million. That $40 million and the premium paid will be booked as a goodwill asset and added to the capital of the merged institution.

"Unfortunately, that goodwill asset is not in any way similar to the goodwill in my hypothetical IBM transaction. In the IBM transaction, the goodwill is made up of an estimate of future earning power. In our transaction, a portion of the goodwill is made up of a calculated future loss. That loss almost certainly will be recognized over the life of the loan portfolio.

"To overcome that loss, Jackson will have to do two things: First, he'll have to grow the combined institutions, based in part upon the equity created by the asset he booked as goodwill, which counts as a part of his regulatory capital under his agreement with the regulators. I would estimate the growth to be about $120 million of new income-earning assets.

"Second, he'll have to invest those new assets in such a way as to earn more than the normal savings and loan earns on its assets to overcome the amortization of the future loss he is booking as goodwill. If he doesn't do that, the loss will simply be greater at the end of the day. Jackson is no fool. He knows that, unless he can grow MSA and make above-market returns on his new assets, he can't survive. If, by some miracle, however, the transaction works the way Jackson thinks it will work, he can survive.

"I'm not as smart as Jackson, and I don't understand the complexity of his investment strategy, but I don't see how he's going to do it. In the end, to mitigate the risk of borrowing short from depositors and lending long to borrowers, the hedging cost has to match the risk. I'm not sure there is any profit left if you mitigate the risk sufficiently to prevent the impact of rising interest rates on the bank.

"In my own simple-minded way, I think the transaction fundamentally violates the commonsense laws of economics. The accounting of the transaction permits something that doesn't comport with reality. Congress and the regulatory agencies are allowing this because they have no choice unless they want to admit that the industry is bankrupt and raise enough tax dollars to recapitalize the FSLIC."

Like Pat, Stephen was accustomed to looking at the facts from different points of view. I could tell that he was both listening and attempting to see the transaction through the eyes of Jackson, the regulators, the SEC, the investment bankers in New York, and a jury and judge who might one day be called upon to rule on litigation that might ensue, as well as through my eyes. There was a long silence.

Stephen seemed to be doing something I had seen him do in the past. During negotiations, a deposition, or even in the middle of a trial, Stephen sometimes straightened his back, closed his eyes, and began holding all the facts before him in his mind, as if building an invisible mental model of what was happening and how it might turn out. Inside his head, he was playing a personal game of three-dimensional chess. In this case, the facts were too complex for him to reach a conclusion during our conversation. He opened his eyes and began the process of closing the meeting.

"You have given me a good bit to think about. I want to take some time to think and maybe visit with Jackson. I will keep confidential everything you have said to me. Do not worry." He then shared with me something I did not know. "I don't have any interest in MSA. When Jackson came back to town, he bought me out. He did not want me to interfere, and I did not want to take time to understand what he was doing. His strategy seemed overly complicated and risky.

All this talk about derivatives, risk-controlled arbitrage, and the like seems like financial black magic. Now, I wish I had learned a little more. Thank you for sharing."

To my surprise, he turned the conversation in another direction. "Arthur, I like you. I have never been sure your future was here at Winchester & Wells, but I like you. I understand something of what has caused a certain partner's concern, but I believe he is wrong. You have good judgment and broad experience and knowledge. When this transaction is finished, one way or another, I want you to join our team. You have the makings of a good lawyer if you can learn to trust your instincts, think clearly from all points of view, and decide wisely but firmly in complicated situations. Lawyers, just like children, mature and grow at different rates. Often, the more sensitive, intelligent, and capable the person, the longer it takes for him to find his feet. I think you are finding yours in a difficult time. It speaks well of you."

This was music to my ears and the answer to a long-time dream.

Stephen then returned to matters at hand. "As I said, I need to think about our conversation before I visit with Jackson. You may not hear from me for a time, but you will."

***

I was flying on high, white Houston cumulus clouds as I returned to my office. I might not make partner this year or ever, but I just might get the chance to work with Stephen

Winchester, and that experience would be worth whatever happened.

When I got back to my office, I had a call from one of the investment bankers involved in the transaction. His name was Lance DuFort. I had known Lance briefly in law school. He was at the University of Texas and graduated slightly before me. After graduation, he practiced law with a big firm for a short time and then took a job as an investment banker in New York. We had reacquainted ourselves because he was working on the transaction for one of the investment firms involved. Lance was smart but known to be overly ambitious and full of himself. He wanted to talk about the transaction.

"Art, those of us up here in New York would like to know what's going on with the transaction. What can you tell me?"

I filled him in on where the transaction stood, warning him that we felt there might be some delay due to the investigation the FBI was conducting. I also let him know that, in all probability, Jackson would take over the presidency of MSA. I tried to be as noncommittal as possible about the future of the transaction, while not saying anything that would be disloyal to Jackson, MSA, or the transaction.

"In the end, Lance, it will take time for things to get straightened out. Anything I might say about timing today would be sheer speculation."

Lance, as always, jumped right in. "I've been analyzing the transaction. If we can get the right amount of federal assistance to take over WISA, there's a lot of money to be made. Jackson is a wiz at trading securities. His hedging operation is well known in New York and around the country among those of us who are in the business. In addition to investment banking fees for placing the securities in the transaction, there will be a lot of trading commissions earned as time goes by. Of course, we also hope to set a standard for how the S&L business might be reconfigured. If the transaction can get back on track pretty soon, our firm, at least, is ready to go forward."

I took a moment to remember that I needed to be helpful but also slow things down and give Stephen and the executive committee time to meet.

"Lance, I can only tell you the following: The team working at our firm has been instructed to go forward with all deliberate speed, redrafting the documents that need revision due to recent events. I would say that the folks in New York will know more by the end of next week. They may even be able to see some documents in a week or two."

Seemingly satisfied, Lance moved on to other matters. "By the way, how is that beautiful redhead associate doing?"

I was in no position to tell Lance anything about Gwynn and me, so I had to let it pass with the observation that she was busy revising documents and responding to requests for information from the various agencies involved.

The conversation ended soon thereafter because I needed to work on other things.

A Visit to Church

AFTER MY CONVERSATIONS WITH STEPHEN and Lance, I needed time to clear my head. I returned to the office and asked Betsy to call Maria, Don Mendoza's daughter, who had spoken to me at the funeral, and ask if we could meet. Maria was anxious to get together and suggested we meet that afternoon at the Church of the Resurrection in the Houston Heights, where her father's funeral had been held. I worked at my desk for another hour or so and then took off for the meeting.

Our meeting was scheduled for about an hour after school was out. I arrived early and was surprised to find the sanctuary doors open. I went in and once again admired the stained-glass windows that had made such an impression on me during the funeral. I sat in the pews for a few moments, remembering my father's churches and how often I had sat in those pews, squirming, anxious for the church to get out, barely listening to the sermon.

My brother enjoyed church. He was active in the youth group, diligent in Bible memorization, and earned a God and Country Award in the Boy Scouts. After college, he went to seminary, and after graduating, he followed my father into the Presbyterian ministry. He was the family's "perfect child." On the other hand, I was a high school rebel and anxious not to be known as a "preacher's kid," or "PK." The stories in our family about some of my antics in and out of the church are famous and often repeated.

I never doubted the existence of some kind of a god. (Somebody or something must have created the universe.) The God who seemed so present and important to my father and brother, however, was a distant figure and irrelevant to my daily life. In high school, I didn't want a personal relationship with God. I wanted to have friends, date cheerleaders, be above average in sports, make good enough grades to get into college, practice law, get rich, and have a good time. God wasn't particularly necessary for any of those activities.

Dad was what we would call today a *theological moderate*. His favorite theologian was Dietrich Bonhoeffer, the German theologian martyred at the end of the Second World War. In point of fact, Dad was moderate in every way. He liked people. In sermons, he was always careful to avoid taking hardline positions that might hurt someone.

He spoke out on a few things—like the civil rights movement—but most of the time, he was careful to

151

encourage everyone and hurt no one's feelings. He was a gifted counselor. In every place we ever lived, he was sought out by people, inside and outside the congregation. He and Mom now were serving a church in Brenham, Texas, a few miles northwest of Houston. I went up once in a while to see them. My brother, who had attended Union Theological Seminary in Richmond, Virginia, on a scholarship, had a church in the Northeast. He was busy caring for people and rarely came home. Mom and Dad hoped that would change.

I was glad to arrive at the church early. I had long since forgotten how to pray but enjoyed sitting, thinking, and meditating in the quiet beauty of the empty sanctuary. For just a few moments, I was able to clear my mind. For some reason, staring at the stained glass, particularly the picture of the Resurrection, through which the afternoon light streamed, was reassuring.

Perhaps there is a God who listens to prayers. If there is, I need some prayers, I thought as I considered Gwynn, the baby, Winchester & Wells, the transaction, and my uncertain future. In any case, it was enjoyable to sit quietly and think in such a lovely place.

Maria arrived a few minutes late, letting me know it took her more time than usual to close up her classroom. That explanation opened up a conversation about her career as a high school teacher in the Houston Public Schools. Apparently, she coached soccer and taught American history. We chatted for a few moments, sharing details about our lives.

I once again expressed how sad I was about her father's death. Then, I got to the point. "I was surprised at the funeral when you suggested that you might like to visit. I did not expect it. Is anything in particular on your mind?"

Maria looked at me with dark, watchful eyes. "I need you to assure me that nothing I say will ever get back to my mother or be attributed to anyone in my family."

It was obvious there was something important she wanted to tell me. On the other hand, I wasn't sure that I wanted to know it. Nevertheless, I assured her I would not disclose anything unless required to by state or federal law. I knew that I might be subpoenaed to testify and must tell the truth if interviewed by a federal agent. This seemed to satisfy her.

"I am not sure my father's death was accidental. My mother and I are close. For several weeks before his death, Dad was acting strangely. When I asked my mother about it, at first she wouldn't tell me anything. Then, she told me that my father was concerned about work. He was thinking about leaving Marshland Savings and finding new work. He was involved in something he referred to as *The Transaction*."

I smiled because that was exactly the emphatic language we used at the firm. The transaction was so complex and complicated that it deserved to be called *The Transaction*! I asked her to go on.

"My mother doesn't understand business. She said somebody named Big Jake, or something like that, bothered my father. Apparently, this person is a businessman with unsavory connections and a bully. My father didn't think the bank should be involved with such a person. After my father died, my mother told me that he had mentioned his concern to people in authority."

Suddenly, my attention was riveted on this young girl and her story. "Did your mother mention whether these persons were at MSA or some regulatory agency?"

"My mother didn't know, but she thinks he visited with federal authorities, perhaps the agencies regulating businesses like Marshland Savings Association. I don't know the names."

"Did your father tell your mother the exact nature of the problems he was concerned about?"

"It had something to do with real estate loans from out of state."

I was beginning to wish I had never called her. She was giving me information that, if disclosed, would almost certainly seriously delay or end the transaction. Such information also should be disclosed to any investors in MSA. It was information that, if I was interrogated by the FBI again, and they asked the right question, I would have to disclose. If that happened, there was no way that Maria and her family could be spared danger. Finally, this was information that the firm ought to know. If things went badly, I would be criticized for not disclosing it. If I said nothing, the blame for any future problems would fall squarely on my shoulders. At that point, my chances of making partner at Winchester & Wells would be zero.

Our conversation went on a few minutes longer. Unfortunately, Maria didn't know anything more than what she had said. I could tell she was worried and possibly regretted having spoken with me. Before we ended our conversation, I gave her my own warning.

"I don't want you or your mother to worry. Please do not tell her about this conversation. I also don't think you should ever mention this to a third party. Of course, if the FBI asks you any questions, you must answer truthfully. Finally, be careful. If anything suspicious is going on—and we can't be sure there is—someone concerned enough to kill your father might not stop with one murder, if challenged."

I did not know how right I was.

***

As we walked out of the sanctuary, a rather tall gray-haired man wearing a clerical collar, probably in his early sixties, walked into the building. Maria introduced him as Father White. In the course of our short conversation, Maria referred me to Father White if I ever wanted to talk to him. The priest indicated that he had time just then, so we said goodbye to Maria and walked back to his office.

I've seen many lawyers' and pastors' offices. Interestingly enough, law offices can look completely different, depending on the character of the person. Some lawyers like modern furniture; others, roll top desks and country furniture; still others, traditional Chippendale furniture. Some lawyers like their offices to be covered with law books. Others like nothing in the office that might distract them from the business at hand.

Pastors' offices, which are called *studies* because they are where the pastor studies to preach and teach the congregation, are different. There is always a bookshelf or bookshelves. The longer the pastor has been a pastor, the more books there are; by retirement, the average study is filled with books. The only exceptions are very small rural congregations, where the pastor often studies at home. Whatever the style of the pastor, the books are always there.

I had a lot of experience with Presbyterian pastors. I understood that people do not become pastors without liking to read books: Books on the Bible. Books on theology. Books on church history. Books on church management. Books on Sunday school classes. Books on small groups. Books on denominational government. Books, books, books, books, books.

Father White's office was no exception. He had a good many books of various kinds, particularly on the Anglican Church and the charismatic movement. Behind his desk was an older typewriter on which he wrote his sermons. There was a table and a couple of chairs where he had meetings. He lit a candle on the table when we entered the room. There was a cross on one wall. His desk was somewhat unusual. It had been built for him by a congregant and had a dove, the symbol of the Holy Spirit, engraved on its front.

We talked about my father and his churches, about Episcopal priests we'd known over the years in small towns in Texas, and about my experiences when I was young. Father White was pretty good at getting me to open up, and before the conversation went on for very long, he was aware I had drifted from my father's faith and was troubled and worried. I wasn't about to let him know anything about the transaction, but to satisfy his curiosity, I opened up about my dream and the unusual figure in it.

"There is something I've been wanting to ask my father," I said. "Since we are here, I would like to ask you. Recently, I've been having dreams. In my dreams, I see a burning black figure. The black figure is almost exactly my size and shape. I don't see any features of any kind on the figure. The figure is humanoid but black as night. Surrounding the figure is a kind of deep, blood-red fire that becomes yellow just at the fringes. In my dreams, the figure is filled with hate."

Father White's eyes looked intently into mine. I could see that he was thinking hard about the dream. When he finally spoke, he was direct. "Do you know anything about psychology, the psychologist Carl Jung, and something that psychologists call the shadow self?"

I shrugged my shoulders. "Very little. Jung is just a name I heard in college."

"You've been having a series of dreams. As a Christian, I believe dreams are revealing. Almost always, dreams are about the inner life of the dreamer. Our dreams reveal things about us that we do not consciously understand or perhaps want to understand. On the other hand, dreams present opportunities to grow as a person. Much of the time, we human beings submerge inner conflicts in the subconscious. In this way, what deeply concerns us does not interfere with our day-to-day lives. When we sleep, however, our capacity to submerge worries and anxieties is lessened, with the result that dreams often reveal something important.

"I don't think you need to be much of a psychologist to understand that a young man in the prime of life who has a dream about a demonic figure of darkness is worried about something, perhaps about something within himself. From a Christian point of view, I wonder if you are concerned about the wisdom and goodness of the path you have taken in life. I even wonder if perhaps there isn't a demonic capacity within you that you fear is seeking to be unleashed. From a purely secular point of view, I wonder if you are not worried about your life, character, actions, and ambitions. I cannot answer what the exact interpretation of your dream might be, but I think it is worth your going to see a professional or at least taking time to think this out for yourself.

"The psychologist Carl Jung called the darker aspect of one's personality one's *shadow*. In my experience, facing the dark aspects of our personalities takes courage. All human beings have good and bad sides. There is darkness in all of us. That darkness results from what we Christians call the fall. We are all anxious and self-centered, desire to succeed, gratified by power of all kinds, and seek our own self-interest to the detriment of others. Finally, we are all fearful about the future, especially about the prospect of our own deaths.

"You seem to be a young man who is ambitious and wants to please. These are good qualities with a darker reverse side. In the attempt to get ahead by pleasing your clients, your employer, your friends, your lovers, and others, if you deny your fundamental self, it can lead to nothing but suffering."

We talked for another few moments, as he focused on my need to understand that the dream almost certainly had to do with me.

"It is easy to think of dark powers as outside of us. It is harder to confront the fact that dark powers cannot warp our lives without help—and that help comes when we humans allow our inner darkness to impact others around us: family, friends, colleagues, and the like. In some cases, that darkness can reach the point where it deserves the description of *demonic*. When the darkness in us reaches this point, we can cooperate in our own self-destruction and the destruction of the families, communities, and nations we love. Just look at Nazi Germany as one huge example."

I digested this information as best I could on short notice. I'm not a particularly reflective person. Before Father White's analysis, I did not perceive any deep conflict within myself. Yet I knew that I was not happy about certain aspects of my life and my lack of any effective response. I wasn't happy about working with Roger. I wasn't happy about being involved in the transaction—and a lot less happy after my conversation with Maria. I was happy about Gwynn's disclosure of our baby, but I wasn't happy about putting her in that situation. I wasn't happy about the difficulties we faced in getting married. I could blame others if I wanted to, but any fault was mine.

He asked me to describe my last dream. This involved a bit of a problem. I didn't want my fiancée involved in this. Nevertheless, I decided that I could admit that I was in a relationship of which neither the church nor my parents would approve.

"Well, I've had this dream about five or six times. I was with my fiancée the last time. That time, the black figure was threatening not me but her. I woke up having jumped on top of her to protect her from the imaginary figure. She thought I was crazy and suggested I see someone, which is partly why I'm here talking with you." I thought about what to say next. "I am always protective of my fiancée, but I'm particularly protective now. We think she's going to have a baby, and I wouldn't want anyone or anything to hurt that baby."

He looked at me quietly, as if biding me to continue.

"On this occasion, the dream had a sequel. I either woke up or had another dream in the middle of the night. I don't know which. I saw a thin pillar of multicolored light shimmering in the same corner where the dark figure appeared. It was a kind of comforting quality to the light, so I went back to sleep. Of course, when I woke up, there was nothing there."

The priest now sat up straight in his chair. He looked at me with an intensity I have rarely seen or experienced. "Arthur," he said, "different people can look at what you have experienced in different ways. I am not a secular psychologist. I believe either your subconscious is confirming to you that all will be well despite your inner conflicts or angelic powers are simultaneously challenging and looking after you. Frankly, I think it is both. I am not by any means a fundamentalist. I am an Episcopal priest. I have been a pastor for many years—many years. I believe there is what Daniel called 'a war in heaven,' and that war is reflected in people and events on earth as we allow our hearts and minds to be influenced by ideas, movements, beliefs, and even invisible powers.

"No one in their right mind wants to be drawn into some kind of invisible conflict. We have enough troubles in our day-to-day lives. You haven't told me much about your work, but I saw you at the funeral the other day. I know the FBI is investigating the crash that killed Maria's father. At this moment, I can only think that your work is troubling you. Be careful, but know that someone is looking after you."

When I stopped going to church, I stopped worrying about heaven, hell, and any kind of spiritual conflict. I wasn't in the mood to see my life as involved in some kind of heavenly conflict among powers and principalities. However, I was having these dreams and was in over my head at work.

I considered myself an ordinary person. I am a bit more gifted than most in the practice of law. Life experiences have allowed me to become a leader but never a spiritual leader, though since the events of the transaction, on and off, I have been active in churches and community work. My father and brother, Ahn, and others like Father White have an innate ability to relate to spiritual things in ways I cannot. I have learned, however, to listen and not discount the advice of those with a greater connection with spiritual realities than my own.

I needed to think about what Father White had said. He was correct about one thing: I was troubled about the transaction and not happy at my inability to influence Roger and others to share my concern. I was troubled about Gwynn and did not want her to be hurt in any way.

We visited for a bit longer. He prayed for me, and I left feeling strangely relieved. My head was swirling, but I knew I had to have one more conversation before the day was over.

***

It was late afternoon when I got back to the office. I had enough pink call slips marked "urgent" to spend hours returning phone calls. I didn't return any of them. Instead, I went into my office, shut the door, and called Stephen Winchester. I asked if I could come and see him immediately. He said I could.

When I walked in the door, I knew he was not expecting a visit from me quite so soon after my last one. He even looked a bit disappointed and put out. He asked me to sit down, this time in the cane chairs.

I told him I could not give him the source of the information I would disclose. The source had asked me to keep it confidential and needed to keep the source private because the person felt their family might be in some danger. From my face and body language, Stephen could see that what was coming next was not good, but I sensed it was also not completely unexpected.

"I'm sorry to bother you again today, but I had to talk to someone. This afternoon, I spoke with someone who had asked to speak with me some days ago. This person is not directly involved in the transaction but learned firsthand of a conversation that one of the plane crash victims had with another person. In a conversation several weeks ago, either Frank or Don complained about a person I can only think was Big Al and a participant in the transaction, which I can only think was West Isle.

"There are two parts of the conversation I find troubling. First, the person overheard a complaint about business loans in the institution coming from criminal elements. Second, the person who talked to me believes that Frank or Don was talking to someone in authority. The person did not know whether it was inside MSA or whether it was someone with a regulatory agency. My source thinks it was probably federal regulators.

"Either way, it's bad news. Either Jackson has known about certain problems for some time and has not discussed them with us, or he does not know. Nevertheless, either federal or state authorities probably do know—at least, they know something. This is not good for Jackson, MSA, the firm, or the future of the transaction.

"Humanly speaking, no one else besides Jackson was in authority above Frank and Don. In all probability, the person was bypassing Jackson and talking to someone at a regulatory agency. Either way, this information casts grave doubts on the transaction. If this person did not talk to Jackson, it means the person felt Jackson might somehow be involved. If the person talked to the regulatory authorities, we can assume that there is already an ongoing investigation of the relationship between MSA and WISA."

I stopped. There was nothing more to say that would not be mere speculation.

Stephen was a good trial lawyer. Rumor had it that he was a good poker player in college and the Marine Corps. It wasn't like Stephen to show any response to information, however terrible. Stephen had a good poker face, as do all trial lawyers. It was revealing when he visibly winced as I went through my talk. The most obvious wince came when I mentioned the possibility that Jackson could be involved in something shady. He also winced when I mentioned there was almost certainly an investigation going on of which Jackson had no knowledge.

"Please don't talk to anyone—and I mean *anyone*— about this." He looked me in the eye as if to be sure I understood that meant someone like Gwynn, Roger, or anyone to whom I might otherwise speak about the information.

"I have a dinner appointment with Jackson tonight. If we can't get together tonight, I promise I will speak with him before the weekend is over. You haven't told me anything I did not suspect might be true. I have friends in the industry outside of MSA, and none of them thinks highly of Big Al, West Isle, or Big Al's business associates and friends."

With newfound courage, I wanted to be sure I said plainly what was on my mind. "I think you need to talk to not just Jackson but to the firm's executive committee. Federal and state authorities may have information about the transaction that has not been shared with us. We now have information that, in some form, must be disclosed in every filing we have made and to our investors. I cannot imagine how this kind of information could be disclosed without delays in the transaction. It is even possible that we have a duty to inform the FBI about our suspicions because it could be relevant to their investigation of the crash. I am already concerned that we need to amend our filings with the SEC to disclose the ongoing investigation of the crash.

"At this point, the best course of action might be for the firm to recuse itself from further involvement with the transaction. Furthermore, we have very little time to deal with this before we risk either confronting Jackson or filing a document that the regulators know is false or at least feel is false. Finally, if the person who gave me this information talks to the authorities, they will know I was aware of the facts we have discussed. As a result, I am personally in a very dangerous situation."

Stephen responded with a nod.

"You are correct. I was going to speak with Pat in any case in the next day or so. I am on the executive committee, and this is the kind of problem we have to discuss from time to time, though this situation is by far the most serious we have ever discussed. I can't tell you what I'm going to say or do, but I can tell you that I completely agree about the need for this information to be discussed at an executive committee meeting.

"I've thought about the possibilities as well as the dangers associated with removing the firm from this matter. In a few days, we will get back together. In the meantime, go on as if nothing were amiss, being careful not to file anything with the authorities until we get some clarity about what is going on here. If Roger or anyone else tries to force you to make a filing, come to see me immediately. I am afraid there is more here than meets the eye."

We went through the status of the transaction and of the parties one more time to be sure that Stephen completely understood the facts and situation. He could not afford any misunderstandings when talking with Jackson or the executive committee. We discussed how long it would take to close the transaction in ordinary circumstances.

We also discussed what delays might be caused by these extraordinary circumstances. It was dark before we left his office.

He was on his way home. I was headed back to my office for a late night of doing most of a day's work after the day was over.

15

Another Death

THE NEXT MORNING, AS SOON as I got to the office, I called Gwynn. The purpose of our meeting was to go over various documents and filings. I could not tell Gwynn what I knew, but I could pump her for information. I also wanted to warn her that we must not file anything with the regulators until further notice, without disclosing the source of my concern or Stephen's orders. We began by going over each document and related filings. Eventually, we got to a matter involving WISA real estate. I began digging for information.

"The other evening, you mentioned that some borrowers at WISA appear to be questionable, as do a few transactions in which the parties were involved. Can you tell me more? We have to be sure that our disclosures are adequate and that risks are properly disclosed in the SEC filings—and we do not want to be on the wrong side of the TSLD and FHLBB."

Gwynn outlined the loan issues that were originally found in the WISA loan portfolio, many of which could be excused as substandard documentation by a relatively unsophisticated bank that was more accustomed to preparing home loans than commercial loans. Next, she described two loans in particular that attracted the attention of the examiners.

"Many of the issues the examiners found with WISA loans were merely failures to fully document loans in the best possible manner. There were a few loans, however, that raised different questions, two of which involved MSA. As I understand it, only recently were these loans questioned by the examiners."

This confirmed that someone had tipped off the regulators and was a partial confirmation of Maria's information. I asked her to go on.

"The first loan involved a shopping center in Lakeway outside of Austin. An Austin-based S&L originated this particular loan. The loan was troubled from the beginning. Two borrowers purchased the property from Florida, both Cuban refugees. MSA originated a loan to take the property out of the Austin S&L. Two days later, the loan was sold to a bank in Louisiana, about which the regulators have voiced concerns. The property was then bought and sold several times in rapid succession, each time with a higher appraisal. Eventually, a loan on the property ended up in a

Dallas savings and loan association and went into default. The regulators are concerned the loan was a part of a daisy-chain operation to hide some kind of money laundering. The transactions also resembled a 'pump-and-dump' fraud, whereby the already artificially inflated value of the property was increased and then left in the hands of a final unsuspecting dupe."

"What does MSA say about the loan?"

"We interviewed Frank. He denied there was anything wrong. He then sent us to Jackson, who said that all MSA did was originate a loan to a qualified borrower who promised to move the loan within a few weeks. An appraisal was received to validate the loan value for MSA. MSA received a pretty big fee for providing the gap financing. In Jackson's view, MSA simply took an opportunity to make a substantial short-term profit on a low-risk transaction. He seemed put out that the regulators would even question the loan."

"What about the second loan?"

"The second loan bore some resemblance to the first. A high-profile Middle Eastern investor had a Houston-area property financed with another Houston S&L. The particular S&L has been in the news recently, and almost everyone thinks it will soon be closed with big losses to the FSLIC. In this case, MSA stepped in and purchased the loan from the troubled S&L with very little documentation. Once again, a few days later, the property was sold to an affiliated entity of the original owner and refinanced by another troubled Texas S&L. The new loan was for a good bit more than the loan MSA purchased. Money apparently went into the hands of a Chicago-based loan broker with ties to more than one troubled S&L and the Middle Eastern investor.

"The bank examiners traced some of the funds as far as an Isle of Jersey account, but then the money was lost in a maze of transfers through places like Cyprus before disappearing completely. Once again, the examiners were concerned that the transaction involved money laundering. When we asked Jackson about the transaction, he gave the same answer as before: 'We saw a way to make a fee from a highly qualified borrower, who happens to be affiliated with an ally of the United States, in a situation where we were promised that our risk would be short-term. We took our fee and were in no way involved with the property after we were bought out, as promised.'"

I thought a moment, then asked, "Were there more transactions of this kind?"

Gwynn answered carefully. "As you know, when we do due diligence on a transaction like this one, we cannot look at every loan transaction in a bank the size of MSA. We have not identified any such transactions, but I think that the FHLBB is looking into the possibility that there were other similar transactions. We recently received a request for information on a couple of other loans, one that finally ended up at Vixette's savings and loan."

My heart sank at the mention of Fred Vixette. I had an answer to the question I had wanted to ask and a way to delay further filings with the regulators. Trying to appear helpful, I shared a practical solution. "Our current risk disclosures to the regulators and SEC almost certainly need to be amended to say something like this:

"'From time to time, MSA may originate commercial loans with an understanding that the borrower will find additional or new financing over a relatively short period of time. When MSA engages in such a transaction, it is primarily concerned with the fees it will earn for its services, although it underwrites the loans, just as if it intended to hold the loan to maturity. To the extent that the borrower does not perform on the assurances that MSA has received, it is exposed to credit and other risks. Recently, regulatory authorities have questioned a few such transactions and asked for additional information.' The exact language will need to be approved by Roger and Todd. Before any filings are made, Jackson also needs to approve the language."

It was my view that there was no way that MSA or Jackson would approve the suggested language, but it would be interesting to see what language they proposed in response.

Gwynn agreed to begin making appropriate changes in the various SEC filings and ask the Banking Department to change the regulatory filings with the TSLD and FHLBB.

I stood up, consumed by an almost physical sense of worry. "Unfortunately, these disclosures do not undo the loss of trust that the regulators may feel in MSA or the risk that the transaction will end up delayed as they investigate to see if there are other transactions with which they disagree. We need to hold up on making the filings until MSA can give us more information about these and any similar transactions. If someone asks you to make any filings, please see me first before you do so.

"More importantly, Gwynn, this disclosure is by no means the only disclosure that may have to be made. The charge of daisy-chaining is serious. If the regulators suspect MSA involvement in such transactions, I have no idea what disclosures might be required. We need to give this some thought."

I had satisfied myself that no filing would be made before Stephen visited with Jackson and the executive committee. It would be impossible for anyone to do the kind of work required in that short a time.

Gwynn agreed with my suggestion and then outlined yet another issue I had not considered. "I think our problem goes beyond MSA. As I understand it from talking to the regulatory lawyers, the regulators, rightly or wrongly, believe that various banks and S&Ls nationally are hiding losses by creating long daisy chains of borrowers, and loans are swapped among various institutions. These transactions have become so complex with all the new players in the industry that it is difficult to see exactly who is behind the operations. Some of the transactions look as if they were intended to hide bad loans from regulatory scrutiny. Some of the loans look like normal interbank transactions. Some of the loans look like intentional fraud. The regulators will be looking for who benefits the most. To date, wherever MSA has been involved, it has benefited the most because it was, consciously or unconsciously, at the beginning of what ended up as a daisy chain."

"The beginning," I repeated.

"The beginning of the daisy chain," Gwynn said, looking me straight in the eye.

It is financially worst to be at the end of the chain," I thought, *but it is criminally worst to be at the beginning if you get caught.*

Jackson had always carefully maintained at least the veneer of being a good guy in an industry plagued with fraud. He had also built a reputation on the fact that, as unusual and complex as his bond trading strategies were, he was fundamentally honest. He made money for MSA by being a brilliant bond trader. If the regulators saw either of these carefully created and maintained reputations as untrue, Jackson was in big trouble.

If it was true that one of his top officers had been cooperating with federal examiners to uncover some less-than-stellar business practices, his days as one of the good guys were over. It would take years to recover his standing with the regulators—and Jackson and MSA did not have years to wait. Whether the FBI had already talked to the FHLBB or not, they would, and when they did, MSA and Jackson might be seen as having a strong motive to get rid of Don, assuming he was the source of their information. All this did nothing but confirm that Winchester & Wells needed to get as far away from MSA and the transaction as humanly possible.

I did not share my concerns with Gwynn. Before our meeting broke up, she and I discussed the need for her to ensure that Todd and the banking section kept us up-to-date on the regulatory issues, especially on any further questions about loans about which the regulators had concerns. I asked her to ask Todd not to make any new filings with regulators without my knowledge so that I could effectively coordinate the transaction (and delay it long enough for Stephen to act). I told her that I would call Todd and emphasize that no filings should be made until everyone agreed on the language to be included.

Finally, we made a date to meet for dinner at Ouisie's Table on Sunset near Rice University, later in the evening. That date would be the high point of a long week and an even longer week to come.

***

The next morning, a Friday, I received an invitation from Stephen to have lunch with him, Roger, Todd, and Gwynn at the River Oaks Country Club in the River Oaks area of Houston, near where Stephen lived on Avalon. It was a popular meeting spot for those who lived in the area and had businesses downtown because it could be as little as a ten-minute drive to or from a breakfast, lunch, or dinner meeting. We were to gather in the Hunt Room at noon.

When I asked Roger about Gwynn's presence at the meeting, he responded that Stephen wanted her there. She would keep notes to be sure that we all had the same understanding of what was said and not said. He obviously dreaded the meeting. Stephen notoriously kept out of the affairs of MSA or Jackson to the maximum extent possible, which was normally entirely. The list of invitees indicated that the subject of the luncheon conversation was going to be the transaction. Stephen Winchester was not a man to be crossed when he had determined to act, and it seemed as if Stephen was going to act.

To me, it was clear that Stephen had made up his mind about what to do regarding the transaction. I expected the meeting would be short and to the point. I puttered around the office, having no real incentive to put a lot of effort into the transaction before hearing what Stephen had to say, and left the office with Gwynn a few minutes before noon.

When we arrived, Stephen was already at the table. Roger arrived shortly after we did. We all ordered lunch, which for me was always gumbo on Fridays. The seafood gumbo at ROCC was particularly good—loaded with crab meat. Gwynn ordered a salad with chicken. Stephen and Todd joined me with the gumbo. Roger ordered the special of the day.

With the formalities over, Stephen opened the discussion. "We all know that the transaction between MSA, GSA, and WISA has been challenging from the beginning. It is highly complex—a tribute to my brother's ingenuity. If completed, it might be a great success. Unfortunately, for a variety of reasons over the past weeks, I have come to doubt whether it can be closed, especially if WISA continues to be a part of the transaction. I asked you all here today to hear what I have to say and to get any feedback you can give me before an executive committee meeting later this afternoon, at which the transaction will be discussed."

Roger looked at me with suspicion in his eyes.

There was a long moment of silence before Roger gave his analysis. "Stephen, you don't do as much transactional work as I do. This *is* a complex transaction, but two of the finest investment banking houses in the country are part of the deal. They have a lot of resources. In addition, Jackson believes the regulators have substantial reasons to approve the transaction. The problems with WISA are actually positive for the deal. Whereas before, the regulators had three institutions to supervise, they will now have only one. The combined institution will have the benefit of additional capital raised on Wall Street. In the end, the transaction will be approved because it is in the interests of everyone to see that it is approved.

"Right now, the regulators are covering their asses with questions so that, if anything goes wrong, they cannot be blamed. Once they have accomplished their goal, you can be sure they will fold their cards and approve the transaction. If we were to recuse ourselves from the transaction at this point, the blame might fall upon us if the transaction failed to close or if any of the institutions involved later got into trouble. Frankly, I do not think that the executive committee should discuss the transaction without Todd and me being present."

Stephen seemed to take in Roger's words.

Todd broke into the conversation. "Roger, while I agree with you that we are in a phase of the transaction where regulators commonly ask a lot of questions, this particular transaction has developed features that go deeper than just ass-covering. Even before the plane crash, we received some inquiries about specific loans. In the beginning, the inquiries were only about WISA. In recent weeks, however, we have received requests for explanations of loans made by MSA. It is as if the regulators have developed a theory about why this transaction is being undertaken, and they do not like the implications of their theory."

Todd paused long enough to let the implications sink in. "In my opinion, whatever the explanation of the plane crash, it has done nothing but make their suspicions grow deeper. To make things more complicated, we now have the FBI to consider in addition to the regulatory agencies we commonly handle. My staff is concerned about the transaction and what happens if it closes or doesn't close. We feel that the various investigations are bound to continue for some time. Our standing with the regulators will be harmed if anything goes wrong."

Stephen nodded and looked at me. "Art, what is your feeling?"

In my mind, that question was the exact reason why I should not have been invited to the luncheon. I had several choices. I could agree with Todd, which I did, or I could support Roger, my boss in the transaction, with whose views I did not agree. Finally, I could back Stephen and hope for the best. In the end, hoping for the best seemed the best strategy.

Being very careful with my words, I said, "There is merit to both points of view that Roger and Todd have expressed. There's no question that this is a complicated transaction. I can tell from some of the questions we are getting from the regulators that they are having difficulty understanding some of the complexities, particularly as it involves the investment strategies of MSA and how the financing is being put together. These strategies are very complicated and involve risks that I am not sure even the investment bankers fully comprehend. I certainly have difficulty understanding the strategies or risks.

"In addition, we have this latest round of new questions. Unfortunately, the latest round of questions has implications that, I believe, will certainly delay the transaction. MSA is a large institution and has made a lot of loans. Some of those loans have been sold to other institutions, and MSA may have purchased loans from the same or other institutions in the ordinary course of business. Responding to regulatory inquiries will take a lot of time. The regulators suspect a lot of fraud in the industry, and they will investigate to see if any of that fraud involves MSA or WISA. Frankly, as to WISA alone, that investigation would take months.

"Finally, we've mentioned the plane crash. We all originally operated on the assumption that it was a simple crash. There was some pilot error or equipment malfunction. When I talked to the FBI, however, it seemed to me that they were probing a theory that the crash was intentional. We know their investigation is continuing. Frankly, if the FBI was convinced that the crash was caused by pilot or mechanical error, I don't think the investigation would be continuing. As for me, I think that they suspect foul play."

I looked at Stephen, who seemed satisfied with the answer. Then I looked at Roger, who was obviously angry, and then at Todd, who looked horrified.

"If the transaction fails," I said, "we have to look at the possibility that the firm will be implicated in whatever causes that failure. If the regulators suspect wrongdoing, we have to deal with the fact that they may suspect we are part of the wrongdoing. Finally, if the FBI suspects that the crash was part of a murder plot of some kind, they cannot help but suspect that we might know more than we are saying or that we might actually be a part of the crime. In the end, while I respect Roger's point of view, I do not think it likely that the transaction will close."

All in all, I was proud of myself. I had not disclosed that the FBI currently was operating under the assumption that the crash was intentionally caused by a party or parties unknown. I also had not disclosed that a family member of one of the dead officers of MSA thought that her father was the source of information to the regulators. I did disclose, however, the potential problems those two facts raised. Stephen seemed appreciative of my analysis and of my discretion in phrasing my response.

Gwynn was given a chance to express her opinion, which was short. "I can verify that the due diligence team is having to respond to questions asked by regulators about certain loans. On a couple of occasions, the answers have not been what we might have wished. I think additional due diligence by the regulatory agencies will delay the transaction, but I can't say by how long."

Our food arrived, and we ate quietly. The conversation turned to the beauty of the golf course outside the glass windows that formed one wall of the Hunt Room, the excellence of the food, and a tropical storm that had become a hurricane headed for the Gulf of Mexico.

After lunch, Stephen said, "I want to thank everyone for their opinions. My brother already knows my concerns. As a member of the executive committee, I want you all to know that at this afternoon's meeting, I'm going to suggest that the firm take steps to recuse itself from further involvement. In any case, while I will consider Roger's objections and transmit them to the executive committee, my own mind is made up about this matter. It is too risky for us to continue to represent Jackson concerning this particular piece of business."

Stephen signed the ticket, giving his number to the waiter. We walked slowly to the parking lot. Roger continued to press Stephen to reconsider or at least allow him to address the executive committee.

Stephen, as always, was considerate but frank. "I will think about all you have said, but I do think my mind is made up. As to your addressing the committee, I will suggest that you be invited to give your views to them, if not today then before a final decision is made. In the meantime, you might want to stay at the office until the meeting is over so that we can reach you, if need be."

Todd was not with us. He had parked in another place. Stephen, having arrived first, was parked closest to the front door. We dropped him off at his car and said our goodbyes. Gwynn was walking slightly in front of me and Roger just behind us as we walked toward our cars.

Suddenly, I experienced one of my strange moments. I lost my orientation toward the ground beneath my feet, went off balance, and fell against Gwynn. She was already off balance, having just turned to say something to me. My weight was such that we both fell to the ground. Just then, there was a tremendous explosion. I was thrown down on top of Gwynn, somewhat protecting her from the explosion by falling over her body. Behind me, Roger caught the full force of the blast and was thrown over our falling figures into a nearby automobile. Shards of glass and metal embedded themselves in most of the back of Roger's body, one fairly substantial piece of metal from the car cutting deeply into his leg.

16

Watcher's Journey

THE WATCHER MADE HIS WAY toward the US border, stopping a few miles south of Reynosa in a small village, where he had relatives on his mother's side of the family. Hospitality was important in Indian and Mexican culture, and they enthusiastically welcomed him. The wife immediately prepared a feast. The wife also offered to call a doctor to treat his wound, but Mirador declined. He didn't want witnesses that might tie him to his family. He slept well for a few days, rested, ate the wonderful (if simple) meals the family provided, talked to his distant cousin, regained his strength, and pondered his next steps.

Initially, he intended to go to the United States and Fort Hood to find out who had betrayed him. In the end, he decided it was foolish to cross the border. Whoever had betrayed him would be watching. If he went home, he would be trapped. Mirador had an idea that if the bomb on the plane had misfired (as he thought it had), and there were problems with the authorities, whoever was behind the bombing would arrange for him to be blamed. After all, he was on the scene in Mexico, in the military, had the right skills, and was missing in action. He had already figured that his being unmarried and an orphan meant that no one would look out for him or mourn his passing.

While resting, Mirador read newspaper reports about the crash on the American side of the border. From the press reports, he learned that the King Air was returning from Mexico when it crashed about twenty miles north from Presidio on the US side of the border. Some articles indicated that authorities were searching for a former Special Forces operator who was believed to have had some role in the crash. This confirmed that he should not return to the United States.

As he spoke to his cousin, a different plan began forming in his mind.

"I have a will on file with the authorities in the United States. If it is determined that I am dead, it is likely the authorities will begin the process of probating that will and perhaps stop looking quite so carefully for me. I am going to write a letter to my commanding officer, seemingly containing the dying words of John Mirador."

He wrote the letter that night. In the letter, he denied responsibility for the plane crash, spoke about being wounded by an unidentified shooter while on a mission, and asked his unit commander to undertake an investigation. He never said but implied that the wound was serious.

His cousin sent the letter to a distant acquaintance, who posted it in a post office in Veracruz. It was impossible to trace the letter from a mail station in Veracruz to anyone in his family, miles and miles away. Mirador and his cousin then continued to talk about the situation until they decided on the next step.

Mirador's cousin came up with the final plan.

"I have a brother who is the abbot of a monastery located just outside of San Miguel de Allende in a rural, isolated area. I will write to him. I believe he will agree to receive a visitor and allow that visitor to remain at the retreat, at least for a time. From there, you can decide what to do next."

Mirador agreed, and his cousin wrote the letter. Naturally, the details of the situation were not given, nor was Mirador identified.

Upon receiving the expected invitation, Mirador made his way to San Miguel de Allende, where he was greeted as a traveler entitled to monastic hospitality.

***

The monastery was relatively new, the dream of a hermit who had lived on the property for many years after leaving another monastery in the United States. It was small, consisting of a chapel, the hermitage of the monk who had founded the monastery, a small refectory, the cloister for the few monks who lived an isolated life of silence, and a small retreat house.

The monks who lived there were Benedictines and devoted themselves to prayer and worship, while seeking to build the small monastery into a retreat center for the surrounding area. They prayed for Mexico and the area near the monastery, fulfilling their vows, as had generations of monks all over the world before them.

On arrival, Mirador was put into the hands of one of the monks, shown to the guesthouse, and given basic instruction on the terms and conditions for his stay. He was welcome to stay for as long as three months. He was welcome at all the worship services and was expected to be at the morning, noon, and evening services before meals. He would work in the garden and take care of the grounds surrounding the abbey. From time to time, he would be given other responsibilities in the in the kitchen and other places. He was to respect the monks in their silence and service to God and speak to no one outside the monastery.

He agreed.

Mirador's room in the guesthouse was small and consisted of a bed, a dark wooden chest of drawers in the Spanish style, a chair, and a table. On the front wall was an icon of the Virgin of the Guadalupe. Behind the bed was a picture of St. Benedict, the founder of the order. There was a small bathroom, more than adequate for his simple needs. The building itself was made of concrete with the walls painted white on the interior and a dark rust color on the exterior. He settled in to his new life quickly and without complaint.

A day or two later, Mirador was summoned to the abbot's office. The abbot was a short, muscular man with dark, piercing eyes—eyes that seemed to look into people's souls, as well as paying close attention to any words they spoke and their practical meaning. He obviously shared the Indian background of Mirador's family. He also shared their athleticism. Even his monk's habit could not entirely conceal his broad shoulders and large arms and muscular thighs. He was friendly but guarded, seeming to know a great deal more than he let on. In common with all those who lived in quiet seclusion, a certain contemplative peace emanated from the abbot's person.

"I want to hear the entire story of what has occurred," the abbot said "Tell me everything, John Mirador, because I already know that the authorities in your country are looking for a rogue Special Forces officer by that name."

Mirador had given a false name when he entered the monastery, not wanting anyone to guess his true identity. The realization that he was known confirmed what he had expected when he set out: He would have to tell the truth to the abbot in order to build trust and protect himself and everyone else involved. For one thing, the monastery would be in danger if his presence were discovered. He did not want to be the source of danger to his family. He must tell the truth, for the abbot would easily discern a lie, and only the abbot could protect the monastery and its inhabitants.

"It is true that my country is looking for me," Mirador admitted. "Everything else you might have heard or read in the newspapers is false. I was sent to your country on a mission and was betrayed by my own countrymen. I'm hiding until I can either begin a new life or return home. My mission had nothing to do with the crash of the plane. I was sent as a forward observer to report to my superiors what I observed and, in particular, when the meeting ended, which I did. I was never near the plane in question and could have had nothing to do with its crash.

"In my opinion, something went wrong with a plan, of which I knew nothing. Now, the authorities are looking for a scapegoat. I have been chosen to fill that role. It is conceivable that my name will be cleared, and I will be able to return. Given the services with which I worked, however, and the situation as I understand it, that is not likely. There is some dark intrigue at work, a plot that I do not fully understand. Once a deception like this begins, there is no turning back. Those who betrayed me cannot end their betrayal and lies without danger to themselves and their families. There is danger to me—and to you, if I stay with you too long, and I'm discovered. If it becomes known that I am here, you can be sure agents will be sent to apprehend or kill me. I am, therefore, in your hands."

The abbot nodded his understanding and prodded Mirador to continue.

"I can tell you this much about the mission I was on. In North Central Mexico, there is a hunting camp frequented by wealthy Mexicans and Americans. A few weeks ago, I was asked to watch that hunting camp and report on activities within it. In particular, I was to report when certain guests left the camp to return home. I was inserted in your country by air and did as I was told.

"In the last days of the mission, Hurricane Fey came ashore in your country and began its passage toward the Pacific Ocean. As a result, the meeting was cut short, and those involved left hurriedly. The persons in the plane that crashed left first. After the plane took off, a series of unusual events took place. In the beginning, as the plane began to cross the mountains, the storm seemed to rush forward with an odd kind of lightning flashing within the hurricane. To my eyes, it was almost as if the darkness of the storm reached out for the plane. Just as the storm reached the plane, there was a burst of light and then an explosion. The plane appeared to survive the explosion; it went through the light and darkness and emerged on a path toward the American border.

"I was startled by the unusual storm and the strange lightning, one bolt of which seemed to go through my body with no effect, other than I suddenly stumbled and fell. As I fell, I was shot in the shoulder. Because of the storm and the fall, the assassin missed his shot. I survived with a minor injury and escaped. The assassin was not so lucky."

Mirador did not clarify that last statement but then said, "I had nothing to do with the explosion. My duty was to observe the camp and report my observations to my superiors. In particular, I was to let them know when the plane left the camp. I did all this from a reasonable distance, just as would have been the case if I had been an advance observer in the time of war, which I have been many times in the past."

"Did you know any of the men at the meeting?" the abbot asked.

"No. I now know that two of the men, the two who were on the airplane, were banking executives from Houston, Texas. That fact has been reported in newspapers. Apparently, the plane survived an initial explosion but later crashed a few miles across the border in South Texas, near Ojinaga in your country and Presidio in mine. I think the other men were two Mexican nationals, and one American, an average-looking man. During my surveillance of the meeting at the camp, I took pictures, which I can show you."

Mirador placed the pictures in front of the abbot and identified them by the nicknames he had given them during his mission. The abbot stared at them intently and was immediately and visibly startled.

"The American, I do not know," the abbot said. "But nearly everyone in my country would know the other two. The shorter man is known as El Capitán, the apparent leader of one of our drug cartels. He's known to be violent and unstable. He is a former Special Forces officer in the Mexican army, and his cartel is more than capable of blowing up a plane. In recent months, El Capitán has become more violent than ever. There are rumored threats to his leadership. He has ruthlessly killed many people. It is my own opinion that this tactic will backfire, and the people who control him will eventually have him killed or arrested.

"The tall man you have called 'the Hawk' is actually called by that name in our country. He is El Halcón, the leader of a wealthy family with many business holdings. He has been a high-position public official, once serving as the foreign minister. He has long been friendly with high officials in your government, and he has intelligence contacts all over the world.

"In Mexico, there are very few public officials about whom one can say, 'This man is not corrupt.' During El Halcón's time in office, he became even more wealthy, one of the wealthiest men in Mexico and in all the world. He is feared by all and hated by many. This man is more powerful than El Capitán. I suspect he might even be more dangerous."

Mirador needed time to think and plan and so made his request to the abbot. "You can see that I am in over my head. You can also see that my life is in danger. If what you say is true, it is unlikely that I will ever be able to return to my country. There was a time in my country where one could say that public officials were honest. That is no longer true. I have been in our military Special Forces since Vietnam. I can tell you that my country is not the country of my childhood.

"No one knows exactly when it began, but there is a corruption in my nation as well as yours. Drugs are a part of that corruption, but so is the desire for power and wealth. Desire for wealth and power is, of course, behind the worst corruption. There are also times when our intelligence agencies have partnerships with criminal and other groups in the search for information. They even work with our enemies from time to time. In the dark world of intelligence, there often are operatives we privately despise. In some cases, it is easier to get in bed with the devil than to get out.

"I have worked for many years as a Special Forces operator. I have been in many countries, particularly in Latin America. Much of the time, my work has required that I partner with intelligence officials. I have come to know them well. If I am not mistaken, the American, whom I call the Bureaucrat, is an intelligence operative. I have seen his type many times in the past. If you allow me to stay here, I promise you that I will leave if it appears, at any time, that the monastery might be identified as harboring a fugitive criminal. I also promise I will eventually leave so that you will not be in continual danger." Mirador then concluded with specific requests. "I have some experience in similar matters. I will need a new identity, papers, a Mexican passport, and time for a new identity to take a root."

The abbot nodded. "No one, not even my closest associate who manages the business affairs of the monastery, has heard your true name. From today, you will no longer be John Mirador but *Juan de la Cruz Bardero* —my associates already know you by the name John. You are going through a dark time, a dark night of the soul, and so we will call you *de la Cruz*, for like Christ and John of the Cross, your wisdom comes through suffering. We will call you *Bardero*, for you were a bully for your government in your former life, though perhaps not in the heart—where it matters most."

Mirador smiled and said, "The name is but the beginning. I still need a life history and a Mexican passport. That history needs to be one as far away as possible from my family here in Mexico. It will be convenient if I come from Chiapas or some other area in the poorest regions of Mexico, not from Northern Mexico. Perhaps we could explain to the brothers of this monastery that I am a novice who began training in another place but fell away. Now, I desire to renew my faith and calling and have come here.

"I am sure a monastery is like the army, and rumors will spread. Some of them are likely to reach villages nearby. If gossip is repeated, it is necessary that it not have any relationship with the events we have been discussing. I must be given many tasks involving hard work to perform on behalf of the monastery. In this way, the other brothers will not resent me. I must also be required to make confession to you personally on a regular basis. This will explain our time together.

Mirador paused but then said, "As I said before, I need three things. I'm going to need that Mexican identification card and passport. I may need to travel, which I cannot do with my US identification papers. Second, I need you to see if you can discover, through your sources, the identity of the

American in the picture I showed you. Finally, I need to do some research while I am with you."

The abbot nodded quietly. "This is a good beginning. We will begin with the name and the news that you are originally from Tabasco or some other poor area far to the south. For now, we will say that you are interested in becoming a brother, but we will not use the remainder of the story you contrived. I will see that you have much menial work to do. I will also use my contacts to obtain the necessary papers. I assume that the beard you now have is new and that Juan de la Cruz Bardero will not look like John Mirador to anyone who sees your photo."

"The beard is new. Nearly all pictures of me that my government possesses show me clean-shaven and in uniform. I have lost some weight in the past weeks and will be careful to keep it off. It is important that my picture is not taken, if at all possible, except as needed for a new passport and identification papers. I must rarely leave the monastery. In this way, few people would even wonder about my identity."

The abbot nodded again and made arrangements to meet with the newly named Juan de la Cruz Bardero in the next day or two.

For those not used to life in a monastery, the first few days of residence inspire a gradual and growing sense of relaxation. The quiet that pervades monastic quarters eventually finds its way into the busy soul of a visitor. Long hours of silence create an inner quiet that does not depend on the absence of physical noise. Mirador enjoyed this time of quiet meditation.

For Mirador, who was accustomed to a short night's sleep, the monastic routine of prayer, work, meals, and sleep came easily. He rose for matins and lauds, early in the darkness of morning and again at sunrise. He worshipped and prayed with the community without complaint, which earned him a degree of acceptance. He worked hard, a fact that did not escape notice. Eventually, he was given the responsibility to go into the city to acquire groceries, medicines, and other items for the monastery. He was always careful on these excursions.

San Miguel de Allende was one of the loveliest cities in the world, with its cobblestone streets, many churches, perfect temperature, and ancient homes. The center of the city was 250 years old. Mirador fell in love with the city and with its signature church, La Parroquia de San Miguel Arcángel (the Parish Church of St. Michael the Archangel), the parish church for the entire city, which was visible from almost any angle. La Parroquia, as it was known, was built in a unique style for Mexico and was the emblem of the town. On his visits, Mirador tried to take time to sit in the quiet of La Parroquia and meditate on his past, his present, and his future. Slowly, a plan began to form in his mind.

His mother had been religious, so the monastery's routine of religious readings at meals and at the worship services during each day reconnected him to the faith of his childhood. He found himself thinking about his family, his upbringing, and his career. For the first time in many years, he missed his parents and the ranch. It was obvious that his military career, a career that had formed his life since late adolescence, was over. He would have to make choices about his future. He could not return home, at least not for some time. His future would have to be in Mexico or elsewhere in Latin America. He found himself often meditating about the choices he needed to make. It was somehow comforting to do this work of planning his future within the walls of a place of quiet, reflection, and faith.

17

More Revelations

A FEW DAYS LATER, JUAN de la Cruz Bardero was again asked to visit with the abbot. He was a bit surprised. He had thought it would be a somewhat longer time before he was asked to see the abbot again. He presented himself at the abbot's office when the day's work was over and before vespers.

Their conversation began informally, and then the abbot moved the conversation toward deeper and more important matters.

"I have made inquiries as to how you can receive papers and a passport. It is by no means an easy matter and will take a bit more time. We have begun the process of getting your identification papers, which will not take much longer to accomplish.

"In addition, I have made inquiries through members of our order in Mexico City concerning the identity of the gentleman from the United States whose picture you were kind enough to loan to me. I believe he is an economic attaché at the United States embassy in Mexico City. His name is Edward John ' E.J' Mueller, a graduate of Yale University in your country. His résumé states that he was an officer in the United States Army in Vietnam. After his first tour of duty, he returned as an employee in the American embassy there. Since the end of the Vietnam War, he had many postings all over the world, particularly in Venezuela, Columbia, Central America, and Mexico. I have a dossier on him with his picture, which you may study at your leisure."

One glance at the picture in the dossier confirmed that Mueller was the man Mirador had seen. Mueller's history and postings were consistent with his being either in the Central Intelligence Agency or some other intelligence branch. He didn't want to reveal his suspicions, and so he simply responded, "I see."

The abbot then looked down at his desk, gathering his thoughts.

"I want to ask you some questions about one more part of your experience. I have studied carefully the pictures you took at the sight of your betrayal so that I could accurately describe the person for whom we are looking. When I looked at the pictures closely—in particular, the pictures you took of the plane as it entered the unusual cloud formation—I noticed something that I believe is more unusual than perhaps you suspected."

He asked Mirador to come around behind him as he placed one of the pictures on his desk before them. "This picture is quite interesting. You can see that the main body of the storm has not yet reached the plane, but the front edge of the cloud formation has extended itself until it almost reaches the plane. Inside that formation, you can see unusual lightning, flashing in the darkness of the oncoming storm. Can you see it?"

Mirador nodded.

"You see beams of light, beams that appear to be within the storm?"

Mirador nodded.

"If you look closely—it is hard to see—you'll notice that these beams of light are brighter and of slightly different colors. In fact, they are of many different colors. These beams of light are also unusual in that they are neither completely vertical with reference to the ground nor completely horizontal within the sheet lightning. They appear to be moving or appearing at an angle from the earth and from the clouds that contain them. Finally, there is an almost humanoid shape to them, perhaps *slightly rounded* would be a better description. I think these are not bolts of lightning, at least not any kind of lightning bolts I have ever seen."

Mirador nodded.

"I noticed that oddity at the time the pictures were taken. It seemed to me that there was an unusual quality to the lightning or at least to the strange bolts of lightning within the clouds to which you refer. For one thing, it seemed to me as if one of them went through me just before the shooting and pitched me off balance. The light did me no harm. But I stumbled and fell, saving my life. After the fall, I had no burn or other evidence of having been hit by any kind of lightning. Like you, I have never seen or experienced anything like it before."

The abbot looked at Mirador quietly. It was as if he was trying to formulate in his mind whether or not Mirador would accept or understand anything he said from that point forward.

"In my younger years, I was a scholar. I still write a bit for our order in preparing materials for prayer and other aspects of the spiritual life. At one point, I was able to go to the Vatican to study. While I was there, I wrote a dissertation on the subject of angelology, or the study of angels, in the writings of the Church Fathers. I was reminded of something I once read when I saw these pictures. The Church Fathers described angels as beings of divine light or 'heavenly fire,' created by God as ministering spirits.

"The Hebrew word for angel means messenger. In the scriptures, angels are messengers sent from God and their direction—if that is even relevant—is always to and from God. This is why the angel Gabriel in the Annunciation speaks of himself as 'Gabriel, who stands in the presence of God.' Gabriel, while appearing to Mary, is still oriented toward his presence with the God of Israel, whom he represents to Mary as he gives her a message from God.

"Angels cannot be circumscribed or controlled by any physical force, for they are not physical. They are divine messengers sent to illuminate the world in some way. They reveal themselves only occasionally to worthy persons who are called by God to perform some particular function."

"I am not sure that I follow you," Mirador said. "Can you repeat what you just said?"

The abbot nodded. "According to the ancients, the angels were created by God without bodies, purely mental—what we call *noetic*—beings, capable of being in different places with great rapidity—instantaneously. This is because as creatures of divine light, they move outside of space and time, even more swiftly than physical light. On occasion, they are described as 'pillars' or 'beams' of light. When I saw those almost humanoid light beams in your pictures, I wondered what they might be. The odd angles attracted my attention. As I mentioned, the character of angels in their orientation is always toward God, not toward any created element of our universe. This means that they do not necessarily appear to us as we expect. Angels may appear in human form so that a person might see and hear them, and they may stand upright in their appearance, but their actual orientation is not up or down but toward God and away from God.

"Finally, angelic beings may act at variance to the divine light by which they were created, for their light is not uncreated light but created life. The scriptures and the ancients believed that there were and are fallen angels; that is, angelic beings who have fallen away from their original wisdom and goodness and are now opposed to the good and inclined to harm the human race. In them, the divine light has become impenetrable darkness. In this case, I believe the angels you may have seen are of the former unfallen, not the latter fallen type, but the darkness of the storm might well hide such beings from your camera."

Mirador was accustomed to assimilating new information to choose a course of conduct during military operations. In this case, he sat in mute stupefaction, trying to assimilate the abbot's ideas into any worldview or plan for the future he might make. At first glance, it seemed ridiculous. He had experienced something, however, and that something needed an explanation. If any of what the abbot was saying was true, then the world that he was accustomed to inhabiting was not as solid or predictable as he had always thought. If the abbot was telling the truth, the material world of his day-to-day life was permeated by an immaterial world of pure mind that lay under the surface of experience, a substratum from which angels and demons could and did appear and disappear upon the earth.

He voiced his confusion to the abbot. "I barely understand what you're saying. Are you saying that in this visible world, there is also an invisible from which our world emerges, a world of pure mind or spirit? And if so, that invisible world, which includes angels, is capable of entering into our world at any place and point in time, and for some reason, it entered Northern Mexico during the time I was watching the meeting at the hunting camp."

The abbot nodded. "Precisely. That is what I believe. But there is more. If angelic beings appeared in that storm and prevented the plane from crashing during the first explosion and then allowed it to crash later in your country, then heaven itself and the universe we inhabit did not want that plane to crash in Mexico. For some reason, the plane was intended to reach the United States, which it did. If angels intervened to save your life, you were intended to see the strange lights. The nature of the storm and the appearance of the extraordinary light we have been discussing caused you to stumble, saving your life. Your life was saved, and you are a distant cousin of mine, sent to me because of the fear our family has for your safety. This means that you too were meant to be saved, Juan de la Cruz Bardero—and you were meant to arrive in this place.

"Angels do not appear for no reason. Angels appeared to Abraham to warn him about the destruction of Sodom and Gomorrah. An angel appeared to Gideon so that he might rescue his people. An angel appeared to Daniel so that he might be encouraged to serve his people. An angel appeared to the father of John the Baptist so that he and Elizabeth might know that the new Elijah, the forerunner of Christ, would be their son. An angel appeared to Mary so that she might learn that she would become the mother of the Messiah. If what you saw was angelic, you can be sure that you have something left to do.

"I believe the storm itself, with its strange darkness, gives us a clue to another aspect of your story: a storm has come into your life. That storm is connected to another storm, a storm that has come into my country and yours. In his letter to the Ephesians, Saint Paul reminds us that there are powers, principalities, and rulers of the darkness in our age and every age. These powers are capable of wounding and destroying human life and human civilization. Violence, corruption, addiction, and death all involve a kind of spiritual darkness. The storm, I think, was a visible symbol created by nature, a true and real symbol for a battle we cannot see but in which we are engaged, whether we want to be or not. Drug lords and drug use are a kind of darkness. The corruption in our country and yours is a darkness. The misuse of power by the mighty in business and government is a darkness. This darkness must be faced. The corruption is too large and powerful for us to face alone, and so messengers have been sent to give us aid.

"One last thing. I do not think it by chance that you were spared death by an assassin's bullet. Your life has been spared for a purpose. I cannot tell you what that purpose is, but I believe there is a purpose to your being alive and here."

Mirador looked down, hands folded, and quieted his racing thoughts, as he had many times before as a mission began. "I will give some thought to all that you have said.

I am no scholar and am barely religious. It has been many years since I attended church. I am a man of action and have given no thought to this kind of thing for the past many years, if ever. I had no reason to do so. Now, I must think. I saw the beams of light, the plane escape certain destruction, and my own life spared. It has some kind of meaning. I will think about everything that you have said."

With that, the bell rang the call to vespers and prayer, and they left together for the service. Mirador had much to ponder and meditate upon during the vesper prayers and in days to come.

A Fugitive's Journey

A WEEK OR MORE PASSED. Bardero, as Mirador was now accustomed to being called, learned of a car bombing in Houston, in which Stephen Winchester died, from newspapers that American tourists bought and left behind while staying in San Miguel de Allende. He noted the possible connection between the car bombing and the deaths of persons in the doomed King Air. The King Air had belonged to a savings association owned by Jackson Winchester, the brother of the lawyer who was the apparent target of the Houston bombing. Certain pieces of the puzzle were coming together in his mind, though their meaning and his possible future role were unclear.

He was certain that the bombing of the plane was somehow connected with the bombing of the car. People with some connection to an entity known as Marshland

Savings Association were killed in the plane crash. The airplane was owned by that bank. Bardero noted that this savings association was involved in a major transaction involving two other savings associations in Texas.

The articles noted that the victim of the car bombing, Stephen Winchester, was the brother of Jackson Winchester, the chairman of MSA. The dead brother's law firm was representing MSA in the transaction. Interestingly, it was reported that Stephen Winchester had no financial interest in MSA. He also noted that Winchester was survived by an elderly mother in a nursing home in Houston and a wife, whose name he recognized as Vietnamese, Ahn.

He decided to do a bit of research. When he researched the family, he realized that he had briefly met Stephen Winchester at Khe Sanh, where Winchester gained a reputation for quiet courage. He remembered that the man had been wounded in battle and airlifted out. He did not recognize pictures of Ahn. From what he gathered, neither Stephen Winchester nor his wife was the kind of person to be involved in something like the murder of three people in a bombing. Mirador's vague recollections supported that conclusion.

There was not a lot of detailed information available to the public concerning the transaction in which MSA was involved. An investigative reporter for the *Houston Post* wrote a couple of articles about the transaction, neither overtly critical. Both articles mentioned the names of Vixette Savings Association and West Isle Savings Association as thought to be part of a group of savings associations, possibly indirectly controlled by a shadowy Louisiana figure. Neither article was backed by sufficient facts to convince Bardero. Neither article mentioned drugs, drug lords, or federal agencies, except to note that the crash and bombing were being investigated by the FBI, who believed that the two events might be connected in some way. One article mentioned a rogue Special Forces operative whom authorities were anxious to interview.

It was time to stop thinking and reading and take action, if for no other reason than to protect himself. He had interrogated Harry Dent thoroughly. Bardero understood some facts about the crash and had a vague description of the person who had hired Dent. Something deeper, however, was going on that he could not yet understand. He decided to make a trip to Mexico City and then to the United States. He now needed those identification papers and a valid passport. It was time for a word with the abbot.

Bardero and the abbot met late on the evening of the next day. Bardero began by thanking the abbot for his hospitality and asking if he might obtain his identification and passport on an expedited basis, by the end of the week at the latest. He needed to make a trip to Mexico City and the United States. The abbot said that he would try. He then made Bardero aware of the limits of his hospitality.

"As you know, we are a monastery and cannot become involved in anything criminal or violent, nor can we run the risk of the Mexican authorities or drug cartels taking an interest in this place. Mexico has a history of persecuting the Catholic Church if it is seen as opposing the government. If you leave, I will want assurances that you are not going to involve us in something beyond our abilities to handle."

Bardero assured the abbot that he had no intentions of doing anything that would expose the monastery or its occupants to danger.

"I need to leave to inform others of the danger we have discussed. I will be outside Mexico when I do this, though I cannot tell you where at this time. If I have a valid Mexican passport and a credible short-term business visa under the name Juan de la Cruz Bardero, there is relatively little danger of my being caught. If by chance I am caught while in the United States, I soon will be recognized as John Mirador. That is your risk. To protect the monastery, it might be best if Juan de la Cruz, which is a common name in your country, is identified as a Mexican businessman checking up on a small investment in San Antonio, Texas.

"Before I go, I intend to write letters to three individuals. They will be posted anonymously in or near Mexico City. The letters will not be traceable to your monastery. I will be sure to write them on paper and ink purchased in Mexico City. If the stationery or ink is traced, it will be impossible to implicate the monastery. I will leave just enough clues for the authorities to believe, if I am caught, that I have been living in Mexico City, not here.

"While I am gone, I do not believe I will be involved in anything violent. I have listened to you carefully and spent many hours meditating in this place. My days as a soldier and man of violence are over. From press reports, I've concluded that the people who ordered the bombing of the plane, and the car bombing in Houston, are almost certainly Americans. The person who prepared the bomb was an American, but I do not know who ultimately hired him to go to Mexico, nor did he know when I interrogated him. I think the assassin was also hired to bomb the plane and kill me. He was not hired in Mexico but was sent here after he was hired by persons unknown. I do, however, believe that El Capitán was somehow involved.

"The bomb was planted by a person or persons within the hunting camp under the direction of the assassin, who was careful to remain out of my sight while I was observing the camp. The assassin did not know who initially ordered the bombing, but I think I may know a way to possibly find out. If I can contact appropriate persons in the United States, over time, they may be able to investigate and discover the persons responsible on the American side of the border, which is why I need to make a short trip to the United States."

The abbot nodded. It would be easy for the monastery to arrange for a lawyer in Mexico City to ask that someone deliver legal papers to San Antonio as a favor. American authorities were certain to allow it. In such circumstances, Mirador would find it easy to get through customs. He would have between forty-eight and seventy-two hours to do whatever business had to be done before returning to Mexico by Aero Mexico. If he intended to go to Houston, it would be best if he did not travel to Houston directly but instead rented a car in San Antonio and drove to Houston. Mirador agreed. In any case, he did have personal business in San Antonio.

A few days later, Juan de la Cruz Bardero left the monastery early in the morning and traveled to Mexico City, where he wrote and mailed three letters before boarding an Aero Mexico flight bound for San Antonio. He was carrying a Mexican passport. A well-groomed, athletic, gray-haired, bearded man wearing an expensive floral Guayabera shirt and linen slacks caused no concern at customs. He explained that he was from near Mexico City and was coming to San Antonio on a business errand. His papers were in order. Upon inquiry, he stated that, in addition to his business, he intended to see relatives if he had time. He would be in the United States for one or two nights at the most before returning to Mexico.

After passing through customs, Mirador rented a car at the airport. His first stop was at a rental facility located in San Antonio. He had cash, documents, and some personal items stashed in the storage facility against any emergency. He carefully boxed and shipped the personal items and some of the documents to an address in Mexico other than the monastery, then drove to Houston, where he spent the night.

The next day, he returned to San Antonio in time to return to Mexico later that same day. When he went through customs, he had nothing to declare. His briefcase, which had been full of papers when he left Mexico, was nearly empty on return, evidence that he had delivered the documents he had been requested to deliver during his visit to Texas. He was back at the monastery within seventy-two hours. He was never examined or searched by anyone.

Awakening

I WOKE UP IN THE hospital. When I regained consciousness, my mother, father, and uncle Ben sat quietly, looking at the bed. Apparently, for some time I had been gradually regaining consciousness. My mind was not clear. I remembered stumbling and falling on Gwynn but nothing else. Every bone in my body was sore, and I could tell that one of my legs was slightly stiff and numb from the explosion.

"What happened? How did I get here?"

Uncle Ben answered with simple clarity. "There was a car bomb."

"I fell on Gwynn. How is she?"

My mother evidently decided it was her duty to answer that question.

"The doctors think she's going to be fine. Your fall on her was a blessing. You protected her from the full force of the blast. Your body absorbed some of the shards of metal and glass that might have been embedded in her, had you not fallen on her. She has a couple of broken ribs and a pretty severe cut to one side of her forehead where she hit the pavement. She has a mild concussion. But...."

Dad put on his best compassionate pastor's face and looked at me, who he knew well. "The doctors are sure that Gwynn will be fine. Her baby is still in some danger, but the doctors are optimistic."

I did not try to hide anything. "We are engaged. We were going to tell her family and you guys soon, maybe this coming weekend, if our work permitted."

My parents did not look particularly comforted by that explanation.

"What about Stephen?" I asked.

"It was Stephen's car that exploded. He was killed instantly."

At that moment, I crossed the Rubicon of my professional life. Stephen Winchester, the best lawyer in our law firm, one of the most decent persons I had ever known, a role model and mentor, had been blown to pieces, probably as a result of a transaction for which I was personally responsible. If I had acted earlier or differently, he might still be alive. I felt a weight of responsibility for his death.

I had drifted through law school, a federal clerkship, my time at the attorney general's office, and more than five years at Winchester & Wells by relying on my outgoing personality and innate intelligence to take me to the next step in my life and career. "Get along and go along" had been my motto, consciously or subconsciously. I always took the easy way out, including with Gwynn. She and our baby were now in danger. My failure to act sooner could have cost her life and might still cost the life of our baby. Whatever happened next, I was no longer going to drift. If I had the chance, I was going to be a partner at Winchester & Wells—and I was going to be as good a lawyer and litigator as Stephen Winchester had been. I was not going to be cowed by Roger Romny or anyone else. I was going to take care of Gwynn and our child. It was time for Arthur David Stone to grow up.

There was one more person to be accounted for. I asked, "What about Roger?"

"Roger was the most seriously injured," Uncle Ben answered. "You fell far enough ahead of him that he barely grazed your back when he was blown over you into a car. Had he hit you square in the back, it is likely that the two of you, perhaps especially Gwynn, would have been more seriously injured. No one seems to understand exactly how that happened."

I knew exactly how it had happened.

"I've been having these spells where the world seems to go topsy-turvy, and I end up feeling that up is sideways," I said. "I've never actually fallen over in the past. Just before the bomb blew up, I had the most serious episode yet. Gwynn had just turned around to talk to me when I fell on top of her. She was already off balance, and I took her down with me when I fell. This happened just a few seconds before the blast. When the blast occurred, we were nearly on the ground. If I believed in miracles, I would say it was a miracle."

My uncle stared in disbelief. My father, who believed in miracles, stared too but not in disbelief.

"In any case," my uncle said, "Roger was hit by glass and metal. His head struck the tire of the car into which he was blown. He has serious injuries, particularly to one of his legs. Because he hit the tire with his head, he has some swelling in the brain, and the doctors are concerned that there might be brain damage. It is too early to say how far Roger will recover or when."

At this point, my mother excused herself. "I think I'm going to leave you boys to visit. I'll go see Gwynn and see how she's doing. We were over there earlier, but she had not regained consciousness. I'd like to be there, if and when she does."

She left, and for a few moments, there was silence. Dad asked if I felt well enough to talk. I nodded, and we three looked at one another.

My uncle broke the silence with a blunt question that completely summed up my feelings about the situation: "Art, what in the world have you got yourself into?"

"I am not sure."

"Since the blast, I've been calling friends in the FBI," Uncle Ben said. "They believe the plane crash in South Texas was a result of a bomb. In fact, they know it was a bomb because they found debris that indicates that the initial explosion came from inside the plane. In addition, they found residue of plastic explosives embedded in some of the fragments of the plane's cargo hold. Three people died in that crash—the pilot, the president of your client, and its chief financial officer.

"The FHLBB has told the FBI that the CFO of Marshland, one of the people killed in the first crash, was a source for them in an ongoing investigation. Your client and its principal shareholder are the focus of that investigation. The bomb that blew up your partner's car contained residue of the same kind of explosive used to blow up the King Air, and the FBI is fairly certain, from forensic data, that the bomb was made by the same person or persons. There is something really dangerous going on here."

Dad sat listening in stunned and stoic silence. It was obvious that he and Uncle Ben had spoken about this; he was not hearing this for the first time. I could tell he was not happy with what he had heard.

It was my turn to talk. "Here's what I can tell you— and you must never tell anyone else, not even Mom. When the FBI interviewed me, they made me aware that they suspected the crash was not accidental. The interview was the first time I suspected anything might be amiss. In the day or so before the bombing of Stephen's car, however, I became aware that the chief financial officer of MSA had shared certain information with the authorities. Stephen Winchester received that information from me the same day. The last time I spoke to Stephen, I told him what I had learned, and we discussed our reservations about the transaction. Stephen promised to talk to his brother about the situation. I assume Stephen told Jackson about the FBI investigation and about the investigation that we feel the FHLBB and state authorities are undertaking, related to MSA and others."

Uncle Ben looked relieved. It was obvious I was telling the truth and not directly involved in the bombings. I don't think he ever seriously thought I would be involved in such a thing. He seemed to hesitate before he spoke. "So, what do you think is going on?"

I gathered my thoughts, knowing that I was talking to an experienced investigator who would see any holes in what I said and look for any attempt to shade or hide the truth.

"The way I see it, here are the facts: Frank and Don were in Mexico at a meeting. We do not know exactly why, what transpired, or how much business was involved. Allegedly, they were in Mexico on a hunting trip. Nevertheless, we all know business is often discussed on these kinds of trips. I am pretty sure that the business was with Frank, and Don was just along to answer financial questions.

"Before the trip, someone in the US or Mexico had already decided to get rid of Don. If I am right, Frank was the person involved in whatever business was to be done at the meeting, but Don was the intended victim of the bombing of the plane. He was the person talking to the regulators. As to Frank, whoever ordered the bombing considered him expendable."

"You're correct that we don't know what happened," my uncle broke in, "but you're not correct that we know nothing. The FBI has been talking to its office in Mexico City, and inquiries have been made. They talked to some people who were at the camp. There were at least five people present as guests. We know that two of them were Frank and Don. I don't think they count the pilot as a participant. One of the men has been identified as El Capitán, who is allegedly the head of a Mexican drug cartel. It so happens that El Capitán's cartel supplies the Houston area with much of its illegal drugs. The other two men appeared to have been businessmen, one American and one a Mexican national. The staff could not identify the final American who was present, but they did identify the Mexican as one of the richest and most powerful people in Mexico."

I started to break in, but my uncle held up his hand so that he could continue.

"One last thing is odd about the meeting, and it sheds some light on the crash. There was some urgency to get the planes in the air ahead of the hurricane. The first plane to leave contained the MSA executives. The plane flew northward, attempting to get over the mountains ahead of the storm. It failed to make it. One of the witnesses, a housekeeper, says that the plane seemed to explode in an odd flash of light at one point, just before it entered clouds in the advanced part of the storm. The plane, however, did not crash at that point. Servants at the hunting camp saw the plane exit to the north. If what they say is true, there were likely two explosions. The first was intended to cause the plane to crash on the Mexican side of the border. It was never intended that the plane would be where United States authorities could examine the debris. The bomb misfired, however, and the plane made it as far as the border before a second blast caused its final disintegration."

It was my turn.

"This explains something. I have not been able to understand why someone would blow up a plane on this side of the border when the option existed to blow it up in a deserted area on the other side of the border. It makes sense that there were either two explosions or one explosion that fatally damaged the plane, which later fell apart in the United States. This explanation, however, does not answer my basic question: what incentive would anyone have to blow up the plane just to kill Don Mendoza? To kill three people just to get rid of one requires either a huge motive, a mad person, or both.

"Jackson, for example—even if he knew that Don was giving information to the authorities—would not have killed the president of his company and crashed his own plane. He would have first tried to buy off Don by arranging a new job and some kind of payment. Jackson is smart enough to understand that a murder would surely cause trouble for a transaction in which he has invested a lot of time, energy, and money. He's always said that this transaction is important for the future of MSA. That being the case, I wouldn't think that he would be the person who ordered the bombing. Furthermore, I do not think that, at that moment, Jackson knew about Don's visiting with the federal authorities. I believe he only learned that information, if he learned it at all, from Stephen just before he died.

"I also can't understand why a Mexican drug lord would order a bombing with a substantial amount of their product on board the airplane. Any drugs found on an airplane would immediately cause suspicions in Mexico and the United States. The drugs point to someone wanting the authorities to think that drugs were the reason for the crash to cover up someone else.

"On the whole, I cannot understand the motivations of the person or persons behind the two bombings, unless someone was acting outside of normal behavior or for some reason yet to be discovered. The clue to this mystery remains to be uncovered."

My father and uncle stared at me with new respect. My father was seeing a part of my character he had never seen before. In particular, both of them seemed impressed by the logic behind the notion that the drugs on the plane might have been a cover for someone or some persons who wanted drugs to look like the motive for the meeting and the crash.

I think I'm right, I thought. *Whatever the real reason for the crash and bombing, drugs were not the core reason.*

"Two other characters in this little drama should be considered," I told them. "Originally, three savings and loan associations were involved in the transaction. One of them is in Dallas, Vixette Savings Association, which Fred Vixette controls. A few weeks ago, it became obvious that VSA was too large with too many problems to ever gain regulatory approval for the transaction. Jackson was forced by the firm and his investment bankers to have a meeting, at which Fred was informed that VSA was out of the transaction. He didn't take it well and threatened everyone involved.

"Fred Vixette is an interesting character. He is a braggart and a fool. In the meetings we've had, he's boasted about his connections in Louisiana with the Mafia and with the CIA. Frankly, nobody believed him. He may have had some dealings with unsavory characters, but Fred is an average real estate developer from Dallas. He gained control of the savings and loan association, made a bunch of construction loans to his buddies, and got in big trouble. I don't think anybody believes that he's the kind of person to whom anyone with a plan would divulge important information. In other words, Fred might be a 'mustache,' to use the word, but he would not be a principal. He, however, did threaten everyone in the room when he was told that VSA was out of the deal."

Dad broke in to get clarification. "What in the world is a *mustache*?"

Uncle Ben answered. "The intelligence community and Mafia use the word to refer to a person involved in a situation but who doesn't know what's going on. They're kind of a diversion. They have a role to play but don't know what they're doing or why. They are being used. I think Art's saying that this Vixette character is not a good guy but also most likely isn't in the loop if the drug lords or anyone else important was involved in the crash."

I nodded in agreement. "The other character is more complicated. Big Al Renaldi controls West Isle Savings Association in Galveston. We have no firm evidence to prove that Big Al is involved with the underworld, but his family has criminal connections going back to the early days of Galveston. One reason I recommended that the firm recuse itself from the transaction is my fear that Big Al's involvement in the transaction would cause the regulators to never approve it—or that it would damage the reputation of everyone involved if they do.

"Big Al is not terribly bright. He frequently acts on impulse. I'm pretty sure Big Al is capable of anything if he's crossed, even murder. If he knew that Don was supplying information involving WISA to the FHLBB, he is fully capable of ordering a hit in a moment of rage. In a recent meeting, he also threatened all the people in the room if they took any steps to eliminate his savings association from the transaction in the way they eliminated Vixette's S&L.

"On the other hand, as big and unstable a bully as Big Al is, he would understand that blowing up an airplane would cause an investigation and delay a transaction he desperately needs. Therefore, unless he was acting irrationally, which he sometimes does, I don't see Big Al as the person who ordered the bombing. He could have, but killing three people to get rid of one person ... I just don't know. There is more to this than we can see."

Uncle Ben thanked me for filling in some of the blanks in his understanding of the situation. Dad sat in disbelief. The kinds of things we had been discussing were far afield from preparing next week's sermon or a message to the Women of the Church's monthly meeting. He looked shell-shocked. I asked if Uncle Ben would make a few inquiries and keep his ear to the ground for any other rumors.

He agreed and then said, "There is one more bit of information. The FBI has heard from intelligence sources that a United States soldier, a Special Forces operative, was at the site of the explosion for some unexplained reason, perhaps the drugs. Privately, intelligence and law enforcement agencies are blaming the military, and the military is blaming intelligence and law enforcement agencies. In any case, the soldier is missing. Mexican authorities found the body of another former Special Forces operative in a ravine about five miles from the hunting camp. The body was in pretty bad shape. Animals had eaten on the carcass, but they were able to identify it through DNA testing. The military says that the person involved was discharged years ago for misbehavior and they know nothing about him. The military and all other federal agencies deny that they had any involvement with this person, but the name of the dead person also appears on a list of people the FBI suspects of being professional killers—a hit man."

We sat in silence for a few moments, taking in the information. I was getting tired and needed to sleep. Dad and Uncle Ben could see that I had reached the limit of what I could do without rest. They called the nurse, who gave me something to help me rest. The two excused themselves, and I fell into a deep sleep.

My sleep was troubled. Gwynn floated in and out of my dreams. As I regained consciousness, in a dream I struggled to escape hurting her and the baby as I fell before the blast. Mom was sitting at my bedside alone when I awoke, while Dad and Uncle Ben had gone to get something to eat. A nurse was in the room checking my vital signs.

I immediately asked, "How is Gwynn doing?"

"She is improving," Mom replied.

"Can I see her?" This was my first and most urgent need: to see for myself that Gwynn was alright. Nothing else mattered if she and the baby were not recovering from the blast.

At first, the nurse demurred, but after asking a doctor on call, she agreed.

"We are going to let you see her. Your injuries are minor. The doctor says that you will probably be dismissed from the hospital tomorrow with instructions to stay home and be quiet while your body further recovers. You must not, however, stay too long for your fiancé is still weak and needs rest.

Mom indicated that she intended to stay with me for a few days after I was released, just to be sure I followed her sound medical advice. Little did I know just how little of that advice I would follow.

Before we left to see Gwynn, Patrick Armbruster showed up to visit for a few moments. He began by telling me how sorry the firm was that Gwynn and I had been injured. Of course, everyone was in shock about Stephen. I asked about the funeral, which Armbruster indicated would be the next day.

"We've been informed that there's going to be a service at Saint Anne's Catholic Church on Westheimer. The service will be in the late afternoon—three o'clock, if my memory serves. Later that evening, a reception at the Winchester house on Avalon in River Oaks will be held. As I understand matters, the burial will be later and limited to the immediate family. Ahn is being very private. She did indicate that she hoped that you and Gwynn would be able to attend but understands that your attendance is unlikely. The entire firm is invited. You should attend if you are released in time and feel up to the strain."

"I'll make every effort to be released in time to attend the funeral," I told Patrick. "I'm not sure about attending the reception. It's likely that I'll have some restrictions on what I can do after going home from the hospital. My mother will be looking after me, and it'll be difficult for me to avoid good behavior."

He smiled and said, "I understand. As soon as you feel up to it, I want you to come by and see me at the office. Naturally, this situation has everyone upset. The members of the executive committee were to hear from Stephen on the afternoon of his death. We are meeting this afternoon to discuss the matter further. I think we may need someone who understands the transaction to speak with the committee as soon as possible. I don't want to cause you to relapse, but you may be needed.

"To be frank, the doctors are telling us that Roger's recovery will be weeks, if not longer, before he reaches a point where he can be released. Furthermore, he will need therapy for some time after his release. It is not conceivable for us to wait until he returns to address the issues Stephen was going to raise."

I responded in the affirmative, giving him my personal feelings. "At this point, I don't need to hide anything from you. Stephen and I recently talked about the transaction on two occasions. He was aware that I had reservations about the transaction, but Roger and Jackson wanted to press on, thinking that the issues raised could be overcome. Both of us felt the transaction would not be able to be closed in a timely way due to the ongoing investigations and the likely regulatory delays. We both thought that the firm should not continue to represent Jackson if he continued to press on with the transaction.

"Between the two of us, if there was a little chance of the transaction closing before Stephen was killed, there is less chance now. Before Stephen was killed the authorities were investigating whether the crash of the King Air was intentional. Now, there's been a car bombing. It's inconceivable that the authorities will not want to investigate the car bombing, and they'll be looking for any link between the crash of the King Air and Stephen's death.

"The investigation will involve another round of questioning of the people at the firm. It will also involve another round of questioning of Jackson and the leadership team at MSA. I suspect they will interview all participants in the transaction and their employees. This will take weeks, if not months. I don't know that the investigation will uncover anything new, and I don't think for a moment that the investment bankers, law firms, and accountants involved in the transaction had anything to do with the bombing. I cannot think of any reason why they might be involved in such a plot, but I do believe it will take a long time before the investigation is over.

"Unfortunately, my opinion about potential involvement is not true of everyone involved, particularly Big Al Renaldi and Fred Vixette. At this point, as unbelievable as it may be, I don't think we can rule out involvement by Jackson, though I cannot imagine Jackson being involved in such a thing. He is arrogant and greedy but not a killer. One last fact of importance—Todd will verify that the regulators recently began asking questions about MSA. We have to proceed under the assumption that MSA will be a target of an ongoing investigation. If this is true, there is no chance of the transaction being approved and a huge likelihood of disclosures that will embarrass Jackson and the firm.

"Finally, whatever the executive committee decides, I do not believe I can or should continue to be involved. A lawyer whom I deeply respected was killed. A woman of whom I am extremely fond was injured. The lawyer to whom I report at the firm is in critical condition. I was wounded. Frankly, it is only by a miracle that all of us were not killed in the bombing. I am one of the many people whom the FBI will be interviewing about the bombing. I'm a pretty strong person, but there's no way I could keep my mind on this transaction after all that has occurred."

Patrick nodded in understanding if not in agreement. His response was affirming. "I understand your views, and for the time being, I agree. There will be an executive committee meeting this afternoon. After that meeting, I may want to talk to Jackson personally and alert him that the firm questions whether it can be effective in representing MSA at this point. He needs to understand the implications of the likelihood that many attorneys and others involved in the transaction will be interviewed by the FBI. He also needs to realize that, for at least a little while, the FBI may wonder if the party or parties responsible for the bombing are not involved in the transaction in some way. I will inform him that the lawyers in the firm who are involved in the transaction are naturally concerned about continuing, in light of what has happened. Todd has already indicated to me that he is scared, and his wife and family are anxious for him not to be involved any further."

He looked at me and asked one last question.

"Do you know of any reason other than the transaction why someone would kill Stephen?"

I could see that Patrick's trial-lawyer mind was at work, being sure that he had not forgotten any possible angle.

"I cannot think of any reason whatsoever. Stephen and I were not personal friends, and I have no idea what business or other associates he has outside of the firm. I don't know all of the litigations and transactions in which Stephen was involved, but I don't think that any of them would likely cause a bombing of this kind. You should ask other members of his staff to get a better picture."

"I've already asked the same question of all the members of Stephen's team and received the same response," Patrick said. "No one could think of a reason why any client, opposing counsel, or other parties would do such a thing."

We left it at that. After a few more moments, Patrick thanked me for my help, wished me a quick recovery, and excused himself. He stopped at the door and said, "Come to see me as soon as you are able."

After a meal, Mom and a nurse took me up to see Gwynn for a few moments. She was bruised and uncomfortable but as lovely as ever. We had a short visit and kissed each other good night. She was aware that I would be released first and asked me to see her the next day, if at all possible. She hoped to feel better by then. It was obvious that she was not as far along in recovery as I was, and the baby had also had a trauma. She needed to be quiet and sleep. I left after telling her I loved her.

20

New Information

THE NEXT MORNING, I WOKE early certain I would be released before sunset. First, I wanted to see Gwynn. Fortunately, the doctor on call and his nurse came by as I was having coffee and breakfast. They agreed I could go home in the afternoon. In the meantime, the nurse offered to take me to see Gwynn as soon as she and the doctor were able to fill out my release papers. I needed clothing and someone to pick me up. A quick call to my parents arranged for them to be at the hospital at about two o'clock in the afternoon to take me home.

Eventually, the nurse took me upstairs to see Gwynn. She dropped me off and said she would be back in thirty to forty-five minutes to take me to my room for a rest before being released.

Gwynn was awake, and we had an opportunity to talk privately. It was the first time we'd had time to review what had happened in the explosion. I asked her if she remembered anything.

"Not really. I remember turning around to ask you something, and you fell on me. There was a blast as we were falling. My head hit the pavement, and I blacked out. When I woke up, I was here. They told me you were doing well, that Todd had been too far from the blast to matter, and that Roger is in pretty serious condition. When I asked about Stephen, they told me it was his car that had been bombed, and he was dead."

I nodded. "That's pretty much how it was with me. I remember you turning, my leaning forward to listen, then falling, and the blast. Everything else had to be explained to me after I awoke. My parents were here when I woke up, and they explained what had happened to me. Have your parents been by?"

She nodded, tearing up. "My dad and his new wife came by and spent a few minutes. Mom had to fly into town, but she was here yesterday and met your mother. They are busy planning a wedding." She looked at me as if confirming that there still would be a wedding.

I smiled with anticipation. "I hope we can be married just as soon as possible after you are released. I had the feeling that Mom would love to help plan our wedding. If you don't mind, I would like to have it in Brenham with my father and brother officiating. It would mean a lot to my parents. I don't think they will care about anything but the ceremony and my brother having a part in it."

Gwynn nodded and smiled. "As long as you are there for the wedding, everything else is fine. I am afraid my parents will want a fancy wedding venue for a reception, and it may be much larger than you want. Dad has a lot of business friends he will want to invite. We need to invite our friends and people from the firm. Perhaps we could have a small wedding in Brenham, and then a reception in Houston, where our friends and families can relax after the wedding."

That seemed a reasonable proposal. Houston was filled with venues that Gwynn's parents could afford and enjoy. My parents would be happy with any kind of reception. Pastors and their wives go to a lot of wedding receptions. My parents were proven experts at having a good time—or at least appearing to have a good time—on all sorts of social occasions.

Gwynn steered the conversation in another direction. "No bombing is accidental. Someone killed Stephen. Or rather, someone had Stephen killed. Do you know anything?"

It was inappropriate to tell her exactly what Uncle Ben had learned from his FBI contacts. I could not let Gwynn know that Uncle Ben was working on the case in the background, but some of the facts were public knowledge, or Gwynn would easily figure them out.

"Patrick came by to see me yesterday," I said. "We had a long conversation. As you already know, the executive committee was going to meet just after our lunch. Stephen was killed before he could attend that meeting. I think there is a leak inside Winchester & Wells, or Stephen told someone, probably Jackson. You, Roger, Todd, Stephen, and I are the only people who might have let anything slip. You didn't know what Stephen was going to say. Roger was surprised at the progress Stephen had made in laying the groundwork for the firm to recuse itself. Todd was similarly surprised but seemed to suspect as much because of his understanding of regulatory problems. I am pretty sure the leak came from Jackson. Jackson and Stephen had dinner the night before the luncheon. Stephen certainly told Jackson he was going to recommend that the firm recuse itself. Later, Jackson might well have revealed the facts to Big Al or some other person."

"What about Todd?" Gwynn asked. "Todd parked away from the rest of us. It might have just been where he found a parking place. If so, it was extremely good luck. I can't believe Todd would plot to kill Stephen or even be a quiet participant in such a plan. But the FBI will want to know why he parked where he did and with whom he discussed the transaction in recent days."

I nodded in agreement. "Consider the following possibility: Stephen and Jackson had dinner to talk about the transaction. Stephen had already begun the process of calling an executive committee meeting by that time. Suppose Jackson later told someone he was having trouble with his law firm and his brother. Whomever Jackson told reacted by telling a third party or ordering a hasty car bombing.

"For all Jackson's sophistication, he's in over his head in this deal. He has never faced this degree of complexity and regulatory opposition. In addition, he has never dealt with the kind of people with whom he is dealing. Perhaps he let out too much to either Big Al, Sol, his accountants, or one of the investment banking firms involved. He would have asked for advice on how to handle Stephen's objections. Such a person or persons might be the source of the blast.

"If he went to Big Al, Jackson was extremely foolish. He might have visited with Sol Lewinsky, but I don't think so. He would have been cautious about making Sol any more skittish about the transaction than he already is. That leaves the investment bankers, who might have talked to their counselors about problems with the transaction. I cannot believe that any reputable financial firm would consider a hit on a prominent attorney, but you never know. I doubt the investment bankers knew much, if anything. It is unlikely Jackson would say very much to them for fear of scaring them off and dooming the transaction."

Gwynn nodded but then shook her head. "It's not like Jackson to tell others anything significant about his problems. We need more information. We need to know who, if anyone, Jackson spoke to after he and Stephen had dinner. I know you respected Stephen, but we also need to know with whom Stephen might have talked after that dinner. Any slip by anyone might have gotten information into the wrong hands."

I nodded in agreement.

"I'll be discharged later this afternoon. It may be too late for me to attend the funeral, but perhaps I can make the reception as long as I don't stay too long. While I'm at the reception, I will undoubtedly see Patrick. I want to make an appointment to see him first thing in the morning. I don't know about you, but I am convinced the firm has to recuse itself from further representation of MSA." I looked at her and smiled. "For one thing, I don't want you involved with this transaction ever again. You and the baby are too important to take any risks."

She smiled. "You're also precious, and I don't want you involved any more than I want to be involved."

"When I see Pat, I'm going to be firm about Winchester & Wells recusing itself from further representation of Jackson or MSA concerning this matter. I believe he will agree. When we spoke yesterday, he was aware of my views. He wanted to give the problem some thought, but I had a strong feeling he will ultimately decide there is too much danger to the firm to continue. Patrick might sometimes be overly political, but he loves the firm and won't let it be involved in anything that might harm its reputation or future. As soon as possible, I'm going to go see Jackson to find out what light he can shed on how this tragedy occurred. Jackson is a hard nut to crack, but it might work. He might have some information he can share."

I could see Gwynn was getting tired. A few minutes later, the nurse returned. Gwynn and I embraced, and I left, promising to come by the next day.

***

I was discharged on time. Due to rush-hour traffic, it was after four o'clock when I arrived home—too late to go to the funeral. It was possible, however, for me to go to the reception. Mom had indicated that she wanted to spend the night to be sure I was recovering before she returned to Brenham. She wasn't crazy about my going to the reception at Ahn's home but understood it was important for me to pay my respects. I shared my appreciation for her concern, but let her know that I might be late getting home.

"I knew that the doctors asked me to rest, but if I am careful, I think I can make the reception. I will try not to over-exert myself and leave as early as possible."

"If you are not going to be here this evening, I will go see Gwynn while you are gone."

With that, she left for the hospital. I rested, took a shower, put on a suit appropriate for a funeral reception, glanced at myself in the mirror, and left. I was one of the later arrivals and was warmly greeted by everyone. People were surprised that I felt well enough to come.

"I cannot believe you are here!" was a common comment.

I sought out Ahn to give my condolences. She was wearing a classic black Vietnamese *áo dài* dress, appropriate for a funeral. Ahn was happy to see me. She took my hand, coming close to my ear to whisper an invitation.

"Please stay until the end. When everyone has left, I need to talk with you. Stephen left something I want to share with you."

Patrick was friendly, and we made a date to see each other the next morning. For the rest of the reception, I was in a daze—sore, physically tired, and preoccupied with what Ahn wanted to say privately. The reception was scheduled for two hours, and the guests, respecting Ahn, left before the two hours were over.

When we were alone, Ahn invited me into Stephen's study. "Thank you for staying to visit. Stephen left some information, and I would like you to meet a guest."

She handed me an envelope, which I opened. It was a memorandum summarizing what Stephen had intended to say to the executive committee. In it, Stephen listed the objections to the transaction we had discussed at lunch—delay due to the plane crash, the complexity of the transaction, the dubious character of Al Renaldi, increasingly close examination of real estate loans purchased or made on a short-term basis by MSA, and other factors. It concluded with a discussion of the potential for the transaction to unravel in ways that would hurt the reputation of the firm. I had hoped to learn something new that would shed light on his death, but the memorandum contained nothing new.

In the document, Stephen was not so much setting out the facts as he was persuading the executive committee that the firm should recuse itself.

I looked up and shared with Ahn my regret that there was nothing new in the memorandum.

She agreed and shared what she knew.

"I also learned nothing new from rereading the memo this morning. Stephen read it to me the morning of his death. He was coming home to pick it up after the luncheon before the executive committee meeting. It should be shared with Patrick and placed in the firm's files. Stephen told me you and he had spoken and that you knew everything. In his absence, you are the person Stephen would most trust to make any necessary presentation to the executive committee or Patrick. In any case, Patrick needs to know exactly what Stephen intended to say and be told by someone who agrees with Stephen's position. If nothing else, the memorandum may finally move Patrick to have the firm recuse itself. And there is more. This morning, before the funeral, I had a visitor. I asked him to spend part of tonight in our guesthouse. He is here to share with you what he shared with me."

At that moment, a well-built Hispanic male walked into the room. There was something military in his bearing. He seemed prosperous. Ahn motioned us to sit down in two wing-back chairs while she sat on a love seat facing her husband's desk. A black laminated oriental coffee table with a glass top separated us. She motioned to the man, who began to speak.

"My name is John Mirador, or as I am now known, Juan de la Cruz Bardero. If you've read the newspapers, you know the United States government is looking for a missing Special Forces operative. I am that operative. I returned to the United States to give important information to Steven Winchester's widow. She indicated that you are her attorney. She wants you to hear my story. When I have finished, I will leave. I do not believe we will meet again. It would be dangerous for us to be seen together. Do not attempt to contact me. If there is a need, I will contact you."

Mirador recounted what he had observed before the crash and what transpired in the immediate aftermath of the explosion that first damaged the plane. He spoke about the assignment he was given by his commanding officer. He did not believe his commanding officer would have intentionally sent him if it meant becoming involved in anything illegal. His commander, however, would not have been suspicious of a request from another federal agency. Mirador mentioned his original belief that he was on loan to a law enforcement agency that was investigating drug cartels in Mexico. He went into detail about being dropped into the country, the days he watched the hunting camp, the plane as it was prepared for take-off, and its occupants.

"In the beginning, I thought that I had been sent into Mexico at the request of a law enforcement arm of the government. Now, I am not so sure."

Eventually, Mirador spoke of the rushing black clouds, the strange lightning within the storm, and the flash of light accompanying the explosion.

I made him repeat that part of the story. "I'm sorry. I am confused. Could you describe the storm and lightning again?"

Mirador went through the moments preceding and just after the explosion a second time, describing the heat lightning and the strange humanoid-looking pillars of light. He described the storm enveloping the plane and the strange bright light from which the damaged plane exited as it flew toward its ultimate fate in the Chinati Mountains. He explained the belief of the abbot, with whom he was staying, that there were angelic forces at work, a view Mirador was coming to share. He described the attempt on his life, his confrontation with the assassin, and his interrogation of his would-be killer. It was at this point that new information was revealed.

"Dent told me that besides the pilot and the two executives of MSA on the plane, there were three other people at the camp involved. One of them is a person known as El Capitán. This person is thought to be the head of a major cartel in Mexico. Another person is an employee of the United States government named Edward J. Mueller. This man is almost certainly an employee of the Central Intelligence Agency or some other intelligence organization. His involvement in intelligence, and perhaps the drug trade, may go back to Vietnam. Believe me, there is plenty that the public never learned about what went on in Vietnam."

Ahn nodded in agreement.

"The third person is a wealthy and powerful Mexican citizen, Javier Velasco, whose nickname is El Halcón, or the Hawk. He is from an old Spanish conquistador family with large landholdings in Mexico. He has been active in business and government. He is a friend of American politicians and is well-liked by his friends. He is also feared and hated by the common people. Until recently, there was no reason to suspect that El Halcón had connections with drug lords, but the meeting and crash cause me to doubt that he is completely clean.

"There may be more going on here than meets the eye. There have been rumors that our government is facilitating the transport of drugs to the United States to earn funds to fight guerrilla insurgencies in Central America. It may even be to fund activities as far away as Iran. How far up the chain of command this corruption goes, no one at my level could possibly know. There are rumors, however, that high-ranking persons have connections with these activities. From personal experience, I can tell you that not every mission that Special Forces operatives undertake makes military sense to the soldiers involved."

He stopped for a moment to let the implications of his words sink in, giving me a chance to talk and ask questions.

"If what you say is true, I am still not sure why a powerful Mexican national with ties to high-ranking American officials, a mid-level employee of an intelligence agency, and a drug lord would kill two American bankers in a plane carrying cocaine. Such an action would certainly point to involvement in the drug trade. There must be more going on than a drugs-for-guns-or-money scheme. As a result of my investigation, I believe one of the men on the plane was supplying a federal agency with information about certain real estate transactions in the United States. These real estate transactions might be tied to underworld figures in Texas and Louisiana, though, to the best of my knowledge, proof of any such connection is lacking.

"The fact that Don Mendoza was sharing information with federal and state authorities regarding these loans would be a motive for killing him, but it is hard to believe that anyone would order three people killed to get rid of one informer. If silencing an informer was the motive for the killing, one would think those ordering it would conceive another plan to protect the savings and loan associations involved from further investigation. A person ordering such a death would want it to appear unrelated to the transaction our firm is handling. Above all, no sane person would put drugs on the plane. Drugs would point the finger straight back at Mexican cartels and any American partners. Of course, it is also possible that whoever did this wanted the authorities to suspect drug cartel involvement. Perhaps the deaths were structured to give a false clue. On the whole, I believe drugs are not at the bottom of the deaths. The drugs on the plane were planted as a diversion."

Once more, Mirador nodded in agreement, then gave a solemn word of caution.

"I have been a soldier in secret operations for many years. Most ordinary people assume that those involved in a war or criminal activities act rationally, according to the standards of rationality common in American society as you experience it. Nothing could be further from the truth. Evil is never entirely rational. For one thing, mistakes are made. I could not tell you the number of missions I have been on that did not turn out as planned due to human error or even gross negligence of the planners or others involved. The kind of people engaged in covert war or criminal activities are often violent and have no aversion to violence. They are accustomed to lying, believing that a lie told repeatedly will be seen as true. Finally, in times of stress, people act irrationally. The less rational a person is to begin with, the more likely it is that he or she will act irrationally under pressure.

"Let me suggest the following possibility: perhaps an order was given to silence Don Mendoza but without precise instructions. Perhaps no one said, 'Be sure you don't injure anyone else.' We both believe that Henry Dent was, in some fashion, working for or through El Capitán. If the order came from El Capitán, it came from someone accustomed to securing power through horrifying acts of violence. El Capitán is a man capable of great and unnecessary violence. He might have been given an order but did something that the person giving the order would never have imagined possible. In the military, we use the term *fubar* for this kind of thing, which happens in conflict more often than anyone not involved might believe. What happened here might be one giant mess-up."

I was beginning to think that both the plane crash and the car bombing might be two separate instances of an unbalanced person or persons doing something unimaginably foolish and evil under pressure. The deaths might just be what happens when *dark powers,* as my religious friends say, gained control of a bad person, and good people did nothing.

It was past midnight. Mirador was ready to leave. He had a long journey ahead of him. He concluded our conversation by giving a few suggestions about how I might use the information he provided.

"I must leave in just a few moments to return to my place of hiding. Before I left Mexico, I put into effect a plan to deal with those in Mexico responsible for the plane crash. I cannot be of further help regarding those persons involved in the United States. Use the information I have provided wisely. We know that the people involved in these crimes are not entirely stable. When people think they are about to die, get caught, or lose everything, they overreact. Sometimes, they do terrible things. In this case, we are dealing with extremely immoral people.

"In our religion, the devil is described as an angel of light. Sometimes, those who seem like quite well-balanced, normal, and even respected citizens and leaders can be as evil as the devil himself. Be careful. Trust no one. We may never discover exactly what went on or the identity of the most important players. The result is in the hands of God. Keep your mind always open to new or different possibilities."

With that, Mirador thanked Ahn for her hospitality and left by the rear entrance to the house.

Ahn and I sat silently for a long while after Mirador left. She sat, as she often did, with her back as straight as an arrow, her hands on her knees, and her eyes closed, as if meditating on the significance of every word that had been said. I stared at a portrait of Stephen Winchester, wishing I had her faith, wisdom, and spiritual depth.

What a waste for such a man to be senselessly killed, I thought as I gazed at his portrait.

Ahn broke the silence.

"I have long feared that Jackson is involved in something deeper than a mere business transaction. There is a dark spirit hovering around him. In recent months, he has become more difficult to handle than ever before. He rarely sees his mother at the Hallmark. When with the family, he is sullen and withdrawn. He is always distracted and worried. Jackson was always a cynic, but his cynicism has become pathological."

I had questions. "Ahn, you are a special person. On the surface, this is an ordinary murder or series of murders, which, if we investigate long enough, will provide answers to questions we both have. As you said, there's something deeper going on here—something I do not understand but that you might understand. I have seen something like the lightning Mirador saw in that storm. Whether in reality or a dream, I am not sure. I have also seen a dark figure, a fiery dark figure, who appears to me at night in my dreams—at least, I think it's a dream. These dreams are very real, more real than any dream of my life.

"I saw an Episcopal priest recently. He told me about what he calls our *shadow self.* He thinks I am experiencing a deep inner conflict. He also thinks this dark figure may also exist outside me—a dark spirit. I am not particularly spiritual or introspective. My father and brother are, but I have never been like either of them. I am just an ordinary guy. I have no interest or desire to be involved with mystical forces or demonic powers. I am not interested in battling powers and principalities. I believe there is a God, but that is about all—and it's all I ever wanted to know before now."

Ahn listened quietly until I finished my description of my dreams, the dark fiery figure, my periodic loss of balance as the world seemed to shift beneath my feet, and how that loss of balance saved Gwynn's life. Then, she shared her view.

"I know something of the psychologist Carl Jung and what the priest was trying to say. There is truth in his words. The priest's way of describing these experiences is not exactly the way I would describe your experience. I believe there are spiritual forces at work in human lives and human society, and they are not merely projections of our internal state, though that is a part of their mode of existence. Angelic powers exist outside of us, as potentials or invisible realities that can and do influence us when we come under their power.

"When I was young during the Vietnam War, I saw fundamentally good people do terrible things, things that they never would have done except for the demonic power of war. It was as if a beastly spirit had entered them. I saw good men and women reduced to no more than vicious animals. When people opened themselves to the potential for darkness that resides in every human soul, these spiritual realities gained power over them. Worse, the physical power involved was multiplied by the number of people under their dark influence. The result was terrible.

"The fiery figure you have seen is not just a potential within you. It is also a reality outside of you. As to the beams of light, I believe they are spiritual forces of light—angels, if you like. These angelic beings appear to be at war with or opposing the dark forces that have been unleashed in our nation and in Mexico, perhaps even farther. That is the best explanation for their being in the middle of the storm; with Mirador at the hunting camp; in your apartment, guarding you against the dark figure; and finally, at the club, protecting you and Gwynn from the bomb that took Stephen's life.

"Jackson and whoever ordered these killings are, to some degree, incarnating a dark potential. The transaction itself is an embodiment of the darkness in those who conceived it. We must see if we can receive and join with

249

the power of the good light that opposes them. My father was a Catholic, and I was raised Catholic. Before they were married, my mother was a Buddhist. In her way, she continued to practice Buddhism. She lived according to the Noble Eightfold Path of Buddhism: right view, right thinking, right speech, right conduct, right livelihood, right effort, right mindfulness, and right concentration. I do not find these ideals in conflict with the Christian faith. In every religion, there is some good, and God's light is everywhere for those with eyes to see.

"In making decisions, I think about my mother's faith and my father's faith. I imitate both my parents, trying to make a unity of their teachings. I am a devout Christian and practice a kind of Christian meditation. I try to see the world through the eyes of Christ, think about the world as Christ thinks about the world, speak as Christ would speak, conduct my life as Christ conducted his, earn my living honestly, make an effort to do the best I can, be mindful in the present, and concentrated on important things. Sometimes I am successful. On other occasions, I am not.

"We are facing people with a different view of reality. They have a twisted way of thinking. These people are deceitful in speech and evil in their conduct and business dealings. They concentrate on all the wrong things in their daily activities. They are filled with arrogance, greed, and lust for power. Such people are enemies of peace and wholeness.

"You are in a difficult situation. I have more experience in these things, as I grew up amid a terrible war. We must not try to force the future. The world is too powerful to be forced by us. If we are to find out who killed my husband, the knowledge will come to us. For the time being, we must be wise and let the power of divine light guide our steps. One more thing—you must trust yourself and your potential goodness. This situation is a lesson that the good must not compromise too much with the darkness, no matter the cause. Be strong, not just now but in the future."

She saw I was tired and feeling the impact of my injuries. "We both need sleep. Tomorrow, you will see Patrick. You need not call to let me know what was decided. I will find out soon enough."

· It was time for me to speak my last words and go.

"I'll see Patrick in the morning. Please be careful. If you can avoid it, do not see or contact Jackson tomorrow. I cannot be certain, but I believe Winchester & Wells will decide to recuse itself from further involvement in the transaction. I may be asked to convey that information to Jackson. It could be several days before you hear from me, but I will let you know how things are going before the end of the week. Do me one favor. Please look in on Gwynn and my mother during the day tomorrow. I believe it will be late before I will get to the hospital."

With that, I left, exhausted and ready to sleep.

21

Confrontation

THE NEXT MORNING, I WOKE up late. The effect of my injuries and the long night with Ahn and Mirador were evident in soreness, a headache, and grogginess. It took me several cups of coffee and the better part of an hour to overcome the lethargy, soreness, and pain. I had a large cinnamon roll from a local bakery for breakfast with Mom and then went to the office. I suspected the day would bring at least one dreaded confrontation.

Everyone was surprised and delighted to see me. Betsey, who rarely showed emotion, teared up and hugged me. She offered to bring me a cup of coffee, which she rarely did. I thanked her, went into my office, and read the forty or so pink call slips neatly lined up in the order of their receipt on my desk. I briefly sorted out the stack of mail and interoffice memoranda piled on the desk in front of my chair, filled out a bunch of overdue timesheets, and called Patrick's office to make an appointment. I was asked to come upstairs in thirty minutes.

Patrick looked relieved and delighted to see me up and well. He was thankful I was in the office so soon after my release, knowing that the doctors wanted me to remain quiet and rest. He began by asking about Gwynn, and I gave him an update. I had no new information about Roger. He informed me that the doctors were increasingly optimistic about Roger's recovery. Finally, I requested a future opportunity to speak with him about my future at the firm. Then we got down to the business at hand.

I explained my plan to put in a full day, returning calls, getting the accumulated mail off my desk, and putting important papers into my briefcase so that I could read them at home.

"I am happy to help with whatever the executive committee might need me to do regarding the transaction. On doctor's orders, however, I must go home early to rest."

He agreed.

I handed him the memorandum containing Stephen's notes for the executive committee, detailing his reasons why the firm should recuse itself from further representation of MSA concerning the transaction. Patrick read it twice, then laid it aside. He looked at me, prepared to listen.

"I hope that you've had time to think about our conversation at the hospital," I said. "I've been thinking over matters and continue to think it best for the firm to recuse itself as soon as possible. With Roger out of action and me working part-time, the firm can only be so helpful to Jackson and MSA. More importantly, for the reasons we discussed, I believe we must distance ourselves from Marshland Savings Association and Jackson Winchester as fast as possible."

Patrick nodded, looked down, and slowly shoved a letter across the desk. It was on the Winchester & Wells letterhead. "Could you read this and see if you agree?"

The letter read as follows:

> Jackson Winchester
> Marshland Savings Association
> Greenway Plaza
> Houston, Texas
>
> Dear Jackson:
>
> As a personal friend and the managing partner of Winchester & Wells, I hesitate to bother you during a time of personal grief. Our thoughts and prayers are with you and the family.
>
> Last evening the executive committee of the firm met to discuss recent events. It was our unanimous view that the firm should recuse itself from further representation with respect to the merger of Marshland Savings Association (MSA), Global Savings Association, and West Isle Savings Association, together with the creation of the holding company and limited

partnership and other legal actions anticipated by the transaction (Transaction) and regulatory matters related to the Transaction in which MSA is currently engaged.

Your brother and partner in our firm, Stephen Winchester, has been killed. Three of our lawyers, all of whom were important to the Transaction, were injured in the explosion that took Stephen's life. In particular, the partner in charge of the Transaction has been so seriously injured that we cannot predict when or if he will be able to return.

As you are also aware, the FBI and other authorities are investigating both a plane crash involving officials of MSA and now the death of your brother, who was to attend a meeting of our executive committee on the day he was killed. The Transaction was the most important item on the agenda for that meeting. At this time, we cannot but anticipate that those present at the bombing and others at the firm will be interviewed at length and asked to testify, when or if any arrests are made.

Under these circumstances, we could not give the Transaction the attention required for it to be successful. As a result, we believe it would not be in the best interests of MSA if our firm were to continue its representation concerning the Transaction.

Please call me when you have chosen an appropriate firm to replace our firm, and we will arrange for the orderly transfer of our files to the firm of your choice as quickly as humanly possible.

Once again, please accept my personal deep condolences for the death of your brother and our firm's regret that this action has become necessary.

Very truly yours,
WINCHESTER & WELLS

Patrick Armbruster
Managing Partner"

I read the letter several times, made a few suggestions, and expressed my agreement with its contents. Then, I made a suggestion about its delivery.

"Patrick, if possible, I would like to personally deliver the letter to Jackson. We owe it to Jackson to deliver the letter personally and allow him to react. I am the logical person, since, if files are transferred in the future, Todd and I would be the primary persons responsible. More importantly, if Jackson wants to talk about the transaction, or if he wants to argue with the contents of the letter, I'm the best person to initially face him. I am not on the executive committee. Therefore, I can't agree to alter the decision. More importantly, if I say anything with which the executive committee disagrees, the firm will be free to disavow whatever I might say. As an associate, I cannot bind the firm to any course of action by anything I say. In the end, it best protects the firm for me to deliver the letter. If Jackson wants to blow off steam, he can do so at me."

Patrick appreciated my willingness to take on the disagreeable task of delivering the letter and facing Jackson's initial response, which was not likely to be sympathetic.

"I agree. Let me pass the idea by the remainder of the executive committee. If they agree, we will put the letter in final form. I will sign it, and you can make an appointment to deliver it to Jackson this afternoon. We are all anxious to get MSA other counsel at the earliest possible time. I suspect he will not choose a Houston firm. He will want a large corporate and regulatory firm with offices in Washington, DC, to handle the matter. Jackson is no fool. He knows it will be next to impossible for this transaction to gain regulatory approval. He needs a powerful Washington firm if he is to have any chance at closing the deal.

"One more thing—at the beginning of our meeting, you mentioned you wanted to see me about the firm. Let me put your mind at rest. One reason we did not have to wait for you to recover to write the letter is that Stephen had already shared his feelings with me and, individually, with others of the executive committee. Most of us had come to the same conclusion before the meeting. It did not take much to convince the remaining members that recusal is the best course of action. When speaking to me, Stephen gave you credit for acting wisely and in the best interests of the firm.

"Stephen also talked to me about your situation. He and I both agreed that you would be best served to leave a purely corporate practice and join his team. Obviously, his team is going to undergo a change in the future. We currently have no one partner with the ability to manage the kinds of transactions and litigation in which Stephen's team is involved. He felt, however, and I feel that you will become a fine litigator if we put you in the litigation department. At the same time, you have the corporate experience needed to allow Stephen's team to continue with the transactions they currently have underway. Finally, we need you to take over managing the transactions in which Roger was involved before his injury and be the primary person to oversee the removal of our firm from representing MSA.

"For the time being, one of the litigators in the firm is going to take over the responsibility of managing the litigation Stephen's team is handling. Because of your experience in clerking for a federal judge and at the Texas attorney general's office, we don't think it's going to take long for you to gain the required expertise to take on a bigger role. You must make friends among your colleagues and gain their trust in the next months.

"As to your future, I cannot, of course, offer you a partnership in the firm, but there is no reason why you should fear for your future. You are well thought of by the partners and have done very fine work in what has become a dangerous and difficult situation. We appreciate your talent and dedication. We all respect Roger's abilities, but we are also aware of his weaknesses. Does this satisfy your concerns about your future?"

I responded with appreciation for the kind words. "Nothing could make me happier than to follow in Stephen's footsteps. While in the hospital, I decided to try my best to become the quality lawyer Stephen was. I also made another decision: I want to be a partner at Winchester & Wells, if the offer ever comes. There is one other matter about which I need to make you aware. Gwynn and I have been talking about our future. Over the past weeks, we have become attached to one another. Obviously, if we were to be engaged and married, one of us would have to leave the firm. She is the better brain; of that, we are all aware. I can't speak for her, but I believe that she may be leaving the firm soon. We have been talking about getting married soon after she is released from the hospital."

Armbruster smiled. "Frankly, I am glad to hear this news. Some of us have been waiting for the shoe to drop—and the way the shoe dropped is welcome. We could all see that the two of you were becoming close. We will be sorry to lose one of our brightest associates, and you are correct that you will be marrying above yourself, as most wise men do. I wish you well, and so does the entire firm."

We continued to visit for a short time, and then I left. I noticed that there was a difference in the way Patrick addressed me. It was as if he were not addressing an employee but instead a trusted and valued colleague.

***

When I returned to my office, it took some time to sort through all the messages, talk to Betsey, and visit with those who would be required to transfer the firm's files concerning the transaction to another firm. The most important of these visits was with Todd, for it would fall heavily on the banking section to delicately transfer files and information to a new firm.

When I spoke to Todd, our conversation was carefully phrased on both sides. Todd was aware that it was likely that the firm would transfer its files to another firm in the next few days. He had been asked to attend the meeting of the executive committee to give his views on the transaction. He had been forthright that the firm needed to recuse itself from further representation of MSA. At this point, his primary interest was to be sure the firm kept copies of anything transferred to another firm and did not transfer unnecessary files.

"We can't be sure we won't be questioned in the future. We also cannot be sure we won't be second-guessed in some of the decisions we have made in representing MSA. I bet Jackson hires the most powerful and politically well-connected financial services law firm in Washington. Therefore, it's extremely important that we have copies of everything that we have done and carefully consider what we transfer and do not transfer to some other firm."

"I agree," I said.

"There is a strong possibility that there will be litigation between MSA and some other party before this matter reaches a conclusion. MSA and the firm are going to be investigated by the FHLBB, the TSLD, and perhaps other regulatory agencies. The FBI is going to continue to ask questions. We have to be sure we have the information needed to answer any questions and respond to requests for information. I don't think we have any serious concerns regarding the transaction, but we do need to be careful."

I responded thankfully.

"In my case, Gwynn's absence is going to be a serious problem in managing the paper flow. Some other associates in the firm will have to take over the arduous and detailed task of managing the identification, copying, and indexing of documents transferred. It will be a difficult assignment for anyone not familiar with the transaction."

Todd and I agreed that one of his associates, who was familiar with the transaction, would act as the primarily responsible person in managing the copying and transfer of files to a new firm. Todd concluded our conversation with words of encouragement.

"Art, I know that you are not going to be able to immediately give your full attention to this matter. I can see you're still recovering. In addition, you will have new responsibilities that take up much of your time, since we cannot expect Roger to return soon. We in the banking section will try to do all that we can to make this as easy as possible."

I thanked him and returned to my office. On my way, I pondered the difference in how Patrick and Todd treated me compared to in the past.

Late in the afternoon, I was advised that the letter was ready for me to deliver to Jackson. Betsey called Jackson's office and made an appointment. I went up to Pat's office and retrieved the letter, which was sealed. I was given a copy for my files and to read before I went to see Jackson. I spent the remainder of the afternoon before the appointment reading the letter, making notes, and thinking about what to say. When the time came, I packed up my correspondence and documents that I needed to read at home and left for the meeting.

**

When I arrived at Jackson's Greenway Plaza office, I had to wait for him to finish some pressing business. As I sat in the waiting room outside his office, I mentally prepared for a tense confrontation with the arrogant Jackson we had all come to know and dread. I was surprised by the Jackson I encountered upon entering his office.

Jackson was always an elegant and expensive dresser. Now, he looked disheveled. It was obvious he had not slept in some time. There was a haunted look behind his dark, almost black eyes. Furthermore, there was a sense of defeat in his manner, as if he already knew what I was going to say, what was going to transpire in the future, and how the transaction was going to end. He seemed to be coming to grips with an inevitable long period of investigation and litigation. I decided to be kind as well as careful. I began diplomatically.

"Jackson, I know you have talked with Pat Armbruster, the firm's managing partner, and so you probably can guess why I'm here. I have been asked to deliver a letter to you, answer any questions you have, and be of help to you and MSA as best I can. Out of respect for you and your entire family, the firm asked me to do this before I return home to recuperate from the injuries I received when your brother was killed.

"Before we go further, I want to express my admiration for your brother and family. I cannot begin to describe my sorrow at his death. His loss is a personal tragedy as well as a great loss to the firm. He was, without a doubt, the best lawyer I ever knew and a fine human being. He will be missed."

We had a short conversation about the funeral, the reception, his concern for Ahn, and his love for his brother. I then handed him the letter, which he opened and read before putting it down on the table. There was no sign of anger or threats. He just looked tired and defeated.

After a few minutes passed, I said, "As I said earlier, the firm is shocked by the loss of Stephen and sympathizes with your loss of a brother. It is impossible for any outsider to completely fathom the extent of this tragedy for you, your family, and Ahn."

At the mention of Ahn, Jackson looked up in obvious misery.

"She will hardly speak to me, or at least, she has hardly spoken to me. She kept her distance at the funeral and reception, speaking only when necessary. It never occurred to me that something like this could happen. Never in my wildest dreams. Stephen and I were not close, but we were brothers. Since my father died and Mom entered the assisted living area of the Hallmark, Stephen and Ahn have been her primary caregivers. I appreciated their care and concern. Stephen didn't fall in with my business plan for MSA, and he didn't like the transaction. But we were brothers."

I let the words sink in for both of us before asking a question. "I came here only to give you the letter and answer questions. However, if you would like to visit, I would like to ask a question. Stephen visited with you before his death. I assume he mentioned to you that he felt that the firm should recuse itself from representing MSA."

Jackson nodded and gave me a brief review of their final conversation. "Stephen told me he felt the transaction was doomed. He also told me that the firm was not in a position to give the transaction the kind of high-power representation that would be needed, for some of the reasons outlined in the letter. He was of the view that the FBI investigation would taint anything the firm said. Finally, he told me that, on the surface of recent requests by regulatory agencies for information about loans, he felt there was already an ongoing investigation into MSA by state and federal regulators. We argued. The meeting did not end well."

"Did you mention your conversation to anyone?"

Jackson had obviously given the question some thought. "After Stephen and I visited, I made several phone calls that same night. In some of them, I mentioned difficulties with my brother and the firm. I was angry and probably sounded bitter. I had conversations with one of the investment bankers involved. I mentioned the problem to Wendy Ramirez, the new chief financial officer of MSA. She thought that we would be better off with new counsel. I spoke to Sol Lewinsky briefly. He shares Stephen's concerns and would just as soon we call the whole deal off. He may take GSA out of the transaction at any moment, no matter what I do. Finally, I mentioned the problems to Albert Renaldi, who called me that evening. I might have mentioned it on another call to a friend in Washington, from whom I often seek advice."

I could tell that Jackson was trying to be honest but carefully hiding from me the identity of the investment banker and his contact in Washington. He was always careful where the sources of his economic or political power were concerned. In my mind, it was unlikely that Sol had anything to do with Stephen's death. That left as suspects everyone else he mentioned. I thought for a few moments before going on.

"Jackson, someone put a bomb in your brother's car. Whoever ordered or committed that act was and is not stable. Do you think that Big Al or one of the other persons you visited with that evening was unstable enough to have ordered the bombing?"

I was fishing for information. If Jackson pointed the finger at Big Al too quickly, it might mean he was covering for someone else. Big Al was an obvious suspect. He had a motive. He knew of problems with the transaction. Jackson admitted that Big Al knew about Jackson's problems with Stephen. Through his contacts, Big Al probably had the means—or at least access to the means—to arrange a hit. Where Big Al was concerned, opportunity, means, and motive were all present. On the other hand, Big Al also had the most to lose if a murder caused further delays or abandonment of the transaction.

Jackson's response, when it came, was vague and further confused the issue. It was obvious that Jackson was also trying to figure out things.

"Art, it's a complex world. Things are not as they appear. There are wheels within wheels. Wall Street and politics are both occasionally labyrinths of greed and lust for power. You never know who will do what for what reason. In today's world, business, government, and politics are deeply intertwined at the highest levels. This is especially true of regulated industries like banking. There are connections within connections. Big Al is a bully, but I never saw him as a murderer. In addition, I never saw him as a decision-maker, except on a small scale. He is not well-connected in Washington. For the very reason you mentioned—the importance of the deal to him personally—he is not an obvious choice to have ordered a hit on Stephen, unless someone ordered him to arrange it."

It was apparent Jackson was not convinced that Big Al was the person who ultimately ordered a hit on this brother. He seemed to be giving me a warning not to draw conclusions too quickly. I decided to take a detour before returning to the search for the killer.

"I know that you're burdened by your brother's death," I said. "I can see it on your face. I can also see that you're worried about Ahn and others. Is there anything the firm or I can do to help?"

He shook his head. "Thank you, but no. I'm already taking steps to see that my mother and Ahn are taken care of. Ahn will have all the help she needs with Mom. My brother, I am sure, left Ahn well provided for, and I will ensure that she has no real needs in the future, at least any future I can control. My mother and Ahn have been close over the years. Ahn will visit my mother and help care for her. Dad left my mother with enough money to live at the Hallmark here in Houston for the rest of her life. My mother's dementia is getting worse, and the doctors do not think she has long to live. In all probability, the funds my father left for her care will outlast her needs. Ahn will probably inherit at least half of whatever is left when she dies. I am going to try to see my mother tonight before I leave town to think for a while and plan for the future. I need to get away for a few days and think through the next steps that need to be taken."

He went on to discuss the letter. "I understand your firm's desire to recuse itself. It is true there will be an investigation.

It's also true that the regulators might no longer trust your firm if it continues to represent MSA. They would always wonder what the angle might be regarding anything you say or any document you file. It is better that a new firm handles the transaction. I will look for other counsel. Do you think it should be a firm in Houston or Washington, DC?"

I responded firmly. "The firm you choose probably should be from Washington, as the approval process for the transaction will likely be handled from Washington in the future. The transaction is too much of a hot potato to be handled in Dallas and Austin." I gave him a couple of very high-powered names with great connections in the financial and regulatory world. Then the conversation turned back to Stephen's death.

"The regulators will wonder if there's a connection between the deaths of Frank, Don, and Stephen," I said.

Jackson took a moment to formulate his reply. "It is convenient that there was a bomb on the King Air and in Stephen's car. If someone wanted it to seem that there was a connection between the deaths, planting a bomb in Stephen's car would be the best way to cement that thought and divert attention away from other theories. As I said a moment ago, things may not be as they seem. Art, when I was in college, I read a book by the Chinese philosopher Lao Tzu. In one of his sayings, he remarks that knowledge is like the surface of the sea and ignorance is like the ocean depths. I had forgotten that saying until recently. One never knows exactly what is happening, all the connections to what is happening, or all the motives of all those who are acting in any given situation. In this case, something has gone deeply wrong, and things are completely out of control. It is as if someone is deliberately trying to create chaos. If I were a religious man, I would say that the devil is walking about, causing all this mayhem and chaos. More likely, someone with power is pulling the strings. Anything could be true."

Jackson obviously knew more than he was saying. He clearly believed that the use of explosives for both murders was a bit too convenient. He suspected something or someone but did not want to tell me about his suspicions. He shook his head in shame and regret.

"It does not matter who actually murdered Stephen. In the end, I'm responsible. I conceived the transaction. I pushed it despite its problems. I let out my brother's role at Winchester & Wells and the problems I was having with your firm. That information must have gotten to someone foolish enough or evil enough to order a hit."

It was my turn to nod. "Yes. Someone knew, and someone ordered a hit."

Jackson pondered his next words. "I do not know exactly how this happened, but I do have some ideas. If you were to know, your life would be in danger. The hit on my brother was professional, and professional hitmen are rarely caught. We may never know exactly what happened. Of that, you can be sure. In any case, it is probably best for you and your firm to remain in the dark. If I were you, I would let the entire thing drop. If you can figure out what happened in due time, by the time you figure out what happened, you will also know enough to protect yourself, or at least I hope you do. Art, here is a truth: Human beings pushed into a corner are like animals. Things that you and I would think impossible can be done. Big Al is that kind of a person. He is pure instinct and violence, like a tiger shark. There is no rationality or morality in him. He is just a beast with a brain—and there are a lot of other people in this world just like him.

"In my experience, there are also many highly intelligent, calculating people who enjoy creating chaos and hurting other people. Some of them are brilliant and have friends and colleagues with the same character traits. These people are a danger to ordinary people and ordinary life. In their case, making money, gaining power, and triumphing over others are just one big game. They consider themselves supermen or masters of the universe, entitled to do whatever they please because of their wealth, intelligence, physical energy, and power. They believe that they are 'beyond good and evil,' to quote Nietzsche. I know, for I have been one of them. Such people may be behind this situation. I advise you to be careful and keep a low profile."

It was getting dark, and I was beginning to tire. There was a lot more I needed to know and would like to know, but I realized it would take hours to explore everything beneath the surface of this conversation. Jackson seemed to have an idea of who was behind his brother's death but did not want to share complete information with anyone. For the first time, I realized that in addition to exhaustion and guilt, there was a good bit of fear in the way Jackson was answering my questions. He was not just broken; he was haunted.

22

Return to Mexico

EL HALCÓN RECEIVED A LETTER while Mirador was in the United States. The enclosed pictures and note contained the suggestion that he personally had perhaps been involved in the bombing and crash of the King Air. In one particular picture, he and El Capitán were pictured in a deep conversation on the patio of the hunting lodge. The King Air could be seen in the background. There were also pictures of his last conversation with Frank Johnson.

The letter provoked angry phone calls to Mexico City, Washington, New York, and then to a number in Acapulco. A few days later, as El Capitán was leaving his compound, a rocket-propelled grenade, fired from the red-tile roof of a nearby building, hit his car. He was killed instantly. Within a week, his eldest son, "Little Capitán," was installed as leader of the cartel. It was rumored that Little Capitán had ordered the hit on his father. With typical efficiency, the national police rounded up the usual suspects, but nothing was ever proven.

El Halcón was not spared his own date with destiny. Before he was killed, El Capitán received his letter from Mirador. The letter included the information that the writer had been made aware that the bomb in the airplane had been placed in the plane on his instructions. It contained detailed information about the hit that only Harry Dent could have provided. El Capitán knew that if and when El Halcón or his partners in the business received this information, his time as head of the cartel was over. He ordered and paid for the assassination of El Halcón.

An assassination attempt on El Halcón occurred the day after El Capitán's death. It was partially successful. It involved another car bomb. The injuries to El Halcón were serious but not fatal. The blast unfortunately disfigured him. He became something of a recluse, rarely leaving his family compound. He became bitter and vindictive, so bitter and vindictive that his wife and children left him alone, living most of the time in Puebla or elsewhere.

***

EJ Mueller also received a letter with enclosures that, if made public, would prove that an operative of the United States government was at the camp at the time the bomb was placed on the King Air. It also contained a detailed account of Mueller's possible role in the crash. Mueller was worried. He pondered his situation and the wisest course of action.

I cannot be sure I will not be used as a fall guy and made publicly responsible for the inconvenience caused by the bombing. My superiors may decide to blame a rogue agent, with me playing the starring role.

Mueller had been around too long to believe that he was necessarily going to be protected by his masters. He was valuable but expendable. In the end, they might decide he was a dangerous, nonessential liability or a convenient person to take the blame for a scandal.

If there is an indictment or congressional inquiry, or if the press is given the information in this letter, I might be in the no-longer-valuable-and-definitely-expendable category.

Mueller considered informing those with whom he worked of the events as he understood them, but there was danger in that course of action—and it was unlikely to work. It would be best to keep a low profile, go to ground, and allow the future to unfold. He could always reemerge in the event things blew over.

One of Mueller's duties in Mexico City was to handle the money for his principals. The laundering process was Byzantine. Money received for drugs had to be gathered and placed in accounts from which it was later transferred. This was the placement stage of the process. In his case, the laundering process began in the Isle of Man. This could be traced.

To avoid further tracing, there was a second stage involving a process known as *layering*. In the layering stage, the money was broken into many smaller transfers and sent through accounts in tax havens and banks all over the world. This process was called *surfing* and continued until the laundered money was untraceable. In the final stage, the money found its way to the partners in the business.

Mueller was a world-class expert at hiding money. He not only knew how to launder money but each and every tactic anyone might use to find the money he was moving around the financial universe. For a long time, he had been transferring a small portion of the funds for which he was responsible into accounts all over the world, accounts of which he was the incognito beneficiary. If he could get out of Mexico alive, he had a reasonable chance of living affluently for a long, long time.

Mueller was an agent of the United States government and of others outside the agency. In other words, his was a divided loyalty—a double agent of sorts. In his case, his second loyalty was not to another nation but to a group of wealthy individuals and entities they controlled. A person in his line of business needed an escape plan in case of an emergency, and for a long time, he had pondered where he might hide if it became necessary. He knew the steps he would take and the places he would hide.

Of course, his superiors would suspect the worst and search for him. His agency and the others for whom he worked had pretty good track records in finding people they wanted to find, but they did not find everyone. The government and the others would not stop searching until they found him or he was no longer important. As time passed, he would become less and less important. He might be able to disappear for good.

In the past, Mueller had searched for missing agents. He knew the procedures and protocols. He understood his employers' firm policies that every rogue agent, without exception, had to be found, interrogated, and terminated with prejudice. He did not want to become another on a lengthy list of missing persons. Mueller had carefully planned for his disappearance over years. He was ready. The more he thought about it, the more he felt he needed to disappear. He had the hidden wealth to do so and never work again.

There is too much danger in staying in Mexico, hoping things turned out for the best. I need to act as soon as possible.

***

Mueller was nearly finished pondering his course of action when he had a visitor. He lived in a compound with special security twenty-four hours a day. No ordinary person could enter or exit the compound without guards or cameras detecting an uninvited guest. Behind the compound walls, he was safe and could relax his guard. It was unsurprising that he did not see a dark figure who slipped over a wall and slid between detectors just as the power went out in his compound for only a short time. He did not hear an incident that had occurred moments earlier at the front gate, an incident that captured the attention of the guards long enough for someone to enter unobserved.

No security system is infallible. Mirador had discovered the weakness of the compound's security.

Mueller was sitting in his living room, pondering his next move, when the lights flickered a second time. He was plunged into darkness. As he reached for his 9mm Beretta, he was suddenly grabbed from behind, rendered unconscious, bound, gagged, hooded, and taken into his safe room—a secret room built into his house. When he awoke, he realized he had a visitor who was dressed in black with a ski mask covering his face and features. The dark figure did not introduce himself.

"Mr. Mueller, it is good to see you're still alive and healthy. I assume you would like to stay that way."

Mueller nodded.

"I am afraid that staying that way will be a bit complicated. The same letter I sent to you will be sent to your superiors, the press, and others unless we can reach an agreement about your disappearance. I doubt that you will 'stay that way' once those letters are received. You know too much and would be a most unwelcome witness before Congress or a grand jury. It would be impossible to explain why an employee of the United States government was present with the leader of a drug cartel deep in Mexico at a hunting camp, where American banking executives were also present—executives who died in a bombing while returning home. If the press in the United States were to receive this information, you would be viewed as expendable by those for whom you are working. If you add to these facts the murder of the lawyer in Houston, I would say that you definitely would be a liability to those employing you, if my knowledge becomes public."

This was the precise angle Mueller had contemplated in his musings. If it became obvious that a third party knew and intended to disclose his business in Mexico, there was more than a possibility that his superiors would be dismayed at the danger he posed to them and their business. Mueller would immediately become a very expendable liability.

Mueller nodded.

"I hope we can reach an agreement that will spare you any inconvenience," the visitor said. "For inconvenience to be avoided, however, it will be necessary for you to disappear. I am sure you have thought of the possibility that the time has come to go into hiding."

Another nod.

"I assume that you have made arrangements as to how this might be accomplished."

Again, a nod.

"Very good. Tonight would be a good time to put your plan into effect. But first, I think a man in your position can make a few transfers that might help to assist the persons and families injured or damaged in this unfortunate matter. I will see that the funds are used wisely to help the families in question. Is this agreeable?"

Another nod.

"Then let us get to work. You will make the initial transfers. I will make the final transfers. Of the final transfers, you will know nothing. When we finish, this computer will be destroyed, and we will both leave this place. I warn you that I have experience in what we are about to do. It would be a great and fatal mistake for you to attempt to tag any of the transfers in such a way that they might be traced. This would require my acting in a way that I would like to avoid. You already have guessed that I am a man who has killed many people. You do not want to become one of them. Do you understand?"

Mueller nodded his agreement.

The two got to work. Over several hours, they made the transfers necessary to get the funds into the accounts Mirador had selected. Then, Mirador made additional transfers. Mueller also made his personal transfers.

Just before daybreak, there was another brief power failure, and Mueller's visitor disappeared. About the time of the power failure, Mueller's car was seen leaving the compound. He was not seen again.

23

A Second Storm

IT IS RARE FOR HURRICANES to form in such a way as to enter the Gulf of Mexico and hit the Texas Gulf Coast in the late fall. Most late-season hurricanes end up in the North Atlantic. It is a matter of folklore, however, that such hurricanes, when they do occur, tend to be large and destructive. It had been a long, hot summer, and the Gulf of Mexico was still roiling with heat stored in its waters that had yet to dissipate. This fall would see another hurricane threaten Texas.

Once again, off the coast of Africa, at almost exactly the same spot as Hurricane Fey had begun, a tropical low-pressure area formed and began to organize in the favorable conditions of the Cape Verde Islands. As it tracked westward, it became a tropical depression. It strengthened and began to develop a strong center, the eye of the hurricane around which the storm could organize itself and gain force.

Conditions were favorable, and by the time it reached the Leeward Islands, Nemesis made her first landfall as a Category 4 storm near the Bahamas. Nemesis weakened somewhat after her initial landfall but was once again a significant storm by the time it passed between Hispaniola and Cuba. By the time it made its way into the Caribbean in mid-October, it was a Category 4 hurricane with great destructive potential.

Like Fey, Nemesis had a mind of her own. After entering the Caribbean, she drifted westward into the Gulf of Mexico after hitting the coast of Cuba. Again, the storm was downgraded. It paused briefly in the Gulf of Mexico, drew strength from its warm waters, and then set course for Galveston Island. In late October, Nemesis made landfall with sustained winds of 140 miles an hour, making her one of the largest hurricanes ever to hit the Texas Gulf Coast. As might be expected, the damage was severe.

***

After his brother's death, Jackson decided it was time for a break. He needed to get away and think. The Winchester family had long owned a large, contemporary beach house in Pirates Beach, a subdivision on the west side of Galveston Island, an area known as the West Beach. It had been his father's special place of retreat. His mother loved the beach

281

and spent her time there cooking and entertaining in the large home they built.

It was a place with fond memories for the entire family. The boys had spent endless hours, swimming and playing on the beach. Jackson always felt relaxed when he exited the causeway, seeing the oleander blooming on the esplanade as he drove toward the seawall. Most of the time, the family turned at Sixty-First Street and drove to Seawall Boulevard. There, they turned right and traveled west along and beyond the seawall that protected the city of Galveston from hurricanes, until reaching Pirates Beach. This time, Jackson took a longer route, turning left instead of right and stopping for dinner at the Pelican Club in the back of Gaido's, where the family had a membership.

Later, after unloading the car, he sat on the deck of the house with a margarita in his hand, pondering the rolling waves as they came ashore. He walked on the beach, filled as it was with memories. His walks and time on the deck continued during the following days.

Jackson Winchester stayed in his family's beach house beyond the weekend, even as Nemesis approached. He had taken refuge in a place filled with memories. He remembered his parents. He remembered playing golf with his father and brother at the Galveston Country Club and deep-sea fishing trips offshore. He remembered chasing girls down the beach and running to stay in shape. He remembered playing football and volleyball with his now-dead brother.

He remembered long, delicious family meals of red snapper, shrimp, and crab. He remembered nights playing Monopoly as a family. He remembered his first kiss on the beach below. He remembered all the things he had forgotten in the quest for money, power, and influence.

He kept in touch with his office by phone. His personal law firm in Houston delivered and then picked up documents, including a revision to his will. He kept up with the situation involving Marshland, which was consuming his life and reputation like quicksand in a grade-B movie. He noted that he was making the papers in Houston, New York, and Washington. The articles were not flattering. His "friends" in Washington and New York were deserting him with alarming speed. Few people who did not work for him returned his calls.

As he sat on the deck of the beach house, pondering his future. *Most of my friends are not friends at all. They are business associates. They are friendships of temporary convenience and mutual advantage. They are politicians who needed my money, investment firms that want to invest their profits and participate in my deals, lawyers and accountants who want to charge for my business, and employees who want to keep their jobs.* He realized he had few, if any, remaining human friendships.

If I lose my wealth as a result of the problems of Marshland, all my so-called friends will disappear. There will be no one left, not even family," he reflected. *"I have given my life to a false god."*

The problems of Marshland took up a great deal of his time. His partners on Wall Street and his sponsors in Washington wanted answers. Unfortunately, Jackson had neither answers nor any idea of what would happen next. He managed to get a prominent Washington firm to take over representation of MSA, regarding "the transaction and any matters that might arise in the future concerning the transaction." That language assured him that the firm would represent Marshland and him in any administrative or legal actions the future might bring.

The letter from Winchester & Wells had been suitably vague, disclosing nothing that, if made public, would harm Jackson or Marshland. Nevertheless, between the lines, Jackson knew Winchester & Wells felt the transaction had little or no prospect of approval. He read the letter many times. He reviewed the list of documents regarding the transaction and especially the list of steps to be taken that Arthur Stone had prepared at the very beginning. He looked for a solution to the problems he faced. He could not see a way forward and doubted that the new firm would either. Although he was not ready to inform his sponsors, partners, or investors, he knew in his heart the transaction would never close.

On several occasions, he tried to talk to Ahn. She was never able to take his calls. He was reduced to leaving a message on her answering machine.

"Ahn, this is Jackson. I am so terribly sorry for Stephen's death. Please know that I had no idea this would happen.

If there is anything I can do, please contact me. I am in Galveston at the beach house for a few days."

He was too prudent and unsure of the future to admit in a recording that he might have had any part in the tragedy.

In his heart, he knew the words of someone who had set in motion a chain of events that resulted in the death of her husband would be of little or no comfort to Ahn. For much of his life, he had resented his brother and the ease with which he made and kept friends. He had long resented the fact that Stephen was married to Ahn, toward whom he felt an attraction, made more difficult by her indifference. *Indifference* might not be the correct word; *caution* might be better. Jackson realized Ahn never trusted him and would not in the future—and for good cause.

He spoke several times to Sol Lewinsky, who believed that the transaction could not be resurrected. He and Lewinsky talked about other possible plans that might work, in the event the transaction was not approved. Sol, however, was unwilling to agree to anything.

"Jackson, I have no idea what's going on or exactly how this is going to turn out. I can't commit to anything until I know it's going to be a doable deal that makes money for my investors. It is way too early to talk about a new or revised transaction. Frankly, I don't believe you have the credibility left to put a deal together. One thing is for sure: West Isle cannot be a part of any new transaction. My friends and investors tell me they believe that Big Al was somehow involved in Stephen's death. I do not want anything to do with that guy. Period."

Jackson understood. He tried to make peace. He did not call Big Al again. *Let him stew in his own juice*, he thought.

The management of MSA was in shock. Like most people in shock, they either did not react to events or overreacted. The new chief financial officer called with a list of loans that the FHLBB and the Texas Savings and Loan Department wanted to examine. It was long. Though she was upset and concerned, Jackson knew that most of those loans were made in the ordinary course of business. A few, however, might be a problem.

Jackson couldn't remember exactly at what point he decided to stay in Galveston and ride out the storm. It was one of those erratic decisions he had been making in recent months. His mind was operating in constant overload and was in danger of freezing up at any moment. He was no longer able to react prudently to new information. On occasion, it was as if he were not fully in command of his will, which was now operating against his reason and not guided by it.

He thought *I must be going crazy, or I'm possessed. I can't think clearly. I have been swept into a dark place from which I see no escape. I am afraid I have lost the ability to see my way.*

Like everyone else on the island, Jackson heard the news that the authorities had issued an evacuation order as the storm moved closer. He watched the Houston news on television, with their solemn admonition that everyone on Galveston Island should leave immediately. At one point, the Galveston police came by to warn him that he needed to leave the island. He nodded in agreement but stayed.

***

Galveston Island is connected to the mainland by a long causeway. The land on either side of the causeway is barely above sea level. Once the causeway is closed, no one can leave the island. Galveston Island is isolated and cut off from the mainland until the causeway can be reopened. Jackson was still in his home when the causeway closed, and the island became the isolated target of the coming storm.

Darkness and rain engulfed the island and the beach house. As the waves grew larger and the sky darker, Jackson sat on the deck, then moved inside, looking through the large windows that faced the beach. He made himself a large margarita on ice and watched the approaching storm with a strange detachment. At one point, he considered putting up the hurricane shutters, as if that would matter much if the storm struck the house with any force.

Remembering his childhood faith at another point, he considered praying to make it through the storm. But he did not. As the huge waves began breaking over the beach in front of the home, he sat on his deck thinking, *I am going to die, and it is for the best.*

Jackson could see strange lightning and light in the darkness of the oncoming hurricane, but the darkness in Jackson's heart would not allow him to open himself to the beckoning light. Of course, no one can know for certain what occurred before the storm tore into the shoreline in Galveston Island at Pirates Beach. No human being can see into another's heart. Perhaps at the last minute, the darkness in Jackson's heart lost its grip on him, and the light engulfed him. Perhaps even after the storm hit and he was dying, he opened his heart to the light. No one can ever know.

As Nemesis approached landfall, it seemed to reach out with an express purpose, this time of hitting Jackson Winchester's family beach house with its full force. In the end, nearly twenty-foot waves hit the wood-frame beach house. The wind tore off its roof and most of the siding, a tornado ripped through the center of the house, and the great waves of Nemesis swept over it until the house was utterly destroyed, engulfed by the storm, and swept away. The beach house was ground zero of a Force 4 hurricane.

The next day, an advance guard of the disaster relief personnel surveyed the damage in Pirates Beach. The leader of the party took one look at the devastation and reported to his superiors by radio phone.

"Jesus, I have never seen anything like this. There is almost nothing left of the entire Pirates Beach subdivision on the beach side of the island! The place is nothing but rubble."

There was nothing left of the house where Jackson Winchester died, except a few pilings driven into the ground far enough to withstand wind and water. As the days went by, there was little information as to exactly what had happened. His family and employees hoped for the best, but no one really believed he had survived. Eventually, what was left of his body washed ashore on the Galveston Bay side of the island. In due time, his remains were identified.

***

The funeral was a small affair to which only relatives, a few people from his businesses, and a few members of Winchester & Wells were invited. Arthur Stone attended, as did Patrick Armbruster. Ahn attended to take care of Mrs. Winchester, who was in a wheelchair. She did not seem to understand that both her sons were dead.

Ahn was surprised when Arthur Stone called a few days later to say that the firm had been given the task of probating Jackson's will, in which she was named independent executor and sole beneficiary after his mother died. She already had been made administrator of Stephen's will, of which she was the sole beneficiary. She went about her new duties with quiet efficiency.

Another casualty of Nemesis was the original branch of West Isle Savings Association. The bank's original office had been located near Trammell's Convenience Store on West Beach, near the entrance to Pirates Beach. The shopping center in which the office was located was also near the dead center when Nemesis came ashore. The hurricane completely destroyed the building and its contents. It was never rebuilt.

Along the entire Gulf Coast region from Galveston to Houston, there was little power, much-contaminated water, massive flooding, many closed roads, and extensive damage to houses and property. The original site of Marshland Savings Association near the Houston Ship Channel, which the family had preserved over many years, was completely destroyed by wind, water, and a huge tornado that went directly through the building. Even the Houston Space Center, including Clear Lake City and the surrounding area, were not spared damage. When it hit that area, the winds of Nemesis were still over one hundred miles an hour. Many buildings and rooms were seriously damaged. The Seabrook Yacht Club was destroyed, and most of the boats were damaged beyond repair. Nearer to Houston, Ellington Field, where NASA had a fleet of airplanes, sustained substantial damage.

The storm was not without consequences for the city of Houston. Including Jackson, nearly one hundred people in the Houston area lost their lives. It was by far the most destructive hurricane in the history of the Texas Gulf Coast, which had seen some large storms. Parts of the downtown, including the parking garage of Winchester & Wells, were flooded. Some of the tunnels that connected the great skyscrapers of downtown Houston flooded and were damaged. Many skyscrapers that dotted the Houston skyline sustained damage to glass and façade. One hundred thousand people were without homes. Several tornadoes hit Memorial Park near downtown Houston, and massive tree damage resulted.

In an unusual event, the bayous that made up the water-drainage system of the Houston area, including Buffalo Bayou, which was part of the drainage of the downtown area, became clogged with trees and debris. Water began to flow backward, causing the bayou to overflow its banks, resulting in massive flooding. The area experienced a massive electrical outage, and the city's water was contaminated.

As the storm moved north into Montgomery County, it weakened but still caused significant damage. In fact, it was still a considerable storm when it passed through Memphis, Tennessee, more than a day after landfall. Eventually, it made its way into the Midwest and dissipated over the Great Lakes.

***

Eventually, Houston and the surrounding Gulf Coast returned to normal. However, it became increasingly clear that Marshland would not survive the past few weeks' events. The FHLBB, the TSLD, the SEC, and other agencies launched a series of investigations. The FBI made a public announcement that the plane crash near Marfa and the car bombing at the River Oaks Country Club were somehow connected. Their press releases indicated that they were treating both the crash and the car bombing as intentional acts. The state of Texas launched its own murder investigation. The heat on Congress was such that the House of Representatives and Senate began an investigation of Marshland and its business connections. This led to other, more productive investigations.

Everyone concerned, especially the politicians who had been close to Jackson and solicited his generous contributions, became anxious to see Marshland as a part of history. It was ultimately announced that Global Savings Association of Bellaire, Texas, would acquire Marshland in a transaction in which Sol Lewinsky's GSA would receive substantial federal assistance.

It was announced separately that West Isle Savings was being put into receivership by the FSLIC and would be liquidated. It turned out that the records of West Isle had been substantially lost or damaged in the hurricane. Unraveling its business and selling its assets took more time and money than anyone expected. Losses to the taxpayers also were more than expected. At about the same time, Vixette Savings in Dallas was closed. This particular closure led to other closures around Texas and Louisiana, creating the largest single loss to the FSLIC in its history.

The failure of Marshland, West Isle, and Vixette was a turning point in the Texas savings and loan crisis. Formerly, regulators tried to work things out with mergers and acquisitions of troubled associations. Congress now appropriated the required funding to simply shut down insolvent institutions. In the end, it was probably the only rational course of action—and it should have been done years earlier, before the crisis created the level of losses it finally reached.

Jackson Winchester and others were painted as villains by a Congress anxious to place the blame somewhere besides on politicians. It was convenient to place the blame on someone dead and without the means to defend himself.

The political results were also dramatic. One United States senator and more than ten representatives, all of whom had connections with failed institutions, either retired, did not run for reelection or were defeated. The president did not win his reelection bid, partly because of public anger over how the savings and loan crisis had been handled. Before the dust settled, there was plenty of blood on the streets of Washington, DC.

Most of the real estate in the closed institutions was eventually turned over to the Resolution Trust Corporation, formed by Congress to take over the assets of troubled S&Ls. Many of the same folks who had borrowed what became terribly underwater loans, secured by assets worth less than the loans on the property, ended up purchasing foreclosed real estate on favorable terms. Fortunes lost became fortunes gained.

Winchester & Wells eventually became a primary litigation counsel for the RTC in litigating certain closures. The business kept the firm busy for many years, earning Winchester & Wells large fees. One of those cases concerning a California institution made Arthur Stone famous in the legal community of Texas and beyond. It was the second stage in his emergence as a force in the area of complex litigation.

Renewal

NOT ALL THE NEWS WAS bad. Gwynn recovered completely from her injuries, and our first child, a boy we named Murray, was born healthy. There were no long-term health consequences related to her injuries. Two months after the hurricane, we were married in the little white wood-framed Presbyterian church in Brenham, Texas, where Dad was currently the pastor. My father and brother officiated. The wedding day was the happiest day of my life.

After we married, Gwynn formed her own practice, which she continued until three children—two of them active little boys—and her other social responsibilities made practicing law full-time impossible.

Just before the wedding, my brother and I spent time together with Dad as guests at a small farmhouse near

Brenham. It was a family substitute for a bachelor party. We were able to reconnect after some years of distance in time and life.

One night we spent together remains vivid in my memory. My father, brother, and I were alone after dinner. They asked me to recount the events of the past months, which I did. When I got to the dark figure and strange lights, Dad and my brother got very quiet. Finally, they asked me what I thought my experiences meant. I had a hard time answering.

"I don't really know what to think. I make my living not believing what people say unless it can be proven in court. However, that kind of proof is unavailable when it comes to personal perceptions of a spiritual reality. I know what I experienced. I know what I saw or dreamed. I know what happened as a result. I do not think it was simply an illusion or false delusion. I am not sure I need to know more."

My father seemed to think that was a pretty good answer.

"In the ministry, I have seen a lot of things that an unbeliever might explain as a coincidence, supernatural answers to prayers, the intervention of God, or chance. I have always thought of them as something spiritual. I never felt it necessary to know or understand more. In the end, it is a matter of faith how one interprets experiences like those you recently had. Personally, however, I also think the experiences were real."

My brother listened carefully, then gave his take on what had occurred.

"When I was in seminary, I had a class on, of all people, John Calvin. One day, as we were discussing Calvin's views about angels, someone in the class spoke dismissively about Calvin's premodern worldview. The professor, who was by no means a fundamentalist, paused thoughtfully and then said, 'I think it is a great mistake not to believe in angels.' He never explained his meaning, but I have always remembered that class.

"During my seminary days, I was often asked to preach in churches with which the seminary wanted to sustain a relationship. During those times, I habitually asked pastors what they thought about angels and demons and whether they had ever experienced things that seemed mystical in origin. The answers were interesting. Across various theological orientations, the answer was almost invariably that they believed in the demonic and in the angelic in some form. They had seen and experienced things in ministry that were difficult to explain on any basis other than supernaturally. They did not agree on the explanation, but they did agree on the existence of what I would call a *trans-material dimension* to the universe. I have experienced things as a pastor that are hard to explain without postulating an element of the divine or demonic.

"Art, it seems to me you have had such an experience. Your visions could just be dreams, but in the case of the angelic lights, your experiences were shared by others who saw the strange pillars of light. These experiences do not seem to be some kind of mass delusion. You will have to decide for yourself what you believe. As for me, I believe the world is stranger than we know."

My father chimed in. "One interesting development in philosophy in recent years has been recognizing that reality is multilayered. At the bottom of material reality lies the principles of physics, from which chemistry and biology emerge as independent areas of reality. The human race emerged in a long process of biological and social development, with the result that religion, psychology, sociology, law, and other disciplines also developed, due to the capacity of human beings to create human societies and institutions. Each level of reality depends on others, yet has its own degree of independence. While other levels are relevant and may impact higher levels, they do not determine them. In my view, beyond the created order, there is a vast, invisible order of spiritual reality. This order may well include an angelic order of being. You may have had some kind of contact with that reality."

Our conversation shifted to the wedding and the excitement it generated in the family. We never returned to the subject of angels. In the intervening years, until recently, I rarely encountered anything like what I experienced during the final days of the Marshland transaction. As the years passed, the vividness of my experience faded, and with it, my curiosity and interest. I was busy as a lawyer, husband, and father. Yet it was in those days that I found my true vocation, the great love of my life, and a kind of center from which I have lived since.

Ahn remains a calming influence and a constant source of quiet wisdom. Winchester & Wells represents her from time to time in her many business and charitable ventures. Stephen left her well provided for, and the addition of Jackson's fortune made her very wealthy. She spends much of each year as a guest of a Benedictine monastery in the New Mexico desert, which she loves. The remainder of the time she spends in her condominium in Houston. She sold the Winchester family home, feeling it was too large to reside in alone. I enjoy living there. It is filled with memories.

Roger was eventually released from the hospital. He had some residual physical issues, but his mind was as clear as ever. Interestingly, his time in the hospital changed his outlook on life, which was never quite the same. We are good friends and colleagues.

Patrick remains a close friend and adviser. Even though elderly and retired, he is still as wise and practical as ever. I visit him often. His advice always is important in my decision-making.

A year after Nemesis, I was made a partner in Winchester & Wells. After a time, I became the head of the team that Stephen led. His old office became my office. I never completely redecorated it. It reminded me of his wisdom and goodness. It gave me a place to reflect daily on his example, the quiet influence of Ahn, and the destiny that found me in the mid-1980s.

I never had a moment of physical instability since the day I fell on Gwynn and saved her life. I still dream on occasion, and my dreams sometimes are filled with warnings, which are surprisingly helpful in the life of a busy trial lawyer. In the years since Nemesis landed on the Houston coast, however, the dark, fiery figure who haunted me for so long was not a part of my dreams—until recently. But that is another story.

As a lawyer, my life is dominated by what can or cannot be proven in a court of law. Over the years, I have learned to doubt myself, others, and even events right before my very eyes that might turn out to be an illusion.

It often happens that when a lawyer takes a case, he or she conceives that the facts will take a certain pattern of meaning, only to find out that the case's underlying meaning is quite different. A good lawyer learns to adapt to changes in perception of the facts and the best interpretation of those facts.

As a human being, I saw and experienced unusual things. My opinion is that a wise person does not decide too quickly about important matters.

Epilogue

A few months after Nemesis struck the Texas Gulf Coast, a short phone call was placed from a townhouse in Washington, DC, to a home near New York City.

"Good morning, sir. I understand that you would like an update on things in Texas."

"Yes."

"On the whole, we believe things have been resolved satisfactorily. It might not be how we originally intended, but the resolution seems acceptable."

"Just tell me where things stand."

"As you know from the press reports, Jackson Winchester died in Hurricane Nemesis. After his brother's death, he went to the family beach house in Galveston and stayed through the storm. The storm made landfall almost exactly where the family house was located. Only a fool or a suicidal person would have stayed in that house through a Level 4 hurricane.

"After the storm, it was impossible for the transaction to continue. WISA has been closed by the regulators, and its majority shareholder is dead. We know Big Al received a call shortly before the hurricane hit, asking him to attend a meeting in Louisiana. He decided to avoid Nemesis by visiting associates in Louisiana. He went to a motel in Metairie, hired a prostitute, and drank heavily. He was seen being removed from the hotel by three men, early the next morning. Apparently, the three men put him in his car and drove him away. The lady who owned the establishment involved later told authorities that Big Al was violent and drunk. He hurt one of her girls. She assumed the three men with him were friends. She did not recognize them.

"A few days later, Big Al's car and body were discovered in a bayou in South Louisiana. It appears to the authorities that he drove off the road while speeding under the influence of alcohol. The FSLIC has taken over the institution he controlled and will investigate the losses, but without a majority shareholder to sue, they will not look very hard at its transactions.

"In any case, in preparing for the proposed transaction, most of the evidence of any wrongdoing was obscured or destroyed. Just before the hurricane hit, many of the files related to WISA loans were sent to the branch at Pirates Beach in Galveston, Texas, where the savings association began. The location was almost precisely where the hurricane made landfall. Most of the files were lost or damaged beyond recognition by the water and wind. Based on all this, we do not believe there will be any public disclosures of significance to us as a result of West Isle's closure."

"What about MSA?"

"When it became obvious that the transaction could not close, MSA approached a third party about an acquisition, a businessman in Texas named Sol Lewinsky, the chairman of Global Savings Association. It is fairly solid for a Texas S&L. Some of the investment strategies that Winchester used have been used by Lewinsky, though Lewinsky is a conservative and careful guy. The odds are that Global survives the crisis. Lewinsky is not one of us, but he is smart and doesn't want trouble. He's going to force the FSLIC to take over any bad assets within MSA. Whatever is left will have nothing to do with us. We can handle the assets that end up in the hands of the regulators. We don't think we have anything to worry about there.

"One curious fact: Jackson Winchester was unmarried and his father and brother are dead. Apparently, the widow of Stephen Winchester—some Asian beauty queen—is the executor of his estate. She wants to liquidate Jackson's company as soon as possible and have nothing to do with any of the businesses of her husband's brother. She's liquidating San Felipe Investment Partners and all the assets it holds that we might have concerns about. We're told she's kind of otherworldly. Doesn't seem to have much interest in business or money. I think if one of your people makes a decent offer for the assets of San Felipe, in which we have an interest, she will take it."

"Could she become a problem during liquidation?"

"We don't think so. Although she might become aware of the names of a few investors, we don't think she'll recognize any names, nor will those names be names we desire to remain unknown. A good number of the investors in San Felipe, including you, invested through offshore companies and nominees. The real parties in interest are invisible. That is certainly true of our interest.

"One of our contacts in the Houston legal community actually talked to the lawyer handling the estate for her, one of the attorneys who was injured in the second bombing, a guy named Arthur Stone. He indicated that Ahn Winchester's sole interest is to liquidate the partnership as soon as the sale of its assets can be closed. When that's completed, distributions will be made to the partners in the names and to the addresses on the books of the partnership. That's all he felt he could say, but it is enough to know that we have nothing to fear from the Jackson Winchester. Actually, it's probably a good thing he died."

"Speaking of Winchester & Wells, what does our contact say?"

"Our primary contact within the firm is still in the hospital. Unfortunately, he received serious injuries in the car bombing. Frankly, sir, we ought to distance ourselves from him. He was never an important source of information. He doesn't know much. He certainly does not know about you or any of the principals in our operation. Jackson only used him to convey information to me if he could not directly communicate the information. What little information he knows came from Jackson and no one else.

"Our understanding is that his injuries are significant enough that he will not be of any use to anyone for some considerable time, if ever. It might be in our best interest if he were to leave the firm, have a long period of recuperation, and end up doing something else. In any case, if he stays at the firm, he cannot possibly hurt us."

"What about the investigation of the plane crash?"

"As you know, it was our hope that the plane crash would be seen as an accident, and the crash site would be in Mexico. Unfortunately, the plane did not crash in Mexico. The authorities know it was no accident, but they do not know who ordered it or why. They believe El Capitán ordered the bombing. He was killed in what appears to be a power play in Mexico. Javier has felt for some time that El Capitán was becoming an erratic liability. It was time for a new front man, which we now have.

"The authorities are currently playing with the theory that El Capitán, acting on his own, had the plane blown up. With Big Al dead and El Capitán dead, there's no chance that the authorities can reach any definitive conclusion as to the bombings or their relationship with any third party. There is no possibility that any connection with us could be proved. If anyone suggests it, we will call them an unbalanced conspiracy theorist, which is exactly what most people would think they were. The investigation will come to a dead end, with everyone involved suspecting it was one or both—El Capitán and Big Al—who blew up the plane, and both of them are dead."

"And the car bombing?"

"Using the same plastic explosives on both the plane and car was a mistake. The authorities know there must be some connection. On the other hand, the facts point the finger right back to the people we hoped would be blamed, both of whom are dead, Renaldi and El Capitán. That's part of what I meant when I said things are working out, not as we planned but satisfactorily."

"What about the girl who was injured?"

"The male attorney with whom she was involved is already back to work. He's the attorney handling the estate for Stephen Winchester's widow. He recently received a promotion inside the firm and is handling a great many matters that Stephen Winchester and our contact formally handled. He and the girl recently married. She is in the process of setting up a pro bono practice. Neither she nor her husband knows anything important. We don't believe Jackson talked to anyone about anything before he died."

"What about Mirador?"

"We are pretty sure Mirador is dead. It's hard to put together the exact pieces of the puzzle, but it seems Mirador was badly injured during the original assassination attempt. We think he was making his way back to the United States, probably intending to take revenge against those he felt betrayed him, when he died in a small town southwest of Reynosa. By the time he got near Reynosa, his wounds had become infected. He was weak and beyond help. We verified that there is a grave with his name on it in a cemetery in North Central Mexico.

"We had no idea he had relatives in that area, but apparently, he had some distant cousins. Our people contacted them. They verified that a man fitting his description showed up at their home. He was seriously wounded and dying of exposure and his wounds. While they mourn his loss, they never really knew him. Our sources are fairly sure their story is true. Once he died, the family notified the authorities and buried him. A certificate of death was sent to his unit at Fort Hood. The unit has begun the process of taking care of the formalities associated with the death. It's been decided to give him a posthumous medal to satisfy any lingering questions. The story is that he died in the line of duty in an anti-cartel operation.

"Mirador had almost no assets. He owned a small house, a four-year-old Camaro sports car, a few hunting rifles, and personal belongings. His will, which was on file with the military, gives everything to a charity for the dependents of Special Forces servicemen who die in the line of duty. Mirador was chosen for the mission because he had no family. His parents are both dead. He has no siblings. He's been gone from the ranch on which he was raised for many years. Hardly anyone even remembers him. He was a person with no real human connections and no one to grieve his loss. There's no one to ask questions."

"Anything else?"

"Yes, sir, one thing of which you are already aware. As you know, around the time of the hurricane in Houston, amid the confusion, our agent in Mexico City disappeared. We have not been able to contact him since. What's more, when he disappeared, about $10 million of our money also disappeared. As you know, for us to distribute money between the various partners, we keep a common bank account in the Isle of Jersey, from which monies are laundered, then transferred to the person or entity to which they are due. Before we realized Mueller was missing, a series of transactions took place out of that account.

The money went all over the place. It went to the Cayman Islands. It went to South Africa. It went to Luxenberg. It went to Switzerland. It went to Jersey. It went to the Isle of Man. It went to Cyprus. It went to Poland. It went into Russian banks and Hong Kong banks. It went to Singapore. The money went all over the globe to places where it cannot be traced, especially through Africa and Asia. I have looked at the series of transactions, and it is the most complex scheme I have ever seen. The guy must be a genius. We were able to trace some of the initial transactions—about half of the second set of transactions, almost none of the third transactions, and none beyond the third set. The money was broken into small units and went through so many various laundering sources that we lost the trail. Frankly, I don't think we'll ever uncover the money, but we can try."

"Ten million dollars is not a lot of money, given the scope of our operation. However, we must try to find him and the money—and deal with him in the usual way. Otherwise, in the future, there could be others who think that they can betray us."

"I understand and completely agree. Nevertheless, I must warn you that I'm not confident we'll be able to find him or the money. It's interesting. He only took $10 million. That happens to be just a little more than we estimate it might cost us to trace the proceeds and find him, a process that will take years, a lot of work, and many informers. After all, the reason he was given the task had to do with his experience in laundering funds in untraceable ways. He knew exactly what he could get away with stealing and where to send it. As I said, he seems to be a genius at this. We can try to find him, but it's probably a losing proposition. It's as if he thought through exactly what he could take without it being worth our while to find him or the money. Wherever he is, he knows we're looking for him and always will be looking for him. Therefore, he will keep himself well hidden. One day, we may find him. If we find him, we will find what is left of the money. In the meantime, I propose that the loss be shared among the partners proportionately. Since he was our man, we might take a bit more of the loss than our share. That should make everyone happy. We can pay ourselves back when we find him."

"What does Javier think about this?"

"Javier was the subject of the assassination attempt ordered by El Capitán. The Hawk was seriously injured in the attempt but will recover. He is not back to his old self, however. Javier is upset but understands and will go along with splitting the loss. He's happy to be rid of El Capitán and knows that no investigation in Mexico or anywhere else will ever get back to him."

The man on the New York side of the call thought for a moment, pondering the information. "I can't say that I believe the resolution is satisfactory. We're out a lot of money and have a rogue colleague on the loose somewhere in the world. Nevertheless, if it's the best we can do, it's the best we can do. It does look like we have tied up most of the loose ends. Eventually, we will tie up whatever loose ends remain."

"Yes, we will. Is there anything else I can do for you?"

"Not right now. We appreciate your work, despite the disappointments."

"It's nothing. I hope to be of service to you in the future."

After the phone conversation was over, a young man in Washington, DC, changed into his jogging suit. It had been a difficult several weeks. He needed to sweat out some tension and a few extra pounds.

Another runner found his body a week later in Rock Creek Park.

***

In a monastery outside San Miguel de Allende, Juan de la Cruz Bardero quietly prayed. He had made his confession before the abbot, and now he had made his confession before God. He was sorry for his past life and many of the things he had done. He could not, however, be entirely sorry about what he had done most recently. After all, the Bureaucrat, the Hawk, and El Capitán had been partners in crime. He had not actually killed them, although he put into play the circumstances that led to injury and death. He did not think that El Capitán had any involvement in the Texas bombing, but contacts of El Capitán might have reacted to information he gave them and had Big Al killed. The assassin had tried to kill him. In any case, his death was in the line of duty and before his new life. Before he died, the assassin had told him about El Halcón—the Hawk—and his business operations with El Capitán. The Hawk, El Capitán, and the assassin had earned their fates.

He might yet have to find and deal with the Bureaucrat, as he still called Mueller. Mueller had no idea of Mirador's true identity, where he was, or what he was doing. Mirador had worn a mask during the entire time they were together, transferring money, and arranging for Mueller's departure to parts unknown. All Mirador knew about Mueller's whereabouts was that the first stop was Pretoria, South Africa. By now, Mueller was in another distant country, with no extradition treaty with the United States, probably getting a good bit of plastic surgery.

Mirador had wasted a lot of his life in violence, serving masters who turned out to be unworthy of his loyalty and sacrifice. It was time to serve another and more worthy master. Whatever he decided to do, he had a nest egg. He had been a careful man, and his wants were few. For the time being, he loved the peace of the monastery and the life of a lay brother. It might not last forever, but it would do for now.

As he continued to pray, the sky became dark and night began to fall. He could not see it, but in the corner of the little chapel was a dark figure. Between Mirador and the figure, there was an invisible pillar of light.

Afterword

Many readers will recognize a thematic resemblance between portions of *Marshland* and C. S. Lewis's *Space Trilogy,* which includes *Out of the Silent Planet, Perelandra,* and *That Hideous Strength.* The connection between the characters of Ransom and Arthur Stone results from the fact that each is drawn from Arthurian legends. Arthur Stone, however, is nothing like Lewis's character, Erwin Ransom. Arthur Stone is a "Duke of Battles," as any historical Arthur might have been. Unlike Ransom, while Arthur Stone is respectful of religion and faith, his life is a practical life of representing clients and winning lawsuits. Like a historical Arthur probably would have been, he is no saint. He is a man of action with the virtues and flaws of such a person. Unlike Ransom, the bachelor, Arthur Stone has his Gwynn, with all the complexity that relationships between men and women entail.

There are descriptions of potential angelic beings in *Marshland.* Lewis's *Space Trilogy* contains many references to angelic beings, what Lewis calls *oyarsa* and *eldila.*

Many years after reading the *Space Trilogy* for the first time, I encountered the description of angels in the early Church Fathers and was struck by how much Lewis must have internalized from their writings. When I decided to write a murder mystery with spiritual overtones, it occurred to me to revisit the issue of the reality of angelic beings but with a twist, in that more than one explanation is given in the novel.

I hope readers of *Marshland* are free to see the angelic presences as spiritual realities, as projections of the internal mental state of the characters, or both. That is, it's up to the reader to decide what to make of the angels who seem to interfere in the lives of Arthur Stone, Gwynn, Mirador, and others. Stone sometimes sees angelic figures in private dreams, but Mirador's angelic figures were seen publicly. For example, people at the hunting camp saw their light which was reflected in photographs taken of the event. As to their reality, I have my own views, but they are only mine.

The existence of angelic beings, both good and evil, servants of God and fallen enemies of God, are part of the rich heritage drawn from the early centuries of the Christian faith. I have drawn my own description from John of Damascus and others of the Church Fathers. In the Christian tradition, angels are beings of pure intelligent light created by God to reflect God's own divine light into creation. Angels are often referred to as "pure mind," which is created as a part of an invisible, noetic creation, of which the Nicene Creed speaks. Finally, angels have the power to inhabit both the heavens and the earth and to travel between them and places within them at an unimaginable speed. The notion of their orientation being always toward God is my own inference from scripture. As messengers of God, the angels appear to me to be simultaneously present with God and as recipients of this divine wisdom and counsel but also capable of presenting themselves to human beings with messages, information, and even illumination.

Others have noted that Lewis's notion of angels has roots in St. Thomas Aquinas and his ideas on the subject. Aquinas says in his *Summa Theologica*, Part 1, Article 51:

> Some have maintained that the angels never assume bodies, but that all that we read in Scripture of apparitions of angels happened in prophetic vision—that is, according to imagination. But this is contrary to the intent of Scripture; for whatever is beheld in imaginary vision is only in the beholder's imagination, and consequently is not seen by everybody. Yet Divine Scripture from time to time introduces angels so apparent as to be seen commonly by all; just as the angels who appeared to Abraham were seen by him and by his whole family, by Lot, and by the citizens of Sodom; in like manner the angel who appeared to Tobias was seen by all present. From all this, it is clearly shown that such apparitions were beheld by bodily vision, whereby the object seen exists outside the person beholding it, and can accordingly be seen by all. Now by such a vision only a body can be beheld. Consequently, since

the angels are not bodies, nor have they bodies naturally united with them, as is clear from what has been said (Article 1; I:50:1), it follows that they sometimes assume bodies.[2]

I think my representation fairly attempts to represent this description in the form of a novel.

In the beginning, I did not intend to write a novel with Arthurian roots. That aspect of the novel emerged as time went on. What I did intend to write was a novel inspired by the work of the least known of the inklings, Charles Williams, who wrote what he called "spiritual shockers." My wife likes mysteries and spy novels. Therefore, I originally set out to write a mystery novel with spiritual overtones—a kind of contemporary version of what Williams did so well.

In common with other authors, I created characters that took on lives of their own. For example, Patrick Armbruster was originally created with the notion that he would not be particularly likable and might easily become one of the darker characters in the book. I was mistaken. Much to my surprise, of his own accord, when visiting with Arthur Stone, Patrick Armbruster became a kind of Merlin figure, giving good advice to a young and inexperienced Arthur. One of the mysteries of writing is learning that the characters may be imaginary, but they still have lives of their own and control a good deal of what unfolds in the author's mind.

---

[2] Thomas Aquinas, *Summa Theologica*, Part 1, Question 51, Objection 3, accessed Nov. 9, 2022, https://www.newadvent.org/summa/1051.htm.

While the human characters in the novel are my own inventions, as is the transaction that forms the center of the novel's plot, the spiritual forces are not. They are eternal realities with which we human beings must struggle. Love, attraction, greed, ambition, fear of failure, a desire to succeed, faith, hope, the struggle of good against evil and of order against chaos—these are the invisible realities that guide this and every novel, for they are the motivations of the human spirit and the invisible realities that power human history for good or for evil.

In the novel, John Mirador becomes a resident of a small monastery on the outskirts of San Miguel de Allende. The city, which I visited while writing the novel, is one of the loveliest in the world. A few kilometers outside the city, there is today a small Benedictine monastery, Monasterio de Nuestra Señora de la Soledad. The monastery did not exist at the time of the novel, but its founder had a lovely hermitage on the site, where he lived a life of solitude and prayer. The setting, as I visualize it, is much like the monastery that exists today. If you have the opportunity to visit San Miguel de Allende, I recommend it and thank our hosts for such a wonderful visit. If one is inclined (and speaks Spanish), the monastery accepts visitors for a small charge. All of the daily services are in Spanish, so it helps if one has a working command of the language. Fortunately for me, my wife does.

I hope readers enjoy Marshland as much as I enjoyed writing it.

Printed in the United States
by Baker & Taylor Publisher Services